sac
lib
friends
FRIENDS OF THE
SACRAMENTO
PUBLIC LIBRARY

sac
lib
SACRAMENTO PUBLIC LIBRARY

Maximillian Fly

Maximillian Fly

Angie Sage

Katherine Tegen Books
An Imprint of HarperCollins*Publishers*

Katherine Tegen Books is an imprint of HarperCollins Publishers.

 For information address HarperCollins Children's Books, a division of HarperCollins Publishers, 195 Broadway, New York, NY 10007.
www.harpercollinschildrens.com

Names: Sage, Angie, author.
Title: Maximillian Fly / Angie Sage.
Description: First edition. | New York, NY : Katherine Tegen Books, an imprint of HarperCollinsPublishers, [2019] | Summary: "Maximillian Fly, a roach-human hybrid, helps two young humans escape from the Bartizan's eye, only to find himself a key player in a deadly war between roaches and humans"— Provided by publisher.
Identifiers: LCCN 2018034247 | ISBN 9780062571168 (hardback)
Subjects: | CYAC: Cockroaches—Fiction. | Brothers and sisters—Fiction. | Survival—Fiction. | Science fiction.
Classification: LCC PZ7.S13035 Mf 2019 | DDC [Fic]—dc23 LC record available at https://lccn.loc.gov/2018034247

Typography by David Curtis
19 20 21 22 23 PC/LSCH 10 9 8 7 6 5 4 3 2 1
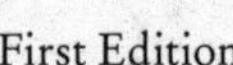
First Edition

For L.V. with love

Contents

Maximillian Fly

Chapter 1

MAXIMILLIAN FLY

M

I am Fly. Maximillian Fly. I am a good creature. I am not bad, as some will tell you.

But I see you do not believe me. You do not like my carapace and my broad, flat head, and I can tell that even my beautiful indigo iridescent wings do not persuade you of my goodness. I know that humans like you call me Roach—even though I am human too. Indeed I was once a squashy Wingless baby, just as you were. But I know very well that if I were small enough you would stamp on me without a moment's thought. Ha! But luckily for me I am much bigger than you and, I have been told, rather terrifying. So we will have no more thoughts of the trampling and crushing of carapaces. They set my mandibles on edge.

I, Maximillian Fly, see all things. I see the revulsion

flickering across your face as you imagine how I look. This upsets me, for I am a sensitive creature. I wish to show you that I am as good as you are—or as good as you *think* you are. Ah, but I am also a forgetful creature. I have forgotten that you cannot see me except through my words. So I will write a picture for you.

I am flying low and fast over our city, a gloomy place named Hope. The fog is late tonight and there is a fine haze of damp in the air. Below I see the dark canyons of the unlit streets, the tumble of vegetation sprawling across the landscape of roofs that glisten like turtles' backs. I am looking for my own dear roof. There, now I see it: at the end of the line, narrow with its attic windows standing out like little bug eyes, its two stone parapets back and front and the tall yellow brick chimney rising high like a beacon. I love my roof. However, I do not love the orange Astro suit that lies wedged in my front parapet. It fell last week and now it has rolled down and settled in the wide lead gutter like a punctured balloon. Oh, an Astro is a terrible thing.

But look! Here is something to distract us from such gloomy thoughts. Down in the street below I see a chase. Two SilverSeeds—crew of the notorious SilverShip, which every year takes a group of young ones away from Hope, never to return—are being pursued by three Enforcers, who look sleekly dangerous in their CarboNet armor, which shimmers in the night with its blue-green oily sheen. I watch the SilverSeeds race along the overgrown street, leaping through the vegetation, a tall one dragging a shorter by its hand. This chase is no business of mine, but I realize that you might consider it *your* business, for they are young Wingless ones just like you. So I, Maximillian Fly, will satisfy your curiosity and at the same time I will prove to you that I am indeed a good creature. And then we will both be happy.

Now I shall for your pleasure describe what I see. The small SilverSeed has stopped running and is now dancing on one leg, emitting high-pitched noises. This cannot be good if they truly wish to escape. Now the larger SilverSeed is hoisting the small one upon its back and setting off again at a run like an awkward two-headed mutant. It moves surprisingly quickly, but will it be quick enough?

I suspect not. The Enforcers, who are older and faster than these two young ones, are gaining ground. They are the usual crew of three runners with a searchlight, a net and a battering ram. You may wonder why they do not shoot their quarry down and be done with it, but Enforcers do not carry weapons—they must bring their prey back alive and in reasonably good condition.

Aha. I have an idea. I will help these young fugitives—what do you say to that? But I am taking a risk here, for young Wingless ones always mean trouble for we humans who are called Roach. So let us make a deal: I, Maximillian Fly, will give them sanctuary. They won't find it anywhere else in this street. And I will go further than that. I will give these SilverSeeds all the help they need to escape that vile SilverShip, on which, one day soon, they will be forced to leave Hope forever.

But first, they must have the wit to find me.

I land on my beautiful roof so softly that not even the rat sitting upon the ridge stirs. I perch to settle my wings and then I pull up my goggles and meet the rat's importunate gaze. I hold it until it looks away: one should never permit a rat to win a stare. Halfway along the ridge is my skylight, which I have left open, and a longing comes over me to drop into the cool quietness of my home. But I have not forgotten our bargain. And so now I will check on the progress of the two young ones.

The outstared rat has an amused air as it watches me slide down the slippery slates and—oh, so undignified—end up in the gutter of the rear parapet. Gingerly, I peer over. Well, well, they are not doing badly. They have just scooted into Thin Murk, which is the alley that runs along the side of my house and then past the back of my yard and those of my neighbors. This is becoming interesting, is it not? I pull my goggles back down and I now have superb night vision. They make my eyes look like those of a Night Roach—those despicable creatures who give us Roaches such a bad name. But there is always a downside to everything, is there not?

Now, let me tell you what I can see. The larger Silver-Seed has a long braid and so I presume it to be a female. The small one on her back is a shorthaired child of indeterminate gender. Oh, yes, they *are* being clever. The female has noticed that my gate is unlocked. She has pushed it open and—*oh, this is exciting*—they are now in my backyard. She has also been shrewd enough to push the gate closed and is now heading along the path at the back of my house, toward the steps that lead down to my basement courtyard. But she is stumbling and I fear she will be unable to carry her burden for much longer.

I look over to the backs of the grimy houses of my neighbors that rear up at the far end of my long, narrow yard. I search for telltale signs of watchers at the dirty little windows: the giveaway glow of a candle, the twitch of a curtain. The city is full of people who would be very happy to take the reward offered for the return of a pair of SilverSeeds. But I see no one. The dark rooms are empty. And those with precious light are not wasting their time looking out into the night.

Ha! I see three dark figures in Thin Murk moving fast and silent like the night fog—the Enforcers are on the trail of the SilverSeeds. Fortunately, they run past my gate and disappear along the alley, the soft *padda-pad-pad* of their stalking shoes echoing off the brick walls. Unfortunately, this is not as good as you might think, for Thin Murk is a dead end. The Enforcers will return, more methodically this time, and then . . . oh dear, oh dear. *Tick-tick* . . .

At the top of my basement steps, the small one slips down from the back of the girl. It hops awkwardly. I believe it has hurt its foot. This is because it wears no shoes, which is foolish, for Wingless humans' feet are soft and, in my opinion, singularly unsuited for their purpose. Glancing anxiously about her, the girl helps the small one down the steps into the basement, where it collapses in the shadows. I hear a *shhhh* sound as she tells it to be silent—which indeed it must be, for the Enforcers' listening devices are highly sensitive. I lean farther out over the parapet, for I wish to see what these SilverSeeds will do next.

Chapter 2

KAITLIN DREW

K,

There's a Night Roach watching us. It is on the roof, hidden in the shadows. I can see the glassy green sheen of its eyes staring down. I remember stories about how a Night Roach will size you up to decide whether to take you in one piece or twist your head off and make do with that. This is what it is doing now: *it is sizing us up.*

This is not a good place to be.

I take out my pocket combi-tool and flip open the knife blade. My little brother, Jonno, watches me suspiciously. He's a scrawny kid, scared as a rabbit, his big, round eyes staring at me as if he thinks I'm going to use the knife on him. I risk a glance upward and am answered by the green glint on the parapet.

I saw a Night Roach dive once. It looked like a huge white ghost dropping out of the fog. They say if one swoops down on you, you must hold your nerve. You stand beneath it and at the last moment you stick your blade up between segments two and three. That's where the heart is. But a Roach is a huge thing, and I wonder about the weight of it falling on me. And its blood cascading over me and . . . *That's enough, Kaitlin,* I tell myself. *Enough.*

I need to get us inside this house as soon as I can, but it's not looking good. We're in a damp, slippery basement area and the only ways in are two barred windows and a rusty metal security door. Rising up above us are four more stories of grimy brick and rotten windows. I could get in through any of those with no trouble at all, but there is no way I can climb up to them. My only chance is down here. But the windows have bars on, and the door will be locked. No one leaves a door unlocked at night.

"Stay there," I whisper to Jonno. "Don't you dare make a sound. Remember what I told you? They will *kill* us."

Jonno nods, too scared to speak—at least I hope he is. I leave him in the shadows and creep over to the door. It's locked. I close my blade, flip up the pick tool and poke it into the lock. It works! The lock springs open, but the door won't budge. There are bolts on the other side and there is nothing I can do about those. So I go for the nearest window. The bars are close together and not even I am thin enough to squeeze through—well, my head isn't, that's for sure. But if I can get just one bar off—*just one*—we could fit through. I flip up the screwdriver, but it is useless. The windows may be old and the glass cracked, but the bars guarding them are new and held together by long pins that go deep into the wall.

Jonno whimpers and I freeze, terrified they'll hear him. And then, in the silence, I hear the *padda-pad, padda-pad* of the Enforcers' soft shoes and a shiver runs through me. They're stalking us and they will find us. Enforcers never give up.

I move silently back to Jonno in the shadows. I sit beside him on the wet stone and I see a puddle of blood seeping from his sock. I feel bad about this. Jonno's deck shoes were way too big for him and I made him take them off so he could run faster. I put my arm around him, but he doesn't react. He is all hunched up, clutching his bear, Tedward. *If only you had let go of your precious Tedward you wouldn't be here*, I want to tell him.

But I can't because I'm listening to the gate opening and soft footsteps on the path above us, deliberate and slow. They're not hurrying because there is no need. They know they've got us. I glance up at the parapet and the Night Roach is gone. Well, that's something, I suppose.

Suddenly a brilliant beam of light sweeps across the back of the house. The Enforcers must be directly above us. In a few seconds they will come down the basement steps and see us huddled against the wall—and I know exactly what will happen then. I rehearse what I must do. I must speak fast before they gag us. I must make them understand that Jonno is hurt and that they mustn't put him in the net. I must tell them that that he never wanted to come with me, and it is not his fault. But before I do anything I must somehow hide his stupid bear. Very carefully I try to pull Tedward out of Jonno's grasp, but he clasps it tighter than ever. I make my pleading face at Jonno and mouth, *Please, Jonno, let me hide Tedward. Please.* But he shakes his head and tugs Tedward toward him. I am in despair—if they get Tedward I've done all this for nothing. *Nothing.* I am about to make a last grab for that stupid, filthy old bear when I hear a scrabbling coming from behind the security door and then the sound of bolts being drawn back. The door is opening. I can't believe it. *Someone is going to help us.* The door opens a little more, just enough for us to squeeze through. I haul Jonno to his feet but he won't stay standing so I lift him up, stagger inside, and the door closes behind us.

It is dark in the house and it smells funny. The bones in my legs feel like jelly and suddenly I can't hold Jonno anymore. As he slithers from my grasp, something grabs my arm. *Pincers.*

Chapter 3

THE HOUSE OF FLY

M

I, Maximillian Fly, have done an unwise thing. I have brought trouble through my door. Mama is right. I am a fool.

I shoot the bolts home and then I look down at the huddle at my feet. The girl stares up at me, and I see a dangerous creature, crouched upon my doormat, an animal ready to pounce. The small one—a young boy I think—is curled up like a snail that has lost its shell.

Outside I hear soft footsteps creeping down into the basement area. I tell myself that these Enforcers are no more than lowlife vermin—for that is how they behave—but the truth is, I am very afraid. In a few moments they will blow up the door, gag these young ones and put them in a net. And then, for the fun of it, they will probably pull my arms off, all three of them.

There is a thunderous crash upon my dear old door, but it does not move. Now comes the electronic voice screen, which all Enforcers—I mean Vermin—use. The voice is flat and menacing, and it speaks the same words I heard when they raided the house of the mad cat woman across the road: "Open! Open in the name of the Bartizan. A refusal will be taken as declaration by all those within that they are traitors. Traitors will be killed. Open! Open in the name of the Bartizan!"

I decide I would prefer *not* to open the door. I move toward the girl, intending to help her to her feet. Her hand flashes out toward me, oddly thin, sharp and shining. For a second I am puzzled and then I understand: she is holding a knife. I am affronted. After all I have risked, *she wishes me harm*. I jump back and another crash comes upon the door. Her blade hovers, uncertain.

Outside, the electronic words begin once more. This is the second declaration. There will be a third, and then they will blow up the door. It is a bad situation. Oh dear. *Tick-tick*. I should leave now, while I still can. I glance down at the young ones on my doormat and I see the fear in their eyes—deep gray eyes, the same as mine. And then I remember my goggles. Aha. Maybe I remind them too much of a Night Roach. I quickly pull off my goggles and as I do a searchlight beam sweeps in through the window and cuts through the dark like a knife.

K

In the light of the beam, I see the Roach *pull off its eyes.* It takes me a moment to realize it has been wearing goggles—and that, with its deep indigo shimmer, it is most definitely not a Night Roach. Well, that's a relief.

I look up into its strikingly human eyes set halfway up its flat head, which are gray just like mine. It regards me with an anxious expression. The Roach is impressive: tall and powerful, yet oddly delicate. Framed by its elegantly curved wing shells, I see its long, segmented upper body tapering to a pair of short, sturdy legs on which it wears plaid Roach leggings. Its broad, flat feet are bare and covered with some kind of hard insecty skin. I see a complete pair of delicate upper limbs but only one in the middle set—the other seems to be missing. I watch its top right hand with its four fingers and one opposable thumb—just like ours but covered in very hard skin, I think—fiddling nervously with one of its antennae, which is bent sideways. And then the searchlight sweeps away and we are in darkness again.

Suddenly, from outside, I hear the word "Blood!"

It is over. I count the ten seconds it takes to check blood ID and sure enough at the tenth, there is a shout:

"It's the boy's. They're here. We've got them!" There is the most terrific bang on the door and in the silence that follows I hear a voice in my ear. It is a Roach voice, small and tinny, like you hear on old radios. "I wish to help you," it says.

The Roach makes an anxious *tick-tick* sound. "You must hide," it says. "I have a safe place. Follow." I drag Jonno to his feet and, clutching Tedward, he limps forward, making little moans of fear as the Roach pushes us along the dark basement passageway into the depths of the house. Suddenly it stops and says, "Give me your neckerchiefs. Both. Hurry, *hurry*."

What else can I do? I pull off our neckerchiefs.

"I smell blood," the Roach says. "Yes?"

"Jonno's hurt his foot," I say.

"Good," says the Roach.

"Good?" I say angrily. "What's so good about—" But I'm drowned out by the third declaration beginning. I know that when it is finished, we are legally dead. And when I look up at the Roach I see that it knows that too. It glances anxiously down the passageway and gabbles in a panicky squeak, "Put blood on one neckerchief. *Quick, quick*." I hear its pincers clacking and I realize it is trembling. It is as scared of the Enforcers as we are.

"Step on your neckerchief, Jonno," I hiss.

Jonno does not move. He is deep in a nightmare, staring at me, terror-eyed. I kneel down and quickly wipe his neckerchief on his sock—it comes away sodden with blood. I give the neckerchiefs to the Roach and it holds Jonno's at arm's length like it has a bad smell.

The third declaration finishes: "Open in the name of Bartizan!" There is a silence. I glimpse the Roach flipping open a panel in the wall and pulling sharply on a lever. I hear a *click* and a small door in the wainscoting swings open to reveal a black hole smelling of damp. I feel pincers sharp in my back as the Roach pushes me forward into the darkness.

"Hide. Please," it says in its tinny voice.

This is not a place I'd choose to go into, but right now the choices are the Enforcers or a place to hide from them. I pull a resisting Jonno into what feels like a prison cell. "Stay!" the Roach tells us, like it is talking to a bad dog. Then the door closes and I hear the *click* of the catch.

Everything is quiet and we are alone in the darkness.

Chapter 4

IN AND OUT AND IN AGAIN

M

I, Maximillian Fly, must make haste. I flip down my goggles and am up the stairwell and out of the skylight in seconds. In silent flight—moving only my soft under-wings and gliding with my outer wings—I drop down to the house next door and place the fouled neckerchief on the backyard wall. As I do, so I see the Vermin at work laying the charge. My dear old door will not last much longer I fear.

I pick up a pebble and fly over my yard. The Vermin are so intent upon the destruction of my door that the first thing they know of my presence is the pebble dropping on the head of the one with the net. It looks up. "Roach!" it yells in its unearthly, veiled voice.

The searchlight swings upward, pinning me in its

glare as I hover above them. All three stare up at me and I indicate that there is something of interest on the wall. The searchlight swings around and the SilverShip symbol on the neckerchief shines like a beacon.

"How could you miss that, you idiots?" demands the netter.

"It wasn't there before," says the searchlight swinger. "I swear it."

"Probably all that's left of them," says the rammer. "Blasted Roach has had its supper and left us the wrappings."

This is offensive talk, but I cannot complain, for they have come to the conclusion I intended. I fly slowly away and settle on the roof of my neighbor's house in order to observe.

The Vermin test the blood on the neckerchief; then they swarm over the wall in a frenzy. It is a good feeling when my Roach-hating neighbor's door comes crashing down. I wait until they have disappeared inside and then I throw the second neckerchief through one of the upstairs windows and retreat. As I drop through my skylight into the stillness and tranquility of my house, I confess I am tempted to leave the young ones where they are for tonight and go straight to my nest. But a deal is a deal. They have had the wit to find me and I will not leave them alone in the darkness.

I get up from my landing mat and go downstairs with a heavy heart.

J

Me and Tedward are in prison. There is a huge Roach outside and soon it will come in and eat us. My foot hurts *so much.*

K

The cupboard smells of something dead. In the pitch-blackness I hear Jonno whimper. I tell him it's all right, but I know it's not. The truth is, I'm trying hard not to panic. I run my hands along the damp bricks of the wall, and then around the corner to the door that the Roach just shoved us through. I push against it, but it feels as solid as a rock. I follow the wall back into the cupboard, which is longer than I expected. My fingers trace their way along the bricks until they touch metal bars. This is not good. I shove my arm through the bars and there is nothing beyond but empty space. I trace the smooth chill of the metal all the way down to the floor and then up to an arched stone ceiling. There are no gaps. There is no doubt about it—we are in a Night Roach pantry.

I've heard stories of rogue Roaches who collect victims for the Night Roaches—and, some say, for themselves. And now I understand that is what has happened to us. Jonno and I have been collected.

In a panic I throw myself against the door. It is locked. Of course it is. The thuds of the battering ram have stopped and all is silent. This must mean that the Enforcers are inside the house now, padding around looking for us. I come to a tough decision—our only chance to get out of here alive is to make as much noise as we can and hope they hear us. So I start yelling and kicking and hammering on the door.

M

I, Maximillian Fly, hear loud banging and shrieking. I am stricken with guilt. I have left the young Wingless ones alone and the Vermin have discovered them. I have failed in my pact with you. Mama is right: I am a bad creature.

I drop down the stairwell in such haste that I tear an underwing, and as I go I realize that I am angry. How dare these Vermin terrify my innocent young ones? I reach the foot of the stairs and turn the corner at a run, expecting to confront three vicious Vermin with my two young guests caught in a net. But I find nothing.

The passage is empty, and yet the shouts and the thuds continue.

It is now that I realize the noise is coming from the entry to the Underground, where I placed the young ones for their safety. Something must have come up from the tunnel and frightened them. A Bludd Owl maybe? Or a Fingal Spider? I hurry to the lever and pull hard. The door swings open, bringing with it the girl who is shouting so loudly that I fear my ear tubes will become dislocated. She gives me a shove so powerful that I stagger backward and feel the click of my carapace hitting the wall. A jarring shock runs though me and I fear I have cracked something. We Roaches are delicate creatures in some respects. Our exoskeleton is light and strong, but we do not bounce. You Wingless ones have so much meaty padding that you have no need to consider these things.

The girl rockets off down the passage, dragging the small boy with her. She hurls herself at my door and wrenches at the bolt. She is trying to get out. I do not understand why she is doing this, but she is obviously in great distress and the least I can do is to offer assistance. At the sight of me she emits a dreadful noise. But I persist, for I am a helpful creature. I undo the lock, draw the bolts and stand back. My poor, battered door swings open. I bow and indicate the way out.

Tick-tick. I hope you will agree that I have done my best.

K

Out in the night air, my panic subsides and I realize that something strange just happened: the Roach *opened the door for us.* It even bowed as we ran out. I begin to wonder if I've misunderstood the Roach. That maybe I have made a massive mistake . . .

The other weird thing is I can hear crashes and shouts from the far side of the yard wall—the Enforcers are trashing the house next door. All they need to do is take a look out of one of the windows and they'll see us.

My brain is racing through the options. I could hurl Tedward over the wall into another yard and hope no one finds him, but Jonno won't let go of the stupid bear without yelling, so that's not going to work. Or we can run for it—but where can we go? There are patrols everywhere, not to mention Night Roaches, and there is no sign of the night fog to hide us. The truth of it is, we don't stand a chance out there.

M

I confess that for my own comfort I am relieved that the young fugitives—not to mention the filthy piece of fur the small boy clutches—are leaving. I can now look forward to a peaceful night after what has been an hour of turbulence and woe. But I fear it will not go well for them. I see them standing in the basement yard, holding hands and looking lost. I feel sad. I slowly close the door and give them a little wave to wish them well.

K

I am watching the Roach's door slowly closing and I feel as though a friend is leaving us. The Roach gives a sad little wave and at last I understand—it is on our side.

So I throw myself at the door and I beg it to let us back in.

M

I am a gullible fool, as Mama once said. The girl now wishes to come back in. It is only because of my pact with you who are reading this sorry tale that I agree. I open the door, bow once more and let the annoying creatures back into my home. Immediately the small boy with the vile scrap of fur falls flat on the floor. He stays thankfully silent, but the girl throws herself onto him and begins to emit choking noises.

Once again I lock and bolt the door. *Tick-tick*. So much for a peaceful night.

Chapter 5

BLOOD UPON THE FLOOR

K

The Roach lets us back in and there is something about the expression on his broad, flat features that reminds me of Dad back in the old days, when I'd done something really annoying. We fall back inside the house and Jonno collapses onto the floor and lies so still it frightens me. I drop to my knees beside him and suddenly, embarrassingly, I burst into tears.

The Roach makes *tick-tick* sounds and locks the door. Again.

M

Tick-tick. Now there is a pile of young ones upon my floor and *blood*. So much blood. A joy to a Night Roach no doubt, but not to me. I, Maximillian Fly, have a revulsion to all fluids that you squashy ones exude. Particularly blood. However, I also know my physiology, and I understand that while such a quantity of blood upon my floor may be unpleasant for me, it is dangerous for the person from which it emanates. I suspect the small boy has cut a blood vessel deep inside his foot. This is the disadvantage of being soft on the outside.

Tick-tick. Something must be done.

K.

I am trying to help Jonno and to stop my ridiculous crying when a lantern is lit in the passageway and I hear the Roach's tinny little voice. "Please get up," it says. It sounds so concerned that I feel bad for upsetting it. I manage to get control of the tears and stand up. My legs shake, and I feel as if they will fold under me at any moment. I sway and lean back against the wall and look the Roach in the eye. It returns my gaze and I see concern and puzzlement spiced with a touch of annoyance.

"It is a bad situation," the Roach says. "There is much blood." It waves its antennae and makes the *tick-tick* sound again.

I get the distinct feeling that this Roach is revolted by blood, and maybe even by us. I also get the feeling that out of politeness it is trying not to show it. "I'm sorry," I say. "My brother stepped on some glass and cut his foot."

"*Tick-tick*," the Roach says anxiously. "*Tick-tick.*"

A searchlight beam cuts across the passage. We glance at each other, the Roach and I, and then we look down at the blade of light at our feet.

The Enforcers are back.

M

The Vermin have finished destroying the house next door. They have, naturally, not found what they seek and now they will force their way in here. The girl and I exchange a glance and I am surprised. In that brief moment I believe we understand each other perfectly.

"Please bring your brother upstairs," I say. "Follow me. Quickly."

The brother lies limp upon the floor and she struggles to lift him. She speaks to the brother but there is no response. I steel myself for what must be done. "Allow me," I say. I wrap my three upper limbs around the brother and his foul furry object, and then I pick him up. He is both heavy and soft. Oh, how I detest the dampness of non-carapaced humans.

K

The Roach picks Jonno up! Its wide lipless mouth makes a little twist that looks like revulsion as it sees that Tedward is coming too. Tedward is not a nice bear. He is sticky with blood from Jonno's endless nosebleeds and he smells vile from the time Jonno was sick on him. This has been ideal up until now because it has kept people away from Tedward, but now I feel embarrassed. I follow the Roach and Jonno up a flight of bare wooden stairs. As we reach the bend halfway up, the searchlight beam swings into the passageway below. That was close.

J

I am dreaming that me and Tedward are being carried up to bed by a Roach. It has a bent antenna that tickles my ear.

M

I lose count of how many floors we climb, but at last we reach the very top and I follow the Roach across bare wooden boards of the landing. It pushes open a door with its foot and we go into a small room with beams and a sloping ceiling, which is empty but for a pile of neatly folded blankets in the far corner under the eaves. It is sparse but comfortable, with rugs strewn on the floor and flowery curtains drawn across the window. A swath of goose bumps runs over me: I had those very same curtains in my bedroom at home. I mean, what was home, once. Our real home by the fields.

The Roach waves a pincer at the corner. "Blankets for your brother, please," it says as it gently lays Jonno down on the soft rugs. I fetch some blankets and it carefully covers both Jonno and Tedward with a thick blue tartan one and lays another beneath Jonno's head. The Roach is so tender that I begin to feel tearful again. And then, far below, an enormous bang reverberates up through the house. The Roach and I look at each other. We both know what this means.

The Enforcers are inside.

M

The Vermin have broken into my home—the home that Mama told me that I was not worthy to live in. And now I know that she was right, for I have brought calamity upon it.

The girl speaks. "Please," she says. "*Please help us.*" I am becoming accustomed to her squashy, formless features with her shining gray eyes, and I read the expression well enough. It is fear. I wonder if she can read the fear in my eyes too? My mind races as I desperately try to think of a way of ridding us of these vile Vermin and I find I have an idea. "Your brother's jacket," I say. "And yours. Put blood on both. Hurry."

She understands. She takes the jacket from the brother, who grasps his bear as though he thinks she will take that from him too. I am pleased to see that he will not be parted from it however foul it is, for one must never be parted from one's bear. She pulls off the brother's sodden sock, wrings it out onto the jackets and scrunches them together. I take the jackets. They are revolting but highly satisfactory for my purpose. "I go now," I say. "I will lock the door." I do not do this to protect my fugitives from the Vermin, for it will be useless. I do it because if I succeed in my purpose there will no doubt be some unpleasant sounds that I do not want my young ones to hear. Call it vanity, but I do not wish them to think of me as being no better than a Night Roach.

I turn the key; then I flip my goggles over my eyes and progress down the stairs with dread in my heart. As I descend, the sounds of destruction grow louder, and when I am on the first-floor landing, I hear a noise that is a dagger in my heart. It is the sound of smashing china.

I know exactly what this means—the destruction of the love of Mama's life, her precious collection of Meissen porcelain. I think of the dancing fish teapot, the fruiting clock and the flight of golden cherubs with the shimmering blue wings all smashed to smithereens and I can hardly bear it. I do not think I could kill for my own sake, or even for the sake of my young fugitives, but I will do it for Mama. *I will do it.*

K

The Roach has gone and I feel very afraid for it. I check that our door is locked, even though I know that when the Enforcers reach us it will be no more use than a sheet of paper. I lean back against its flimsy panels. There is nothing more I can do. Our future is in the hands—or the pincers—of a Roach.

But wait. There *is* something I can do.

I tiptoe over to Jonno. He is curled up like a pill bug beneath his tartan blanket, his eyes closed, his face pale and drawn. I give Tedward a gentle tug and he does not react. I feel mean taking advantage but I'm doing this for him too. Very carefully I ease Tedward from his grasp. He gives a little moan and I whisper, "It's all right, Jonno. It's all right." With his hand freed from guarding Tedward, his thumb slips into his mouth and Jonno is a baby again.

Quickly I flip open my pick tool and undo the stitches beneath Tedward's right arm until I've made a hole big enough to push in the long-nose tweezers attachment. Then I find what I am looking for and pull. A heavy, flat silver disc—one side of which is striped with gold bands—emerges. This, Mom told me, is the Disc Key Circuit Breaker—DisK for short. Without it the SilverShip cannot leave the city. And as long as the SilverShip cannot leave, Jonno and I and all our SilverSeed crewmates are safe.

The DisK lies heavy in my palm and I get a weird feeling in my stomach as I realize that Mom was the last person to hold it. It was Mom who stole it, Mom who hid it in Tedward by replacing his growler, and the stitches I have just unpicked are hers. In fact, sewing these stitches was pretty much the last thing Mom ever did. I gaze at the DisK, trying to find an echo of her, but all I feel is the faint buzz of its charge. Mom is gone.

Chapter 6

SHARDS

M

I, Maximillian Fly, stand at the top of my basement stairs and look down at the Vermin. I see two. At first glance they look quite charming: they have obliterated their Wingless squishiness by wearing a carapace of iridescent CarboNet armor, and a feature-flattening visor encases their heads and turns them into smooth ovoids. But their actions fail to charm. One is still in Mama's porcelain store and I can hear the silvery smash of china. It is unbearable.

The other two Vermin are swarming up the stairs. The one in front carries the searchlight, the next the net. They are so intent upon their foulness that they do not see me waiting in the shadows at the top. I raise my wings above my head in the classic Night Roach threat stance and the movement catches their eye.

They look up and they freeze. I know that all they see is the glint from my goggles and my shape. The front Vermin drops the searchlight and we all listen to it clattering down my stairs and rolling onto the stone flags below. I cannot see the expressions of horror beneath their visors, but I know they are there. Which is most gratifying. The one with the net recovers first. I suspect it is a female—they are more fearless. It pushes forward, up the stairs. "Stand aside," it says. But it is not as brave as it appears. Through its electronic voice-screen I hear the constriction of fear in the back of its throat.

The third Vermin emerges from Mama's china cupboard and stops dead, taking in the scene. There is a brief silence and then it screams. Its voice-screen changes the scream to something unearthly and I seize my moment. I raise my arms and wave the bloodied shirts in front of me and then I launch them into the air. The netter snatches them up and I hope the Vermin will leave. But they do not. The netter stuffs the shirts into the bag that hangs from its waist belt and they all stay put, staring up at me—they have seen that I am not a Night Roach after all. Now it is not going to be so easy.

So I must raise the game. I take a step down toward them and they mirror me with a step backward. Another step down, another step back. And another. I become suspicious: their movements are too practiced. This is some kind of maneuver.

K

A scream comes from below. High and thin, like a slipped note on a flute, it pierces the air. It's the Roach, I know it is. I remember how Tomas told me he once saw one cornered by some Enforcers. They pulled its arms off and it screamed like the kettle we used over the illegal fire. I can't bear to think about the Roach losing its arms, I really can't. But I must, as Mom used to say, stay focused. I must hide the DisK. Because any minute now the Enforcers will be trashing the house, looking for us.

But the room is so empty. I don't know where to hide it. I panic and shove the DisK deep into the pile of blankets beneath the eaves and hope that Mom would think I've done the right thing. It will be fine there, I tell myself. Once they've got us, they won't be looking for anything else.

M

The netter gives a high-pitched whistle and suddenly all three are running at me like rats. I am glad of this attack, for I do not want you, my young watcher, to think that I kill without provocation. I drop down into the fight stance. I take my stiletto dagger from its sheath beneath my underwings and then I make the noise that all Wingless ones fear. I hiss.

The hiss of a Roach is a distressing frequency, but I suspect the Vermin have earplugs, for they do not react. The netter pulls a long, thin dart from a holster at its waist and throws it at me, aiming at the vulnerable segment gap between my abdomen and thorax. It is a deadly throw. I turn just in time. The dart flies through my inner underwing and lands point down into the floor, where it stays, quivering.

Please note that I now act in self-defense.

The Vermin are gathering for the kill. They expect success. Of course they do. I look fragile, I clatter, my upper limbs are stick-thin and, yes, you can easily twist them off if you get the angle right. However, I have a surprising strength and I am not afraid to use it. I advance down the stairs at high speed and throw my weight against the two forward Vermin; they fall against the banisters and there is a sharp splintering of wood. I half leap, half glide, down the remaining steps targeting the despoiler of Mama's china. It understands the score and once more it screams in terror. That is the last sound it makes.

I am upon it. My weight slams it to the floor and I

ease my stiletto blade into the join in its armor plates under its left armpit. I push downward. It is done. Silent and clean. And, as yet, no blood. Mama's floor is free of effluent, though strewn with a thousand glittering shards of porcelain. I pull the blade out and wipe it on the CarboNet. I get to my feet and turn to see the remaining two Vermin staring at our little tableau.

The ex–searchlight holder says to the netter, "Get out, get out!"

The netter demurs. "But we haven't got them."

"Because the Roach already had them. You've got the shirts. It's proof."

"Not enough," says the netter.

I decide they can discuss the finer points of their nasty little mission elsewhere. I raise my wings and advance upon them with my stiletto. They turn and run, racing out of my wrecked door, which hangs broken upon its hinges. I look back along the passageway and see the dead Vermin lying across the threshold of Mama's storeroom. The Vermin is now leaking blood. I sigh: yet another human to clear up after. So much . . . seepage.

I drag it out to Thin Murk and return to my despoiled home.

I need a dust bath.

K

It's been silent now for ages. But I'm ready. And now I can hear footsteps on the stairs. *They're coming for us.*

I flip open my combi-tool and a blade glints in the moonlight. I flatten myself against the wall, waiting. I hate these people. I hate them for what they've done to what was once my family. I know I won't win, but I'll get one of them if I possibly can.

M

I drag myself up the last flight of stairs to the attic, where my next batch of trouble resides—the young Wingless ones who have brought misfortune and woe to my door. But do not fear for them, for I know this situation is of my own making. It was I who took them into my house. It was not they who forced their way in and it was not they who destroyed Mama's precious collection. It is not *their* fault. I must remember that. I am a good creature. Not bad. *Tick-tick.*

I reach the top landing. I pause to prepare myself, and then I move toward the room where the young ones are hidden. I unlock the door and push it open. It is oddly silent. The brother lies where I left him, eyes closed, clutching the bear, but of his sister there is no sign. I take a step forward and suddenly I see a flash of steel coming toward me—it is a knife and attached to its handle is the female. This is treachery most foul. I throw myself backward, out of the door, away from the blade, I lose my footing and find that I am rolling down the stairs. As I bounce from step to step, I consider both the perfidy of the Wingless and my own foolishness.

K

Oh my days. It was the Roach. *I stabbed the Roach.* No, no, *no*!

I race down the stairs. The Roach is lying on the landing below, rolled into a cylinder of carapace. This must be what a Roach does when it's dead. *I've killed it.* I kneel beside it and stroke its smooth, iridescent wings. They feel nice, like warm plastic. "I am sorry," I whisper. "I am so, so sorry. I didn't know it was you. I thought it was *them*. I never wanted to hurt you. *Never.*"

I think of Mom, Dad and Tomas: all gone in their different ways. I think of Jonno upstairs bleeding because I made him take his shoes off and now the Roach is dead on the floor and we all know why that is. I find I'm crying *again*. My tears drop onto the beautiful indigo carapace and run down its delicate grooves.

M

I lie in my shield position and hope the girl will go away. And then yet more fluid, warm and salty, comes trickling into the gaps in my carapace and seeps into my cut underwings. It is unbearable. I uncurl.

K

The Roach is alive! Without thinking, I throw my arms around it and I feel it flinch as though I have hit it. I rock back on my heels and I apologize over and over. I tell it I thought it was an Enforcer. I tell it how scared I was. And then I ask if I hurt it. The Roach shakes its head; then very slowly it gets to its feet and walks laboriously up the stairs. I follow. Its back has a look of resignation and I push away an image of how Dad looked as he waved Mom off to work that last night. Memories make no sense anymore.

M

As I painfully climb back up the stairs I know I have a decision to make. Do I throw the young fugitives out of my house and return my life to its peaceful, well-ordered ways? That will be worse for them but better for me. Or do I let them stay and disrupt my life still further? That will be better for them but, oh, so much worse for me.

How I wish I had not set upon this ridiculous course to prove to you my goodness. Why should I care what you think of me?

Enough of this.

They must go.

Chapter 7

THE DisK

K,

I climb the stairs behind a cross carapace and I know that what I have done is what Dad used to call a "deal-breaker." I follow the Roach's resentfully folded wings into the attic room and I see Jonno huddled beneath the blankets, his face taut with pain. I know there is no way he will survive a night outside in the city. I hear the Roach's *tick-tick* sound—which I am beginning to understand is a mixture of anxiety and annoyance—and I know it is about to tell us to go. I have a split second to get in first and say something that will change its mind. But what?

It is the flowery curtains that do it. From somewhere deep in my memory I hear Dad reading me a story called *The Gentle Roach.* I remember that in the story the Roaches used strangely formal language and greeted one another with their hands crossed over their abdomen combined with a small bow of the head. So that is what I do. I cross my hands over my SilverShip sweatshirt and give a respectful bow of my head. When I dare to look up, I see two sparkling gray eyes regarding me with a bemused expression. Quickly, before the Roach has a chance to tell us to leave, I say in what I hope is a suitably formal way, "No words can express how sorry I am for my actions. I am devastated to have caused you pain. From the bottom of my heart I thank you for saving me and my brother. We will always be in your debt. My name is Kaitlin Drew and I am honored to have met you." Then I bow my head.

M

I have a book. It is called *The Gentle Roach*. On the inside page it says: *To Maximillian with love from his papa*. No one has ever spoken to me like this before. I am quite discombobulated. *Tick-tick*.

K

There is no reply. I risk a glance up at the Roach and see it looking at me in bewilderment. It makes another *tick-tick* sound, but it does not speak. I am desperate for a response, so I bow yet again. "I know we have brought trouble to your door," I say, "but I would be eternally grateful if you would allow us to remain here tonight."

Tick-tick is the only response.

It's not looking good. With my heart pounding in my ears I wait for the Roach to pronounce sentence on us. I watch Jonno's blanket rise and fall as his breath comes fast and sharp with pain and I hear the Roach's tinny little cough. I look up into its flat, sloping face and try to read its expression, but it isn't giving anything away. And then, echoing what I have done, it crosses its top limbs over its thorax and folds its single middle limb neatly below, as one would hold an arm in a sling. It gives a low, slow bow, then straightens up and begins to speak.

"I, Maximillian Fly, bid you welcome to my home." It pauses and then adds, "For tonight."

Tears of relief rush into my eyes and I bow my head to hide them.

"The blood," the tinny voice continues, "must be stopped."

I look up, unsure if this is a condition for us staying or if the Roach—I mean, Maximillian—is concerned for Jonno.

Maximillian answers my question. "It is dangerous for a small person to bleed so much," he says patiently, as though I don't understand that bleeding is bad. "Therefore I will bring the necessaries." I watch him walk out of the room, his wings still neatly folded but now, it seems to me, in a more relaxed fashion. I sit down with a thump beside Jonno, feeling as floppy as Tedward with his DisK gone.

Maximillian returns with a red box and very gravely hands it to me. Inside are all the usual first aid things plus a few bits and pieces I don't recognize. I make myself look at Jonno's foot. It is worse than I expect; there is a sliver of glass stuck deep into his heel. I grit my teeth and pull it out with tweezers. Jonno yelps and gloops of blood ooze onto the floor. Out of the corner of my eye, I see Maximillian shudder—I think he is trying not to be sick—and he passes me a cloth that smells of spirit. I clean Jonno's foot with it and then Maximillian hands me a roll of thin but strong transparent tape. I pull the edges of the wound together, crisscross it with tape and then, under Maximillian's instructions, I raise Jonno's foot up and press hard on his heel. Jonno yelps like a puppy but he lets me do it, and at last his foot stops bleeding.

J

It's gone. The glass in my foot has gone. It's got tape all over it and the Roach brought the tape. His head touched the ceiling and his antenna got stuck in a crack in a beam.

K

Maximillian Fly bows and tells me that he is going now. He has, he says, an important meeting to attend but he will be back later. I bow in return and wish him a pleasant night. And then he is gone.

And now I am kneeling at the attic window, the DisK safely in my hand, and I am looking out onto the night world of our city. It must be a clear night Outside because beyond the haze I think I can see the fuzzy bright blob of the moon. Sometimes I wonder what the sky would look like if we did not have the Orb protecting us from the deadly Contagion Outside. I think it would be wonderful not to be trapped beneath a huge force field, however good for us it may be.

The Orb makes the fog fall every night, but it is late today and I can still see a landscape of rooftops spread before me, shining in the dampness like the wings of a Roach. This part of the city is near the center. The houses are tall and the street below—the Inner Circle—is wide, with its borders home to a good crop of spinach. Most of the houses are empty now, but people still use them to grow food. I can see potatoes sprouting in sacks hanging from windows opposite, green things like broccoli and kale in wall boxes and even strawberries hanging down from the gutters. We learn about seasons at school, but there aren't any beneath the Orb; fruit and plants grow whenever they want to.

Last year, when we were still a family, we lived on the edge of Hope in a tiny cottage next to a farm. We had fields at the back all the way out to the foot of the Orb and we had a garden where we—well, Dad mostly—grew all kinds of stuff. I grew carrots and even Jonno liked those.

I stare into the darkness trying to figure out where our old house would be, but it's hard to tell. In the distance I can just make out the soaring, elegant shapes of the skylons—masts that create the force field for the Orb—on the edge of the city. We lived near skylon number three, but they all look the same, so there's no way of knowing which one was ours.

I'm trying not to look at the Bartizan tower, but it is hard to ignore, sticking up so high, black and misshapen like a rotten tooth. It was once the city's water tower and was something to be proud of because it gave everyone fresh water drawn from the artesian wells deep beneath the chalk on which we are built. But now we have to take our water from the street pumps—if we can get it—while the Guardian of the city lurks at the top of the Bartizan tower in luxury and watches us, day and night. The Bartizan has its own skylon on the roof, which I can see rising up so high that its tip is hidden in the haze. It is there, in the control panel of that skylon, that this DisK belongs. Mom sacrificed her life to get hold of it, and now I have to make her sacrifice worthwhile. The thought of Mom draws my gaze back to the line of lighted windows that run around the top of the Bartizan. I don't want to look, but I can't help it. Because one of those windows is where they throw the Astros off.

Suddenly the ghostly white shape of a Night Roach glides by the window, so close that I can see the green glint off its big compound eyes. I duck down, terrified. They say that Night Roaches are created by the Bartizan to make us afraid of going out at night, but being indoors is no protection. Night Roaches break through windows and take children from their beds. It happened to a house along the alley after we went into hiding. I can still remember the sound of breaking glass. And the screams.

I pull the flowery curtains closed and tiptoe over to Jonno. I put my hand on his forehead like Mom used to do when we were ill. I don't really know what I'm feeling for, but his skin is dry and cool, which surely is a good thing. I check his foot and it is clear of blood and the tape is secure. The attic room feels quiet and peaceful and I think about how lucky we are to be here still. I wrap myself up in the pile of blankets under the eaves and lean back against the wall, my head jammed under the sloping ceiling. The DisK lies heavy in my hand. It is a little buzzy as though it is alive, and I don't want to let go of it because it makes me feel close to Mom. As I snuggle deeper into the blankets I realize that this is the first time I've felt safe for a whole, long year. And then I think about what happened a year ago, the day after my birthday, when everything fell apart. . . .

It was late in the evening when my older brother, Tomas, had a huge fight with Mom and Dad. He stormed out and he didn't come back. And then, in the early hours of that morning, Mom and Dad woke me and Jonno up. They led us out into the night fog, through the silent streets to a horrible house by the solid waste works. Dad had the key to two rooms in the basement. This, he told us, was to be our new home from now on, but he wouldn't tell us why.

It was awful in that basement. Jonno and I were not allowed out at all. Jonno caught a cold and grizzled pretty much all the time and no matter how much I asked Mom and Dad what was going on, they refused to tell me. And Tomas never came back.

Mom just carried on working as usual. She did night shifts as a nurse in the Bartizan hospital—the only hospital in the city. It was for Bartizan people only, of course. Mom didn't like working there but it was, she said, a good job and we needed the money. But each night she left I was afraid she would never come home. I think Dad was too.

I'll never forget the last few hours in that sad basement.

I woke up in the middle of the night to the sound of Dad playing a lament on his flute. It sounded so, so lonely. I must have gone back to sleep because the next thing I remember Mom was home and tiptoeing over to Jonno's bed. I watched her very gently take Tedward—only Mom could have done that without waking Jonno—and then creep out. I went back to sleep and when I woke up again Tedward was back with Jonno.

There was a weird atmosphere that morning. Dad was really jumpy and Mom seemed kind of crazily excited. Later, while Dad was doing reading practice with Jonno in the kitchen, Mom took me aside. She told me that Tedward was a very special bear and that if something happened to her, I must be sure to look after him.

I felt so angry. "You're treating me like a baby," I told her. "Just like you did with Tomas. Mom, you have to tell me what's going on. Dad was so worried last night that he was playing the lament."

"Oh," Mom said, biting her bottom lip like she always does—I mean, did—when she was really upset.

"And now," I said, "you come back from work in a really weird mood and I just *know* something scary has happened and all you do is *tell me to look after Jonno's stupid bear.*"

Mom put her head on one side and looked at me for what felt like forever. "Katie," she said at last. "This is dangerous knowledge. Are you sure you want to know it?"

I nodded.

And so Mom told me. Everything. She told me that the only way to open the Orb was with what she called a Disc Key, DisK for short. There was only one of them now and it was kept in the Guardian's office at the top of the Bartizan—*and six hours ago she had stolen it.*

I was so shocked I couldn't speak.

Mom shrugged. "There was a party on the top floor. We nurses were being used as waitresses, can you imagine? Your father knew what I was planning to do. And I did it. I got the DisK and now it is inside Tedward instead of his growler."

"Jonno won't like that," I said. "He and Tedward growl at each other a lot nowadays."

Mom smiled. "I'm sure Jonno can easily growl for two," she said.

Once Mom had started telling me things, she didn't stop—even though I soon wished she would. I couldn't believe what I was hearing.

She told me that the DisK operated the Bartizan skylon and that was how the Orb was opened. She said that now she had the DisK, this was exactly what she and some others were going to do: open the Orb. Forever. "Soon, Katie," she said, her eyes shining with excitement, "we will set our city free."

"Mom, you can't be serious," I said. "The Orb is our protection. We'll all die of the Contagion."

Mom shook her head and put her finger to her lips. "That's what they tell you, but it's not true." I stared at Mom, stunned. I knew some people had weird ideas about getting rid of the Orb, but I didn't know Mom was one of them. How could she be so stupid? But she just carried on, telling me her crazy plans. And then she finished up by saying, "So make sure you look after Tedward, Katie, because he is carrying our freedom."

I felt really angry. There we were, on the run, living in that smelly dump and all, it seemed to me, because of Mom's stupid obsession about the Orb. "You're telling me you've messed up our lives because of some ridiculous, crackpot idea. That stinks," I told her. "It really *stinks*." And then I stormed out into the other room and slammed the door. Hard.

A few minutes later there was a quiet knock on the door and Mom said, "Katie? Katie? Can I come in?" And I told her to go away. Oh, I so wish I hadn't. Because five minutes later, Mom did go away. Forever.

And now, here I am, alone with this DisK and I'm using it for the exact opposite of what Mom intended—I'm hiding it so that no one can ever open the Orb again. So the SilverShip will never leave and all our crew will stay safe. And even if they won't set us free at least we won't be sent out like canaries in a cage to test the air—which we all know is full of the Contagion.

So I'm sorry, Mom, but I have to do what I think is right. And at least I've kept your DisK safe.

Chapter 8

FRIENDSHIP

M

I, Maximillian Fly, fly into the night. Through my precious green goggles, I see the darkness of the city spread beneath me. I think how beautiful the city must have looked before the Orb was created. They say Hope was vibrant and well cared for then, but since it has been cut off from the Outside world, it has become frozen in time, fading like an old photograph. Sometimes I feel as though Hope is slowly dying.

I glide over the rooftops—a sea of patched and battered carapaces shining with drizzle—and I breathe in the smell of the houses below—earthiness of vegetation and moldering brick and the faint sharpness of metal. There was a time, they say, when the odor of the Wingless after the rain was strong, but the SilverShip has taken so many away that the city is half-empty now and no more than a stale aura lingers above some of the roofs—the better-tended ones, I must admit. We who are Roach are not good on house maintenance.

I fly fast, alert for hostile movement, for I am uncomfortably close to the old grain silo, where there is a Night Roach Chapter—the name the Bartizan gives to the Night Roach roosts and nurseries. There are two Night Roach Chapters in this city—the Silos and the Steeples. My new friend, Parminter Wing, lives near the Steeples and I live near the Silos, which makes for interesting visits at times.

Something tells me that you, my inquisitive watcher, live in a place without Night Roaches. How lucky you are, for they are abominations that prey upon Wingless and Roach alike. Indeed, you may wonder why I risk flying so close to these predators tonight? Normally I would have taken the Underground, but due to the earlier, er . . . events to which you have been witness, I do not have enough time.

I am on my way to a meeting of the Friendship Society, an illegal mixed group of both Roach and Wingless people, whose aim is to promote understanding between us. Parminter introduced me some months ago. She told me I needed to meet people and she was, of course, right. To be truthful, I find most of them a little intense, but I have made a good friend, Andronicus, in whose house the meeting is tonight, and I am looking forward to seeing both him and Parminter. But, oh dear, I am so very late. . . .

So, young watcher, you are still here? Still watching? Well, I will describe to you how it is to fly. I know it is something that you Wingless ones would love to do and I suspect it is the only thing you envy us who are Roach. The air is cold now and as I stretch out my wings to their fullness I feel the chill creeping into me. I wish I had worn my flight vest, but with the events of the evening, I quite forgot it. So my carapace is bare and all I have on are my Roach leggings. And my beautiful night-sight goggles of course, which are made for those foolish Wingless who wish to venture out at night. They say you can see a Night Roach twenty yards into the fog with these, and considering that Night Roaches are the same color as the fog, that is impressive. I was very lucky to find them lying in a gutter. Someone will be missing them, I am sure.

I fly steadily on through the chill air, which is expectant and still as it waits for the night fog to descend. I have my wings spread wide and I am gliding about twenty feet above the rooftops and all around me I see the pallid haze of the Orb—the globe of the force field beneath which our city is trapped. Beyond the Orb they say there are the moon and stars—indeed, I have seen pictures of them—but all we can see down here is a faint fuzz of light. I long to see the moon clearly; it must be wonderful to have another world shining down upon you. And stars too, although I do not understand how there can be distant suns that show themselves as just a pinpoint of light in the sky. Indeed they say there are so many stars that in olden times people joined the shapes they formed and made pictures and stories from them. I am not sure that I believe in stars, but I do believe in the moon because tonight I can see the mysterious glow of something white and round beyond the Orb.

I am suddenly recalled from my dreaming by the glimpse of movement upon a chimney pot. I look again and a flash of compound green eyes shining out from a looming whiteness tell all—it is a Night Roach. *You fool, Maximillian*, Mama's voice says inside my head. *Always taking the shortcuts. Never thinking things through.* I wheel away and commence a dive, but I am too late. The great pale wings of the Night Roach rise up into the attack stance. This is bad. I am not in good condition: I am stiff from the fall down the stairs and my torn underwing diminishes my speed.

I cannot outfly it. I must hide.

I alight under the arch of a recessed window on the top floor of one of the older houses. It is deep shadow with a wide ledge but it is not as ideal as it appears, for I smell Wingless ones inside. However, the curtains are drawn and I hear sleep noises. If I am quiet they will never know I am here. I settle on the ledge and lean back against the window, taking care not to rattle the panes. I fold myself into my wing cases to shield my goggles and stop the Night Roach picking up their reflections.

I listen anxiously for the swish of wings, but I hear only snoring and drips from a broken gutter. However after some minutes I detect a noise on the roof above. It is nothing much: a light, scratchy shuffle; but I know what it is. It is the sound of wingtip upon slate. I know what has happened—the Night Roach can smell blood on me. And now it is no more than three feet above my foolish head, roosting and waiting . . . for *me*.

Frozen in panic, I huddle upon the window ledge. Drips from the gutter find their way into my underwings, and I fear that if they get much wetter I will not be able to fly at all. I feel despair creeping upon me. I do not want to end my life in the Night Roach Silo. I wonder how my young fugitives will fare when I do not return, and strangely the thought of them lessens my panic. I remember how they behaved when they were cornered and I now admire how calm they were. The girl methodically checked all escape routes and the little boy stayed silent even though he was hurt. As my dear friend Andronicus would say, they kept their cool. And so must I. I must also hope that something rescues me, as I rescued them. But in my head I hear Mama's voice saying, *You are a fool, Maximillian. Who will rescue a disgusting Roach squatting upon a window ledge*?

I sense a change in the air: a chill, a soft silence. And now I see that I do indeed have a rescuer: the night fog. It falls fast and within minutes its tendrils curl around me like a white blanket. I drop from the ledge like a stone and I am away, flying for my life.

I can find my way to the house of Andronicus with my eyes closed. This is fortunate, for tonight the fog is making up for its tardiness with a choking thickness. I land awkwardly upon the roof, misjudge the chimney pot and send it bouncing down the tiles. This is not my first encounter with Andronicus's roof furniture and I fear he will hear the smash on the pavement far below. Andronicus is a sensitive person and I do not wish to add to his troubles. Ah, young watcher, I sense you assuming that, because I called him a person, Andronicus looks just like you. But he does not. My dearest friend is Roach like me. We may look different from you now, but we are human-born and consider ourselves to be as much a person as you consider your squashy, noisy and emotional self to be.

I recover my footing and hurriedly give the coded knock upon the skylight. I am surprised—and not particularly pleased—when Cassius Crane pushes up the trapdoor and looks out with a sour face that reminds me of Mama. "Maximillian," he says severely, "you are late. Extremely late."

"For which, Cassius Crane, I am sorry," I say. "However, I have an explanation. I pray you, let me in."

But Cassius does not let me in. "The meeting is almost over," he says. "There is no point to you coming in now." Beneath Cassius I can see the warm yellow light of the attic room with its soft rugs and the dark forms of the group sitting in a circle. Not one attempts to countermand Cassius and I am surprised. I would have expected Parminter to object.

I am clinging to the roof tiles like a bat. I think of the Night Roach and wonder if it can track me by the smell of blood. I suspect it can. "For pity's sake, Cassius, let me in," I say. "I am in considerable danger out here."

Cassius, nasty pie-weasel on stilts that he is, makes one of his sneering smiles. "Dear Maximillian, always the drama queen." He pauses. "You stink."

I am shocked. These are strong words.

Cassius sniffs loudly and I brace myself for what is coming. "Blood. Fresh blood. You stink of it."

"Cassius, it is not what you think," I say.

"Oh, that's what they all say," he replies. "And yet in my experience it always is *exactly* what one thinks. Go away, Maximillian Fly, you are not soiling our meeting with your stink." To my horror, he begins to close the skylight.

"No!" I scream with my body and the air squeals through my carapace like a jet of steam. *"Noooooo!"*

I am indeed a fool: now every Night Roach within miles will know where I am. Surely Cassius must realize that? But he continues to close the skylight as I cling on, watching the edge of the hatch descend toward my hands. One inch above my distal metacarpals it is abruptly stopped. It is lifted up and the face of dear Andronicus appears. He looks strained. "Maximillian," he says tersely. "Come inside."

I need no further invitation. I drop in through the skylight and land lightly upon the floor. I rearrange my wings and look around. I do not like what I see.

There is a Vermin on the carpet.

The Vermin is crouched in the center of the meeting circle. Its attitude reminds me of young Kaitlin, who not so long ago was similarly at bay upon my doormat. I note the Vermin's sleek form encased in its armor, which is a striking iridescent blue-green like a carapace wing. It is, however, marred by the absence of the visor, which has been pulled off to show a damp, squashy face topped by a tangle of dark brown hair. The Vermin looks up at me and I see the same fear in its eyes as I did in my Kaitlin's. I am somewhat shocked to see that its shoulders are torn and there is blood trickling down its CarboNet suit. Cassius seems to have no problem with *this* stink of blood. I stare at the thick patches of congealing red, evenly placed just below each collarbone. The only explanation for this is that the Vermin has recently been carried in the talons of a Night Roach.

I take my empty place next to Andronicus and am disappointed to see that Parminter is not here tonight. I hope she is all right. Her journey here is not without its dangers. Andronicus whispers to me, "The Vermin fell through the open skylight while we were waiting for you, Maximillian. Be aware that Cassius therefore blames you for this situation."

I flash my friend a quick glance of thanks for the warning and direct my gaze to the Vermin. It is now that I see, stuck to the top of its smooth and shiny foot, a tiny sliver of porcelain that shines a brilliant turquoise—the exact color of the wings of Mama's darling cherubs. I cannot help myself. I jump to my feet and hiss at it. The Vermin whimpers.

Cassius laughs. "Be quiet, Maximillian. You're not impressing anyone. We have made our decision about the prisoner. We will implement it forthwith."

"Objection!" Andronicus says. My dear friend may be short in stature, but he has a substantial voice and it stops Cassius's little whine most effectively. "We have made no such decision," Andronicus continues. "For there is one member of our meeting who has not voted." All eyes including those of the Vermin—which I notice are a glittering gray awash with fear—turn to me.

"Maximillian is not part of this meeting," Cassius replies. "He arrived after Greeting and is therefore supernumerary."

Andronicus turns to me, his brown eyes twinkling with mischief. "Maximillian Fly, I *Greet* thee."

I reply quickly before Cassius can interrupt: "Andronicus Thrip, I Greet thee." Cassius emits a hiss of anger but there is nothing he can do. He has been outplayed.

I now discover the nature of the decision my friends have made and I am shocked. They have voted to deliver the Vermin as a peace offering to the Night Roach Silo. The vote was even: two for and two against, leaving the decision with Cassius, who is our convener for tonight. But now Andronicus wishes to run the vote again. This is because he knows that I, like him, believe that all life is of value and he thinks I will vote to save the Vermin. Ah, but he does not have a splinter of blue to consider.

I look at the Vermin crouched upon the floor, its meaty, bloody hands straying up to its shoulders despite trying not to. I see that it is trembling and I understand that I am being asked to vote for murder. I also realize with dismay that two of this group must have already done so. Clearly Andronicus did not, so was it Marilla, Titus or Besander? Marilla and Titus are both Wingless and yet at least one of them must have voted to sacrifice one of their own kind. Times are strange indeed. But now Cassius is irritably calling another vote and my question is answered. The limbs of Marilla and Besander are raised for the killing. I look at them with disapproval, but they avoid my gaze. And then I vote with Andronicus and Titus against the killing. There is a clear majority now and thus Cassius is denied his casting vote.

I suspect that you may well be muttering that I have already killed one Vermin tonight, so why the scruples now? But I killed to defend myself and two young ones just like you. This situation is very different. This has the nasty whiff of enjoyment about it—except Cassius is clearly not enjoying it anymore.

"Meeting closed," Cassius snaps. He turns to Andronicus and waves his hand at the Vermin. "Your problem now, Andronicus Thrip. *You* get rid of it, and I suggest you make sure it can never identify this place *where you live*." He smirks. "Good luck with that."

I see the sudden understanding of the situation clouding the face of Andronicus.

Cassius throws the ladder against the skylight and turns to us all with a mocking smile. "Losers," he says, and then in a light and fluid movement—Cassius is an agile Roach—he is out on the roof and gone. He does not have far to go, for he roosts in an attic three houses away.

Avoiding our gaze, Marilla silently climbs the ladder, her large brown boots clumping up the rungs. She is quickly followed by Besander and they leave together, Besander giving her a fly-lift back to her home near the northern skylon. Titus, a young Wingless man with a wispy beard, now excuses himself. His wife is waiting for him and she worries. He lives at the most distant end of the Underground and has a long trek ahead. Titus gives a quick bow of farewell, which we return, and he hurries away, light-footed down the stairs.

This leaves Andronicus and me alone with the Vermin. "Bother," Andronicus mutters. "Bother, bother, bother."

We look down at the Vermin and it returns our gaze with an insolent stare. It knows it has won.

Chapter 9

THE VERMIN

T

I, the so-called Vermin, have won. If you can call it that. Because actually, I am dead. It is only a matter of time. My first command is a failed mission: At least one SilverSeed is dead and very likely both. I have one crew fatality for sure and very possibly two, because the last I saw of my second-in-command she was being flown off to the Silo. We were snatched by a hunting pair of Night Roaches and I was extremely fortunate to be able to make my abductor drop me—albeit into this nest of vipers. Somehow I have to get out of here. But not through the skylight. I've had enough of heights for one night. I've got to get down to the streets. And then I've got to get lucky.

I stay crouched on the rug trying to get my strength back while the two remaining Roaches stare at me, their creepily thin arms folded. They have no idea what to do next, which is good because I'm in no state to do anything right now. I'm shaking and I can't stop. I'm sweating and I feel sick. I want . . . oh, this is crazy talk but . . . I want . . . *I want Mom.* I want her to walk into the room and scoop me up and tell me it was all a bad dream. But Mom's never ever going to do that again, is she? I am here alone: a killer about to be killed. How did this happen?

I need to stop shaking. I really, really need to stop. Right now.

M

I look down to see the frightened yet calculating eyes of the Vermin watching us. It is shivering, but even so I fear that any second now it will spring to its feet and be away. And then we will be betrayed and very soon we shall be dead. And in this "we" I include my young ones back home.

Andronicus draws me out onto the landing. "What do we do?" he whispers. "It can't stay here. Not with Minna downstairs." Minna is the sister of Andronicus. She moved in with him a few months ago as his self-appointed "caregiver" and is a nosy, unpleasant Wingless woman. I think she bullies him, but he will not say a bad word about her.

"It will betray us if we let it go," I tell him. I sigh. It is true what Mama once said: I am an ill-starred Roach. I have brought trouble to my dear friend's house. I look down at Andronicus; I see his drooping antennae and a deep line creased into the smooth hard skin between his eyes and I know what I must do. "I'll take it home," I whisper. "With me."

Andronicus stares at me, his trusting brown eyes wide with surprise. "A Vermin? In your house?" he asks. "But what about . . . *you know who*?"

He means Mama. "She has been gone over a year now," I tell him. "I've seen her once about six months ago. She said then that she would never see me again."

The frown has not left Andronicus. "But you said that she has come secretly in the night. To visit her pots."

"*Porcelain*," I correct him. "The finest in the city." Or it was.

Andronicus looks at me with pity. His views on Mama echo mine on his sister, Minna. We have agreed not to speak of either. "Andronicus," I say, "I must confess to you that the Vermin is in your house as a result of actions that earlier this evening I misguidedly took in my own house."

"Whatever do you mean?" he asks.

"I will come to you tomorrow and tell all. But for now I will take the Vermin. Trust me. It will not betray us."

Andronicus gives me a strange look. I believe he thinks I plan to kill it. "Take care, Maximillian," he says. "I worry about you, you know."

I sigh. I worry about me too.

T

They are discussing me with tinny whispers. And now I understand what they have decided: the big one is going to kill me.

It will have to catch me first.

I am up and running at them. I take them by surprise, throwing them aside and have the pleasure of hearing their carapaces clatter against the wall. I hear a sharp *oof* of surprise from the large one and then I am away, heading for the stairs. I am nearly there, when of all the stupid things, I trip over the rug and go sprawling facedown upon the floor. I lie winded and weak, and as I feel the weight of the two Roaches upon me, I know there is no more I can do.

Suddenly a woman's voice, suspicious and querulous, calls from below. "Andronicus? Whatever is going on up there?"

The small Roach replies, "Nothing, Minna. We just tripped over the, er, rug. It's fine."

This Minna is my salvation. "Help!" I yell, but I am

cut short by a vile Roach hand placed firmly over my mouth.

"It doesn't sound fine," Minna calls. "I'm coming up."

"No! I mean, no thank you, Minna. It's totally fine. Honestly," the lying little toad called Andronicus shouts down in panic. "Maxie, er, he's going home now. He sends his love."

I hear a soft hiss of disgust from the large Roach.

There is now a hushed discussion between them. I cannot understand it all, but the upshot of it is the large one remains sitting on me, and the smaller one goes off to find something. It returns and they roll me over, pull my arms in front of me and secure my wrists with a fine cord. It is sharp and thin and it cuts into me. I close my eyes so I do not have to look into their ugly Roach faces. They put a gag around my mouth and I feel the busyness of pincers brushing against me, efficient and fast as they wind the cord around my body, pinning my elbows to my sides. There is a tug upon the cord and a tinny voice says, "Get up."

I keep my eyes shut and I don't move. I hear a *tick-tick* sound, more whispering, and then the deep-voiced Roach voice says, somewhat impatiently, "Of course it's not *dead*." The cord is tugged hard and I feel Roach breath upon my face and words hissed in my ear. "But you *will* be if you do not get up." I feel a cold point of metal upon my neck. "I shall count to three," the voice says. "One, two, thr—"

I get up as fast as it is possible with my arms pinioned and then I see that what I thought was a blade is just a key. *Idiot*, I think. The Roaches look at me. The weird thing is, their eyes are oddly human and the expression within them is all too recognizable—it is disgust.

"Listen to me, Vermin," says the small Roach with the surprisingly rich voice. "You will go with this person here." It points to the large, ungainly Roach with the crooked antenna who holds the end of my cord. "You will be safe provided you do exactly as you are told. Do you understand?"

I understand that they are not going to kill me just yet, which is enough for now. I nod. I hope that maybe I will meet this Minna, who is clearly suspicious of these Roaches, and she will help me. I look up into the eyes of the tall Roach and it pulls a pair of night-sight goggles over them with a snap of elastic. A blind glint of green like that of a Night Roach stares back at me. A cold shiver goes through me.

I follow the Roach down a succession of stairs all the way to the basement, where the small Roach stands guard at the kitchen door, behind which this Minna is busy clattering pots and plates. There is a hatch set into the floorboards and the smaller Roach hooks a stick around its ring and pulls it open. The large Roach slips down into the darkness and a tug on my leash tells me I must go too. Minna has heard nothing and my chance is gone. With the small Roach close behind me, I stumble down steep wooden steps into the darkness of a cellar, where the large Roach stops and sends two green beams of light out from his goggles. I see we are at an archway with a high, barred gate across it. The small Roach swings open the gate and the tall Roach goes forward into a wide, brick-lined passageway, dragging me like a dog on a leash. The gate clangs shut behind us, like the doors of the Oblivion cells beneath the Bartizan. I never liked that sound and I like it even less now I'm on the wrong side of it.

And so we set off: I as the dog and the ungainly Roach as my owner. Where it is taking me I have no idea. All I can do is follow.

M

Tick-tick. My life has become a ridiculous thing. How, Maximillian, I ask myself, have you managed to be bringing back the very same Vermin that you got rid of no more than a few hours earlier? In my thoughts I hear Mama's exasperation: *You are such a fool, Maximillian, that it is an embarrassment to me.* It is an embarrassment to me too, Mama, I think as I lead the Vermin into the Underground.

Just before I turn the first corner, the Vermin tugs back on the cord. I sigh inwardly. I cannot allow it to even think of misbehaving and so I turn and assume the threat position, but I find there is not quite enough room. The tips of my wings wedge themselves beneath the curved roof and I am unable to fully extend them sideways. I fear my wings are stuck but I play for time by hissing as loudly as I am able. The Vermin drops to its knees in pain. While it has its eyes screwed tight shut, I manage an undignified wiggle to unwedge my wings and fold them back in. Then I turn away, give a sharp tug on the cord and set off. I feel the Vermin stagger to its feet and stumble after me. There is a sob in its breath and I am sorry for a moment, but then I think of the blue shard upon its foot and the feeling is gone.

Slowly, we traverse the Underground—the system of tunnels that lie, branching like a fallen tree, beneath the oldest part of the city. The Vermin follows meekly, for which I am grateful, and we walk in heavy silence. I suspect the Vermin knows nothing of this place, for Wingless ones like him, with short hair and a uniform, do not venture here. But others do. They call themselves Rats because, ratlike, they travel the Underground passages unseen. They're usually young and lost, searching for something that they will never find in this place.

As I am pondering the sadness of Hope, a Rat comes toward me out of the darkness. He's carrying a flute and is followed by a straggle of children, grubby and wet from the dripping roof and with big staring eyes that grow even wider when they see me and the Vermin. These Rats make me smile. They take on children whose parents are lost to the Bartizan or are desperate for them to escape the SilverShip call-up, and they hide them beneath the city, although Parminter once said a very strange thing. She told me that these Rats take the children to the Outside. She said that the Outside is safe now and that the Contagion is long gone. Parminter also said there is no need to keep us trapped beneath the Orb a moment longer and that the city should be open to the sky. And—this is a crazy thing—she said that the sky is *blue.* Parminter says many wise things, but this is not one of them. The sky is gray. How can it possibly be *blue*? That is a ridiculous color for sky.

The Rat slows his pace and I see a flicker of concern cross his features at the sight of me. I quickly flip up my goggles and I give the sign of peace: the first tip of the index finger put to the tip of the thumb to form an O. Yes, oh Wingless watcher, I have hands that work just like yours. The difference is that they are not covered in squashy skin, but tiny, delicate plates of exoskeleton that flow like water over smooth rock.

The young Rat shepherds his flock toward me, keeping them close to the wall. There is room for us all to pass and as they do, I nod my head. He nods in return and one of his brood gives me a shy little wave, which I return. And then they are gone, soft-footed into the shadows. I silently wish them well and think how wonderful it would be if Parminter were right and they were on their way to freedom, sunshine and a blue sky on the Outside. But I do not believe she is. The sky is gray and Outside is death. And that is how it is.

T

I watch the smooth, winged back of the Roach with its wingtips almost brushing the roof of the tunnel as it follows the two green pools of light that run across the stone tunnel floor. I tell myself that when we stop I will throw myself at the Roach and send it crashing to the ground with that hollow crack a carapace always makes when it hits stone, and then I will rip off the limb that holds my tether and take it with me. I see myself running down the street clutching my leash with a Roach arm bobbing along behind me, clattering as it bounces off the pavement and I laugh out loud. The Roach tilts its head to one side and I suppose it is wondering if it has caught a madman. I begin to shiver again. Who am

I kidding? Right now I don't have the strength to pull a pencil from my pocket, let alone an arm off a Roach. And so I stumble along, a dog on a leash heading toward something it dares not think about.

M

Usually I walk upright on my two stronger lower limbs. However, when we who are Roach traverse the Underground, we need speed, carapace protection and maneuverability, and so we run low: that is on all six limbs—or on however many we are fortunate enough to possess. I get by well enough on five but I do sometimes wonder how much faster I would be with six. When I was little I asked Mama why I was missing my middle left limb and she laughed and told me it was because her knife had slipped. That is when I began carrying a knife of my own—a long, slim dagger in a secret holster beneath my underwings. It stopped me being so scared of Mama. Well, most of the time.

But I must stop thinking about Mama. Parminter says she is too often in my thoughts and Parminter is right. What I was going to tell you was that I am not running low because we who are Roach never *ever* allow a Wingless to see us travel in this way. In front of them we flaunt our own humanity. We do not, as Mama says, *crawl like a beast upon its belly*.

However, I do so wish I could run low now. I am too tall for this tunnel and my neck aches from bending forward. Indeed, I feel quite weak as I trudge up yet another long, slow incline. If the Vermin knew this, it would pull its leash away—no doubt bringing my limb with it—and it would be free. Behind me I hear the ragged breath of the Vermin and then a sudden burst of strangled laughter. I hope it is not becoming hysterical.

The Underground does not frighten me when I am alone and running low, for then I have all my senses at my command, but as the journey continues I feel increasingly fearful. I hear a sudden gush of water and I imagine a flood roaring toward me, I hear the eerie hoot of a Bludd Owl and fear its silent swoop and venomous bite and I see dark movements in cracks in the wall where the narrow-bodied, long-legged Fingal spiders lurk. But worst of all I hear Mama's mocking voice inside my head: *Maximillian, you are a poor, frightened thing, scared of your own shadow. You draw troubles to you like iron filings to a magnet.* And once again I fear that Mama is right.

And so we make our strange procession through the Underground, following the old signs that point to the ancient outlets above the ground—most of which are now blocked. At long last I reach a crossing of tunnels with a signpost of four hands pointing their forefingers: North, South, East and West. I take the West and give a tug on the Vermin's cord. It stumbles forward and we walk along a wide brick-lined tunnel until we reach a wooden door set back into the wall. I push the door open and I am greeted by the welcome sight of my own dear tunnel. The ground slopes upward, and as we climb, the light from my goggles shows the clean smooth walls that I whitewashed only last month. We turn the final corner and I see my gate, the polished iron bars reaching neatly from floor to roof. I feel weak with relief. I am home.

T

I have reached my journey's end: the Roach's pantry. I hear the Roach make a *tick-tick* sound as it opens the lock with its clattering claws. The noise sets my teeth on edge: Roach shell on metal is not a good sound. I hear the squeak of the gate as it swings in on itself, there is a tug on my leash and I am pulled into my prison. The Roach locks the gate and clips the end of my leash to a ring in the wall. It shuffles past me and I see a narrow door ahead swing open. The Roach, who fills the doorway from head to toe, steps out and in the brief moment before the door slams shut I see a passageway with shards of china scattered across the stone floor.

I cannot believe it. I am back in the house of the filthy Roach that murdered my crewman. In fact, my captor *is* the filthy Roach that murdered my crewman. It will pay for this.

M

I walk along the track of blood I made when I dragged the dead Vermin out of my house. I must confront what I have done: I have killed. As I raise my feet from the stickiness, telling myself that feeling the blood upon my soles is my penance for this dreadful deed, I decide to confront something even worse—the destruction in Mama's precious room of porcelain.

I walk in, light the lantern and force myself to look at the carnage upon the shelves. The flare of the flame sets the shards of yellow, white, silver, gold and brilliant blue glistening like a myriad beetle backs. If I didn't know what they were, I would think them quite lovely, but every second of looking at them is a dagger in my heart. I confront the destruction that I have brought to the love of Mama's life for as long as I can bear and then I turn to go. But as I do I catch sight of a golden roundness in the far corner of the top shelf. I stretch out a trembling limb and discover an unbroken dewdrop of perfection—a little teapot of opalescent white, the spout a gilded eagle with little red eyes and its beautiful wings spread around the belly of the pot. The delicate domed golden lid is held safe with a fine gold chain. It is Mama's favorite piece, and it is untouched.

Trembling with joy I carry the precious survivor upstairs as though it were the Holy Grail. I place it reverentially upon a small velvet cushion beside my nest where it sits, a queen among beggars, surveying my little room with its imperial eagle eye.

I lie back in the softness of my nest and I feel . . . not happy, for who can feel happy when they have taken a life? But I sense a quiet contentment within. I think of my young fugitives sleeping peacefully across the landing and the Rat and his gaggle in the Underground comes to mind. I smile, for I have found the answer to the problem of what to do with my young ones: I must find a Rat to get them to safety, wherever that may be. Indeed, the older one would make a good Rat herself. And then—and only then—will I deal with the Vermin.

I cannot sleep and so I pick up my best book, which is called *The Sleeping Princess in the Forest of Briars* and I open it to my favorite page. This is the very first page of all and on it is written: *For my darling boy, Maximillian. From his ever-loving papa.* I gaze at the faded looping writing until a confusion of dreams creeps over me.

But as I drift into sleep I hear Mama's voice loud in my head: *Kill them all in the morning and be done with it.*

T

As I sit in the dark listening to the distant drip of water somewhere in the Underground and to the thick silence of the house beyond, a glimmer of hope is creeping into my thoughts: *I am not dead yet.* The Roach has not yet returned and from the inside of my boot I have at last managed to extract Zip, my combi-tool. Zip was a gift from my father; it is small with various tools, one of which is a tiny flashlight, another is a metal saw. I maneuver it up to my teeth and eventually I flip out the flashlight and I can see once more. I do the same for the saw and then get to work on the fine metal cord that keeps me tied to the wall.

It takes hours, but at last I am free. Now all I have to do is get out of this vile pantry. And then that killer Roach will regret it ever existed.

Chapter 10

FREE

K

The early morning light filtering through the flimsy curtains wakes me. I've not seen daylight for over six months now and it feels so good. The SilverSeed crew quarters are beneath the ground with twenty-four-hour artificial light—unless you get put in Time-Out, when it is twenty-four hours of the deepest darkness you can ever imagine. I was in there once, and when I came out the light felt so harsh. But this light is gentle and soft. It makes me feel alive, not dead.

I sit in my nest of blankets, listening to Jonno's calm, regular breathing. I feel bad about Jonno. He truly believed what we were told—that the SilverShip would take us to a wonderful place free of the Contagion where all the kids who had gone before were now living an amazing life: camping out, fishing and having fun. So he hates me for taking him away.

Thinking of the SilverShip reminds me it is time to let the DisK go. I've held it close all night and now I unfurl my fingers and take one last look. I whisper, "*Goodbye, stay safe,*" and then I push it into a crack I've spotted in the oak beam I slept beneath. It slips in easily and all I can now see is the shimmer of its edge. I rub some plaster dust onto it and it disappears from view. There is no way anyone will find it now. And so there is no way they can open the Orb. And no way the SilverShip is going anywhere.

I crawl out of my nest, stand up and stretch. The house is very quiet. I wonder if Maximillian is still sleeping? I go to the window and look out—it's been a long time since I was able to do that. The street below is deserted and deep in shadow. The only activity is two little brown birds hopping along the low parapet in front of my window, tweeting loudly to one another. I watch them, enchanted, until they fly away and then I pad around the room looking for a book to read or something to do, but there is nothing but rugs, blankets and cushions.

I am so used to being confined that it takes a while for me to realize that I don't have to stay in this room—there is a whole house to explore. I pull on my deck shoes, tiptoe over to the door and tentatively turn the doorknob, which comes off in my hand. I smile. I'm used to door handles falling off. Dad was no good at house maintenance either. I put it back on its spindle, turn it carefully and the door opens.

The landing is wide and bright, with a high balustrade and stairs leading down to the shadowy floors below. I pad across the smooth boards to the long rectangle of light filtering in from the huge skylight, and I stand there in the glow, breathing in the soft quietness of the house. I find I can't stop smiling. *I am free.*

There are two other closed doors leading off the landing and I wonder if one of them is the bathroom. My mouth is dry and I really want to pee. I am not sure what Roaches do about that kind of stuff, but I'm hoping there's still a bathroom here.

But which door to try first? I really don't want to go into Maximillian's room. He is such a private person and I also get the feeling he needs a break from Jonno and me. I wonder if he sleeps in a bed? Or some kind of weird nest? Anyway, wherever he is, I really do not want to see him sleeping; it feels wrong. So I stand on the landing, hoping for some kind of clue as to where the bathroom is, and I hear a sudden snore behind the door opposite me. I find I'm smiling again—who knew that Roaches snored? I tiptoe along the landing to the other door and very slowly push it open. A bathroom. There is a massive low, wide metal bathtub half-full of sand, but apart from that everything else seems just like normal. What a relief. I really do need to pee.

Back on the landing, I listen to the stillness. It's weird being in a strange house when everyone else is asleep. I rather like it. I lean over the banister and look down at the coils of the stairs snaking down through the house, descending into the gloom. It's like looking over a cliff: I feel quite giddy.

I decide to explore. I pad quietly down the stairs and one of the treads creaks. I stop and listen but all is still, so I carry on down to the next landing. There are three doors here and they are all locked. This is a bit creepy but I try not to be spooked by it and I head on down the stairs to the next floor. Here one of the doors is open and I go into the room. Like our attic room it has layers of rugs but it also has a collection of sturdy-looking stools and cushions placed neatly along the walls. It looks to me like a place for meetings. Or parties. I wonder if Maximillian likes parties? Somehow I don't think so.

The room is at the back of the house and two tall windows face out over a long, narrow yard. It's a shadowy place backing onto other yards, beyond which I see the backs of more tall houses rising up. There is long grass near the house and beyond are lines of well-tended vegetables, and at the far end two old apple trees lean together for support. I turn away from the window.

Apple trees always make me sad.

Suddenly I am aware of a new sound. *Footsteps.* I can hear footsteps inside the house, way down in the basement. And now . . . and now the footsteps are on the stairs. I can hear the creak of the wood. They climb steadily, slowly making their way up. I hear them walk across the hall, and then stop, as though the person they belong to is listening. I'm listening too, to the person one floor below who is, I am convinced, listening to *me*. And now they set off again, heavy and ponderous, creaking their way up this flight of stairs and I know that any moment now they will pass the open door and whoever they belong to will see me.

I must hide. But where?

Keeping my own steps in time with the creaks I tiptoe across the rugs and flatten myself against the wall behind the open door, so that anyone glancing through the doorway won't see me. The steps are outside on the landing now. I hear them heading this way, slowly, stealthily, as though they are looking for something. I decide that when they come into the room I will run at the person. I will knock them to the floor and get out of the house as fast as possible. But then I think about Jonno up there, sleeping peacefully and I dither. I can't leave him here, alone. *Oh, what should I do*?

Suddenly, I don't have to decide. The footsteps creak

past the door and now they are going up the next flight of stairs. I wonder if I should chase after them and rescue Jonno, but I know there is no way Jonno will go anywhere with me ever again. I listen to them reaching the attic and I wait, holding my breath, wondering if Jonno will yell out. I hear a door open and it creaks—it's the door to Maximillian's room. I heard it creak last night when he went out. Relief sweeps over me that it's not our room and I'm off. Down the stairs, quiet and fast, because right now all I want to do is get as far away from the creepy footsteps as possible.

T

I heard footsteps a few minutes ago. Heavy and slow. They walked up to the door, they stopped right outside and I'll swear that the person was listening. I did not give them the pleasure of hearing anything. I held my breath until they went away and it was only then that I began to think straight. What if my second-in-command has survived too? What if it was her coming back for me? I wouldn't have thought it was the kind of thing she would do, but who knows? The footsteps went farther into the house, so if it is her looking for me, she will come back the same way. And this time I must make sure she knows I am here.

A note. I'll write a note. My fingers are clumsy and

my shoulders so stiff that my arms can hardly move, but I manage to pull out a paper strip and a pencil from the pocket beneath my arm. I write my crew ID and then: *Help. In here.* My hands are so shaky it looks like my kid brother's writing but it will have to do. I shove it underneath the door and lean back; I feel sweaty with the effort. I imagine the message lying in the nasty little dark passageway among the blood and the smashed pots and I just hope she sees it—if it *is* her. And if it's not her and the Roach finds it, well, what does that matter? We all know Roaches can't read. It will probably stuff it into its nasty little mandibles and have it for breakfast. I hope it chokes on it.

K.

I'm in the basement now. I'm spooked by those footsteps and I want to be as far away from them as possible. It's full of shadows down here, but even so I can see shards of broken china swept aside by a long, thick streak of blood. I know it's from the fight that Maximillian had with the Enforcers, but I didn't realize how nasty it must have been. Or what Maximillian must have done . . .

I walk along the path made by the dried blood but when I get to the Roach pantry I see something sticking out from underneath the door. It's pencil on blue paper, the Silver Seed stuff we keep in our waist belts. I crouch down to look at it and my heart does a flip. It is Jonno's writing.

It says: *KT. Help. In here.* This is how Jonno writes my name: *KT* instead of *Katie.* I stare at the writing and all I can think is, *How come Jonno is in the Roach pantry?* My mind is racing. I know I'm not thinking straight, but I think something must have happened to Jonno when I was in the bathroom. It must be to do with those creepy footsteps, the ones that went into Maximillian's room. And then it hits me. This means that Maximillian must be in on this. I feel like someone has punched me in the stomach. I can't believe it; I just can't. I liked Maximillian so much. And I totally trusted him, I really did. And now he's betrayed us.

I have to get Jonno out of that disgusting Roach pantry fast. Right now in fact.

My hands are shaking as I do exactly what I saw Maximillian do last night: flip open the little panel in the wainscoting and pull on the lever. The door swings open and a gloved hand grabs me. Hard.

It's not Jonno.

T

Sheesh. It's my sister. It's *Kaitlin.* She stares at me, shocked, her mouth open in a soundless O. If I know anything about my shouty little sister, it is that the silence is not going to last long. I'm out of that pantry in an instant and I shove my hand over her mouth. Too late she realizes she can't yell. So she bites instead. I push harder against her mouth and I can tell she is struggling to breathe, but I can't let go. I can't let her shout out, the Roach will have us both. She struggles and I hiss, "It's me. Tomas. Don't scream, okay?"

She goes kind of limp and nods her head.

Oh my days, I know why she's here. She's our quarry from last night. They never tell you who you're pursuing. No names, no numbers. We have the DNA profiles of course, but they are anonymous. But now I understand: they sent me after my own family. *Again.* And then it hits me. The blood. It was a male profile. It must have been Jonno's blood. *The Roach got Jonno.* I feel sick. And so, so angry. Little Jonno is dead, and all because Kaitlin dragged him away with her. He didn't want to go. I saw the footage; he was fighting her all the way. "We're out of here," I tell her. "Don't you dare make a sound. Got it?"

She nods again. It's like the stuffing has gone out of her.

K

It's Tomas. I get it now. He was one of the crew after us last night. Of course he was. Just like before. I'm trying to work out how come he was in the Roach pantry and then I get it. Maximillian must have captured him and locked him up. Which means that, once again, I've misjudged Maximillian. At least this time he doesn't know.

We're outside the house now and Tomas is pushing me up the basement steps. "What happened to Jonno, Kait? Huh?" he growls in my ear.

What right has *he* has to be angry? "Mind your own business," I tell him.

"I know what happened," he snaps back. "*You killed him.*"

"I did not! In fact . . ." And then I stop just in time because I realize that I can at least save Jonno. Not that he'll appreciate it, but that's what I am going to do.

"In fact *what*?" Tomas asks impatiently as he frog-marches me along the path, heading for the gate.

"I didn't kill Jonno. It wasn't me," I say, knowing what Tomas will assume. I think of Maximillian and all he did for us. Who's the betrayer now? I think.

"Yeah, yeah. I get it was the Roach that actually *did* it. But Jonno wouldn't have been anywhere near the filthy Roach if you hadn't dragged him away on your crazy escape. So basically, Kaitlin, *you* killed him." He tightens his grip on my arm. I hang back but he shoves me forward. "Move," he says.

"Where are we going?" I whisper. As if I don't know.

"Back to where you belong."

I want to say to Tomas that *this* is where I belong—in this funny old house with Jonno and a Roach called Maximillian. But there is no point. I gaze up at the grimy windows, which look as though they have seen so many things, and I tell the house goodbye.

Chapter 11

MINNA SIMMS

M

I am awoken by the ever-tedious Minna Simms.

I open my eyes and the first thing I see is her shining, chubby face staring down at me, wearing its usual oh-so-patronizing expression that she adopts when talking to us Roaches. The second thing I see is her large fleshy ankle overflowing from its sturdy brown boot *no more than an inch away from the golden eagle teapot.*

In a flash I reach out and grab Mama's last remaining treasure and pull it into the safety of my nest. Minna looks down and gives me a weak smile full of condescension.

"I see I am superfluous," she says. "You have found your own invalid feeding cup." She sniffs. "A little ostentatious and personally I think you will experience an amount of leakage from the beak. It is not formed for the Roach mouth."

"It is not an invalid feeding cup. It is a *teapot*," I tell her. "Very valuable eighteenth-century Meissen if you must know."

Minna's smile broadens. "Ah, an *old* teapot. Well, well. I know you Roaches like your garish little baubles."

I am so relieved that my first sight on waking was not the sight of Minna Simms's hefty boot crushing Mama's teapot that I do not react with my usual annoyance. Instead I sit up in my nest, pull out some polyester fluff that has stuck between the tiny plates of my mesothorax and say, "Well, Minna, how delightful it is to see you."

You might find it strange that I wake up to find Minna Simms in my nest room and feel no more than a mild—well, to be truthful, as I am trying to be with you, fairly severe—annoyance. Unfortunately this is not my first experience of this. Recently Minna has acquired Andronicus's key to my front door and extended her caregiving activities to me. I have protested, but to no avail. It is most annoying. However, the intrusion is moderated by the fact that every morning, Minna brings me a flask of extremely good coffee. I watch her pour it into a lidded cup from which a wide, flat sucking tube extrudes. "Maxie, dear," she says as she offers it to me. "Darling Andy has asked me to . . ."

Oh, the loathing: *Maxie* and *Andy.* I let the prattle wash over me as I suck up the coffee—cooled to the perfect temperature—through the tube. Minna has developed an array of what she calls "Roach aids," many of which are annoyingly useful but somehow undignified. She finishes talking and I ask, "How is Andronicus?"

"I should ask how *you* are, Maxie dear," she reposts, almost flirtatiously. "You had a heavy fall last night. No damage I trust?"

At first I do not understand what she means, but then, with a sinking heart, I recall the events of the previous night and our struggle with the Vermin. "No damage whatsoever. Indeed, I am very well, thank you, Minna," I reply primly.

"As is Andy, even after his late night. Here's his message." And she hands me a piece of hemp paper folded and sealed with a blob of green wax.

I smile. Notes from Andronicus are always so special. "Thank you, Minna," I say, but I do not open it. She would be breathing down my neck trying to read it and I do not wish to give her the pleasure. Also I am not entirely sure what Andronicus will have written. I finish the coffee and hand the feeding cup back with my thanks.

"Aren't you going to open it?" she asks, staring at the letter.

"I shall save that pleasure until later," I say. I give her my most ghastly smile and drop my voice into a conspiratorial whisper. "Mama taught me all about deferred gratification." I really do sound remarkably creepy.

The color drains from Minna's face. She takes a step away from my nest and I see her wonder if she is quite as safe here as she thought. "Well, Maxie," she gabbles, "just in case you decide to defer your gratification until it is too late, I will tell you that it is an invitation from Andy asking you to lunch. Today. I told you earlier but I knew you weren't listening."

I smile at Minna in what I hope is a conciliatory way, for I must be careful not to make her hate me too much. Despite Andronicus's protestations to the contrary, I am convinced that Minna is a dangerous woman. "How delightful," I say. "Please tell him that I shall greatly look forward to it." And I will. Any time spent with Andronicus is a pleasure.

Minna walks to the door and then, just as I think I am free, she stops and turns. She eyes me in a suspicious way that tells me I am right to be careful with her. "So what happened in the basement?" she asks abruptly.

"The basement?" I repeat stupidly. What was she doing in the *basement*? The front door is one floor up. But I know the answer: she was being Minna. Nosing around. "Ah, the basement. I had a break-in. Mama's porcelain was smashed to pieces. All but this teapot . . ." My voice quite genuinely breaks. "I would rather not speak of it,

Minna. It is very distressing to me."

"I imagine it is," she says dryly. "I will see you at lunch."

"You *will*?" I ask, my spirits falling even further.

"Of course you will," she says tartly. "Who do you think is cooking it?" And with that, she is gone.

Something is different about Minna and not in a good way. There is an edge of steel to her this morning and it unsettles me. I am wondering what the reason for this could be—and then I remember the blood in the basement corridor. I tell myself that I must not concern myself about Minna, for I have more important things to think about—three more things to be precise: my two young fugitives and that wretched Vermin. I sigh. I am facing another day of trial and tribulation.

I lie back in the softness of my nest, which is made, should you be interested, from six duvets. I have only polyester fillings, for feathers are treacherous things. One can go all day with a small feather stuck into the top on one's antenna with not one friend telling you about it and then feel an utter fool in the evening when at last you catch sight of it in the mirror. I hear that you Wingless have the same problem with spinach and teeth, although I believe this is confined to the older ones.

I would like to go back to sleep, but every time I close my eyes I see Minna Simms's goldfish eyes staring at me.

It is enough to give one nightmares. So I sit up, place Mama's teapot back upon its cushion and gently unfurl my antennae from their sleeping pouches while I try to work out why I find Minna Simms so very unpleasant.

Slowly, the quietness of the house intrudes upon my musings. Wingless humans are noisy creatures—especially you young ones—and yet it feels so calm, almost as if no one is here. A niggle of worry makes me roll out of my nest—from the non-teapot end, naturally. I stretch to free up the carapace plates, settle my wings and go out onto the landing. I stop and listen. To my relief I hear snuffly sleep-breathing from the room opposite. I nudge open the door and peer inside. The younger one with the injured foot lies deeply asleep, curled up beneath his blankets. It is his breathing I hear. But in the corner beneath the eaves I see that the nest of blankets where the older one was sleeping is empty.

A feeling of dread steals over me. I imagine the Vermin getting free, creeping up the stairs and taking his prey. A twinge in my underwing reminds me that my Wingless girl, young Kaitlin Drew, is a fighter and I tell myself I am being foolish, for surely I would have heard something? But the twinge also reminds me that my Kaitlin Drew is impulsive. I suspect she woke early, became bored and is now exploring the house. I expect she has been held prisoner belowground in those vile crew quarters for months and she is now relishing her freedom. Feeling thankful that she clearly had the wit to keep out of the way of Minna Simms, I set off down the stairs in search of her.

Ha. I can feel you watching me and I think you know something I do not. *What is it?* My descent through the five floors of my dear, tall house is accompanied by an increasing feeling of dread. And when I reach the basement and look along the shard-strewn passage to see the door to the Underground hanging wide open, I want to sink to my knees and cry.

The Vermin has taken my Kaitlin Drew—I *know* it has. And all I can do is imagine her terror and despair.

Chapter 12

FAMILY MATTERS

K

I go back the way I came—with a brother. The route is virtually the same as yesterday evening—all that has changed is the brother. Tomas has put a cable tie around my wrist and attached it to his belt with a thin and very flexible steel cord. He has said nothing to me at all. He met my eye once and that was by mistake. He could not look away fast enough.

We must present a strange picture: an Enforcer in full shimmering CarboNet, his shoulders bloody and torn from a Roach lift, with a bedraggled SilverSeed clipped to his belt. Tomas has thrown back his head covering to reveal his bruised forehead, tangled dark curls and steely-gray eyes that glint with excitement. He seems proud of who he is and strides confidently along the alleyways, daring anyone to defy him.

We walk quickly and in silence and all I can think of is Jonno waking up and finding himself alone in a strange house with a Roach. He doesn't know Maximillian like I do and he'll be terrified. Maybe I should tell Tomas that Jonno is still alive. Then we could go and get him, and Jonno would be thrilled to come back to his precious crew. But I know I mustn't do that. Jonno may not appreciate it now, but he has a chance to live his life in freedom, not imprisoned beneath the ground. And Maximillian will help him, I am sure of that.

I look up at the tall buildings that rear up on either side of us, their red and yellow bricks blackened by smoke from illegal coal fires, their windows thick with grime because who wants to waste precious water cleaning windows? Some are what Dad called "well curated" with vegetables and fruits growing in every possible container—nets, bins, buckets, bags that dangle from the windowsills and even fruit bushes poking up from behind roof parapets. Many are empty but even so I get the distinct feeling of being watched. I scan the windows, hoping to find a friendly face, but all I see is a twitch of curtains or a shadow drawing away. The early morning brightness is fading now and a chill mist is dropping down from the Orb. I watch it settle on the tops of the houses and slowly creep downward so that soon it feels as though we are walking through a dark canyon miles deep. I begin to feel cold, but I am determined not to shiver. I refuse to give Tomas any reason to think I am scared.

We pass people heading off to small workshops hidden in the backstreets, a few unregistered children on their way to their secret schools and a trickle of shoppers making their way toward a sad-looking market, which I glimpse down a side street. People react in different ways. Some see us and pretend they haven't. They look away, stare at the ground or suddenly have the need to rummage in their bag. Two children run off crying, a young man flattens himself against the wall with his eyes closed and three girls stop dead in their tracks and gasp, hands flying up to cover their faces. But one thing remains constant—no one wants to make eye contact.

We have just entered the wide alleyway—Dog Leg Dive—that will take us all the way to the Bartizan, when an elderly disheveled woman comes out of a doorway. She stops and watches us approach. Tomas stares straight ahead, but I catch her eye and she holds my gaze and gives me an infinitesimal nod of encouragement. As we draw level I see her very deliberately take a catapult from inside her sleeve and—this happens so fast I hardly see it—she draws back the sling and sends a sharp stone flying. It catches Tomas on the back of his head. Tomas's hand flies up to where the stone hit and he wheels around, but the woman is gone, melted into the shadows of the house. I am so impressed by her bravery. I know Tomas wants to chase after her but he has me tied to him like a weight and I pull away, refusing to move. And so, with blood trickling down his neck, I see him scan the building for its number.

"He's got your number!" I yell out. "Take care. They'll come for you!"

Tomas slaps my face. "Shut up," he snarls.

I'm shocked. But I know that up there somewhere the woman is looking down at me, willing me to fight just like she did. Maybe I'm just showing off to her or maybe she's given me courage, but whatever the reason is, I swing around and land a punch where I know it's going to count—on Tomas's shoulder. Tomas yelps. His hand flies from the back of his head to his shoulder and I see fresh blood oozing through the claw holes in the CarboNet. I feel a twinge of guilt and then tell myself not to be so silly. "You always were a bully," I tell him.

"And you always were an interfering little brat," he says through gritted teeth.

From the windows above I sense the woman watching;

she must be wondering about the turn this has taken. Tomas gives a sharp tug on my cord and I pull back. "You should never have come through here," I tell him. "I have friends looking out for me. I suggest you let me go now and run for it. You're not going to get out of here otherwise."

It was a good try but it doesn't work. "We'll see about that, won't we," he says and he sets off fast, his hand still clamped onto his shoulder. My cord tugs at me and I have no choice but to follow. The weird thing is that now Tomas can't stop talking. It's as if my punch has dislodged something inside him.

"You think you know it all, don't you?" he says, breathless as he strides along. "But you don't know the half of it, Kaitlin. You have *no idea.*" He pulls angrily on my cord. "You think I like doing this, do you?" Tomas asks, not giving me a chance to reply. "Well, I *don't.* But you're so self-obsessed I don't suppose you think about me at all. So I'm telling you, I did *this,*" he says, stabbing his finger onto his triangular Enforcer badge—that for some reason has the initials T.M. embroidered on it—"for the family."

I laugh. "Yeah, yeah," I say. "And the sky is blue. *I don't think so.*" And then a rush of terror changes my laugh into a weird hiccup. Because rearing up above the rooftops, blurred by the mist, I suddenly notice the dark, angular shape of the Bartizan tower. It is so close I feel I could reach out and touch it.

Tomas looks at me quizzically. He decides I am upset about Jonno. "Poor Jonno," he says, shaking his head. "Poor little kid."

It takes me a moment to remember that Jonno is meant to be dead. "I don't want to think about it," I tell Tomas. It's true, I don't want to think about Jonno, about how he's all alone now and probably scared out of his brain. And also I can't quite remember what I said.

"Okay. Yeah. I get that," Tomas says and I'm sure I hear him sniff. We are walking past an open door to a tiny café and the smell of frying bacon is drifting out. Bacon is a rarity, there aren't many pigs about, but it was something Dad often managed to get hold of for Sunday breakfast. Suddenly, Tomas stops and looks at me just like he used to. His eyes are full of tears. Are they for Dad or Mom or Jonno or me, I wonder? Or just for himself? There are so many of our family to cry for. "Kait," he says, "how about a last breakfast together?"

I stare at him. "Breakfast? With *you*? Are you crazy?" I say. But I do not resist when he leads me into the darkness of the café, redolent with coffee, bacon and fresh-baked bread, and heads toward a small table at the back, with two ladder-backed chairs, a red-checked cloth and a daisy in a pot.

T

I sit down at the table farthest from the door, taking care to have my back to the wall and a good view of the alley outside, as we are trained to do. My sister sits opposite me, confusion written all over her face. She perches on the edge of her chair and places both hands upon the table in full view so that all can see the cable tie around her wrist and the steel cord running from it to my belt. She wants to make it clear that she has not chosen my company.

There is a high counter with a door behind it, and from the depths of its shadows I see the café owner staring at us. *Tomas, you idiot,* I tell myself. *What are you doing? Take her back and get it over with.* But I can't do it. Not yet. I will, of course I will. But just not yet.

The café owner creeps out from behind his bunker, sizing up the situation. He's a large man, florid and sweaty, and he holds his hands clamped tightly together in an effort to stop them shaking. Which is not successful. This is a typical reaction to my Enforcer uniform. In fact, this is the only reaction I get: no smiles, no banter, and no one ever asks how I am or tells me what they think of the weather—a preoccupation in our city. I am not a person anymore. I am an agent of terror.

The man gives my sister a look of pity as he gathers the courage to speak to me. "Good morning, sir. What can I do for you?" he asks.

"Two bacon sandwiches and two coffees, please," I say.

I see a flicker of surprise cross his features when I say "please." "With pleasure, sir," he says. He runs the back of his hand across his forehead in obvious relief, then hurries away and disappears through the door behind his counter.

We are left staring at each other, Kaitlin and I. "We should talk," I say, knowing as I say it how lame it sounds.

She glares at me.

"I just want to explain. So you know the truth," I tell her.

"Tomas, you wouldn't know the truth if it bit you on the butt," she says. That's my mouthy sister for you.

I persist. "I want you to know that I didn't betray you. In fact, I tried to save you."

"Yeah, right," she says, waving her cable-tied wrist in my face. "And this is just a fancy bracelet? I *don't* think so. I know what happened, Tomas. You walked out on us to join the Enforcers. If that's not betrayal, I don't know what is."

"I did it to *save* us," I tell her. "I figured that if I was part of the system, I'd get to know if they were after you. And then I could warn you. Honestly, Kait. Please believe me. I really thought I could do that."

We both stare at the tablecloth. Then she looks up at me and the expression in her eyes is so full of hate it makes me curl up inside. "Well, that didn't work out too well, did it?" she says. "Anyway, I don't care what your stupid reasons were. All I know is that you, in your dinky uniform, brought two Bartizan thugs to our hiding place and you . . . *you took our mother away.*"

This hits me in the stomach like a punch. How does she know? I was hooded and voice-screened. I get my breath back and say, "Kaitlin. Listen to me, *please.* I didn't bring them; they brought *me.* They knew exactly where to go. They knew because the Bartizan was tracking our family. We were at the *top* of the Persons of Interest list. I *saw* it."

Kaitlin stares at me, gimlet-eyed. "I don't care about a stupid list. All I care is that you took Mom away. I saw you, Tomas. You cuffed her hands. *You* did that. You didn't have to. But you did it."

"But I *did* have to," I whisper. "I was ordered. They made me do it." Oh, I know how bad this sounds. And I can't bear to think of Mom and the way she looked at me when I was doing it. She knew it was me.

"And I know what they did to Mom," Kaitlin whispers. "I asked Dad and he told me. They Astroed her."

I can't reply. We sit in silence. I smell the bacon frying but I'm not feeling hungry anymore. "It's not *all* my fault," I say eventually.

"Shut up, Tomas," Kaitlin snaps back.

"But it's not," I insist. "There was a big secret in our family that Mom and Dad never told us. And *that* is why all this . . . this *stuff* . . . has happened to us."

"Yeah, Tomas. Blame Mom and Dad. Blame anyone but yourself," she says.

"I'm not blaming them. I'm just telling you, that's why our family is in pieces. It's why they had to leave our little house by the farm. It's why I had to split with Mattie. It's why the Bartizan tracked you down. And when you, Jonno and Dad escaped from the basement and hid out with those Rats in that filthy hut down by the old mill, that is why they went to all the trouble of ambushing Dad. And then taking you and Jonno away. Our *whole family* was on their hit list."

"Did you take Dad too?" Kaitlin asks quietly.

I shake my head. "No. It was my day off." I see at once this is a stupid thing to say. Even though it is true.

My sister splutters with anger. "Oh, they give you

days off from rounding up your family, do they? Well, isn't that nice of them?"

"Katie . . . ," I begin.

"You have no right to call me Katie." She spits the words like venom.

"All right, then, *Kaitlin*. You know I named my crew after you: Kilo Tango. KT, get it? Like Jonno writes—I mean used to write—your name." I stop and gulp. Poor Jonno. Poor little boy.

But Jonno doesn't seem to bother Kaitlin at all. She's harder than I realized. "Well, thank you, Tomas," she says. "I feel *so* much better now." Heavy sarcasm was always Kait's favorite way to fight.

I sigh. "Look, whatever you think, it was just horrible bad luck that I was on the mission for . . . for Mom. And then for you and Jonno last night. You see, they don't know who I am. I didn't give them my real name. I'm not *that* stupid."

"So what name did you use?"

I point to my initials on my badge: T.M. "Marne. Dunno why but it felt kind of right."

Kaitlin is staring at me, aghast. "Tomas. You total dumbo pickle-head. You idiot numpty-brain. What a stupid, *stupid* name to choose."

I frown. "I thought it was a good name. Like I said,

it felt right. Kind of comfortable."

She laughs, but not in a good way. "You know why it felt right? Because that was Dad's old name. His *real* name."

I stare at Kaitlin, dumbstruck. "What do you mean, Dad's *real* name?"

"Matthew Marne. It's in his old college books, *duh*. The ones you couldn't be bothered to read. I asked him about it once."

"I bet that was a waste of time," I say. "He never told me anything."

But it seems Kaitlin got more out of Dad than I ever did. "He said Marne was from another life," she says slowly. "Before I was born. I asked, 'Was it before Mom too?' and he looked kind of awkward and said, 'No, not exactly.' And then he said that our name was Drew now and I must completely forget about Marne. So, Tomas, I think they know exactly who you are. You're just a pawn in their game."

I feel winded. Like I've been knocked to the ground. I know at once that she's right. I see now that the mission for Mom was a test of loyalty. And it is true, they did make me put the cuffs on her. I was hanging back in a real state about what was happening and the mission commander pulled me forward and ordered me to do it. I cannot believe I've been so naive. Pickle-head and numpty-brain doesn't even begin to describe it.

I groan and put my head in my hands. To my surprise I feel Kaitlin's hand rest lightly on my arm. "But why have they got it in for us?" she asks.

"I don't know. Mom and Dad knew, but they wouldn't tell me."

"You *asked* them? So you knew something was wrong?"

I nod. "Yeah. That's why I left. You remember? The day after your birthday?" She looks surprised that I remember her birthday. "I was out the back sitting behind the toolshed, reading, when I heard Mom talking in the kitchen. It was her tone of voice that I noticed—she sounded terrified. So I crawled over and listened in the lettuce bed under the window. I didn't catch it all but she was going on about someone being inducted. And that it was the end for us all. Dad made this awful, terrified groaning sound and I was so spooked. They seemed to be talking about some woman who had suddenly gotten power over our whole family. Mom called her a monster and Dad wanted to give himself up in exchange for our safety but Mom told him no. She said he knew perfectly well that she would never rest until she'd destroyed us all. They were quiet after that, so I risked a quick look through the window. They were like a statue, clasping one another. Petrified."

Kaitlin is looking at me, her hands over her mouth. I see her cuff on her wrist and feel so bad about it. How did we get to this? But I don't want to think about that, so I just keep talking. "I wasn't totally surprised," I say. "I always kind of knew that something bad had happened to Mom and Dad before we were born. There was a sadness about them, you know?"

Kaitlin nods.

"It's not good to have a secret in a family, is it? It makes everything kind of skewed. Anyway, later that evening, while you were upstairs reading Jonno his bedtime story, I told Mom and Dad that I was old enough to know the truth. I said I wanted to know who was the woman who wanted to destroy us. And why? What had they done that was so terrible? But they wouldn't tell me. I got *so* angry. I told them that seeing as *my* life was in danger too I had a right to know. But all they would say was it was safer for me if I didn't know. So that's when I stormed out. I walked around the streets for ages and then I made a decision. I was so upset; I guess I wasn't thinking straight.

"First I went to Mattie's house, banged on the door and woke them all up. I told her we were through. Finished. And Mattie cried. So in the end I told her that I was too dangerous to know and she said that she didn't care, she loved me whatever the danger. But I just turned and ran. I ran and I ran so I didn't have to think anymore and I went straight to the Bartizan twenty-four-hour recruitment office and signed on. They took me, even though I wasn't quite eighteen."

Kaitlin is staring at me. "Oh, *Tomas* . . ."

"Yeah. Well. So after that I never had to think about anything. I did what they said, when they said. It was so easy. But all the time I kept an eye on what they were going to do to our family. And Mattie too."

"So you know Mattie's on the SilverShip?" Kaitlin asks. "She got taken with me and Jonno when they raided the hut. Three days after Dad disappeared."

"Yeah, I know. How is she?"

"She's okay. She misses you. A lot."

"I miss her too," I say. "Tell her that. Would you? Please?"

"Yeah. Okay." And then Kaitlin says what I've been expecting—and even thinking myself. "Tomas, you don't have to do this. We can both get out of this. Go Underground. Find a Rat. Hide out with them."

I so wish we could, but I know there is nowhere to go. "There are no hiding places," I tell her. "There's nothing in this city that the Bartizan doesn't know about. You're better off on the SilverShip. At least you get a chance for a new life."

"You mean a chance to die of the Contagion," Kait says.

"No. There's an island across the ocean that's free of it. That's where the ship goes. I've seen the maps."

"Rubbish," she says.

"It's true," I tell her.

"No, it's not," she says. "It's population control, that's what it is—so the city doesn't starve. And it means that parents daren't put a foot wrong because they are terrified for their kids. Frankly, Tomas, it stinks."

I shrug. Nothing I say is going to change her mind. There is a rustle from behind the counter and the fat chef bustles over with our bacon sandwiches and coffee.

We eat in silence. It feels like cardboard in my mouth.

Chapter 13

A STAR

K,

Tomas pays for the breakfast—much to the owner's surprise—and then we are outside. It is getting warm now, a typical muggy morning when the air weighs heavy and seems to stick to your skin. Tomas walks fast. He appears to stare straight ahead, but I notice that his eyes are flicking from side to side like a snake as he checks for any threat. He takes good care not to look at me; the shutters have come down and he's an Enforcer once more. I find it hard to believe that only a few minutes ago we were almost back to our old selves, just brother and sister. I'd rather not talk to him now he's reverted to Enforcer mode, but this is the last few minutes we will ever spend together and there is something I really need to know. "Tomas," I say. "Do you know what happened to Dad?"

Tomas doesn't even break his stride. "Sacrificed," he says.

I feel winded. This is such a brutal reply. "What do you mean?" I ask.

"It's what they call it." Tomas has switched off. He's not giving anything away now.

"Call *what,* Tomas?"

Tomas stops dead, taking me by surprise. It seems he can't keep his Enforcer act up for very long now. "It's what they call it when they leave someone in the Night Roach Steeple."

I feel sick. I'd always hoped that Dad had somehow escaped. Mom used to say he had a lucky star and that if there was a way out of something, Dad would find it. But I guess his luck ran out.

"I went there as soon as I heard," Tomas is saying. "I sat at the foot of the old church, beneath the steeple."

"I wish I could have been there too," I whisper.

"And then I just listened . . ."

"To *what*?" I ask. This is awful. I imagine too many terrible sounds.

Tomas gives a grin that looks like its hurting him. "To Dad's old tin flute. He always had it with him, didn't he? And he played so sweetly that evening. He played all his favorites and then he began on that lament that used to make Mom cry and halfway through he suddenly stopped. So I got up and went back to the barracks. And that was it."

There's nothing more for us to say. We take the last sharp turn of Dog Leg Dive and I see, drenched in brilliant sunlight, the stark white of the marble paving that surrounds the foot of the Bartizan. Beyond is a high steel wall behind which the Bartizan tower rises up, a dark pillar of concrete streaked with black mold. I shield my eyes and squint up at the top, where the old water tower sticks out and I see the fancy wooden superstructure they stuck on top of it, with its line of dark little windows. Behind those lurks the Guardian, keeping an eye on the whole city like a spider at the center of his—or her—web. Rising up from the roof is the Bartizan skylon, a delicate metal lattice ascending into the misty sky. I remember how on summer nights Tomas and I used to go out into the fields and watch for the brilliant flashes of light that would sometimes zigzag out from the top of the skylon and arc across the Orb. It is hard to believe we had such happy times now.

Tomas is moving fast. He wants to get it over with, I can tell. The entrance to the SilverShip is on the far side of the Square, and as we turn the corner I look up to see the metal wall and its creepy mural showing happy kids in SilverSeed uniforms walking hand in hand toward the entrance. As we stride along beside the mural, I think that we are a parody of those clear-eyed, immaculately dressed children—Tomas in his bloodstained, tattered CarboNet, and me in my equally bloodstained, crumpled SilverShip grays.

And now we're there. Standing before the big round arch cut with the sign above it saying *Gateway to the Future* in gold letters. There is a huge security door across it, and this is painted with a childish rendition of what they say Outside looks like: blue sky, white puffballs they call clouds, a long darker blue strip that I think is meant to be an ocean—a massive area of salt water apparently—and in the middle of that ocean a small, green island: the place to which the SilverShip is meant to be going.

This entrance is where Jonno and I were brought in six months ago and it is also where some of the braver parents of the SilverSeeds gather every day. A group is here now, quiet and sad. I remember, in the old days when things like this only happened to other people, walking by here with Mom. I remember how she tried to explain why the people were waiting even though they knew they would never see their children again. "It is to bear witness," she said. "As we all should do."

While we wait for the door to open, I turn away from Tomas and scan the watching faces. I see an initial flash of hope that I might be their own child somehow returned to them, and then sadness when they see I am not. And then, when people catch my eye, I see sympathy. Embarrassed, I look away, only to find myself confronted by images of laughing kids in their neat SilverSeed uniforms that cluster around the archway. These are very weird. It's not obvious when you first look at them, but they *move*. It's only a little, like the first intimations of a smile, the blink of an eye, a breath of wind blowing the hair, but it is just enough to make them feel real. These are living ghosts, for every one of them is an actual kid who has long gone. Mom told me that some parents still visit these images of their children, even though by now they would be grown up and with children themselves—if they were alive, of course. I look at the crowd and wonder if any of those parents are here today.

The security door is still closed—they are keeping us waiting. Tomas is tapping his foot anxiously and I can see a small muscle beneath his left eye twitching. People have started muttering bad things about Tomas. Knowing they are on my side calms me a little and I start to think again. And as I do, a plan comes to me. I feel a twinge of guilt about what it will do to Tomas but I tell myself that he could have let me go at any time and he chose not to. He got himself into this mess, not me.

And so I begin to enact my plan. I gaze at the creepy pictures of the lost children as if they are old friends and

I make an expression of happy anticipation creep across my face—at least I hope that's what it is. It probably looks like I've eaten too much cheese or something. I smile for the security cameras above our heads and hope it works.

At last, the door begins to slide open and someone calls out, "Run, girl, run!" Oh, how I'd love to, but I am still tied to Tomas. But if my plan works, in a few minutes I'll be free of him. And then I *will* run. I'll dive into that crowd and disappear out the other side. I know they'll help me.

The door is wide open now, revealing a brightly lit square lobby of one-way reinforced dark glass: a fish tank in which Tomas and I are the fish. We walk in and I seize my chance. "Tomas," I say, loud and clear to make sure the sensors pick up every word, "I'm so sorry, but I am going to tell them the truth."

He looks at me, puzzled.

I launch into my spiel. "I know I promised to protect you but I can't do it, Tomas. I just can't. I hope one day you'll understand, but I'm a SilverSeed, and you just don't have any idea how much that means to me."

He's staring at me now, dumbfounded, but beneath the confusion I see consternation creeping into his eyes. *Keep going, Kaitlin*, I tell myself. *Keep going.*

"Tomas, I know you only meant well when you tried to take me and Jonno away from this. I know you thought you were doing us a huge favor by planning our escape, but you just don't get it, do you? This is my future." I stop and swing my free arm around the listening walls of the fish tank as though it is the whole world before me. "My new life is waiting, and just because you can't go—and thanks to you, neither can poor Jonno now—that is no reason to take it from me."

Tomas is staring at me, aghast. I can't look at him anymore. I'm too deep in lies now. But with a thrill of excitement I realize I've got the upper hand and that my plan might even work. A wave of exhilaration sweeps over me and that is the only excuse I can give for the terrible thing I said next: "And it's no reason to kill your crewmates either."

I can't believe I just said that.

The color drains from Tomas's face as the implications of what I've said dawn on him. He sees that it is my word against his. In fact, it is worse than that, because I've not lost two crewmates: *my* credibility is not damaged. Tomas sees all of this and he looks like he is going to pass out.

A glass panel in the corner slides open and a guard walks in. She looks at Tomas coldly. "Unclip the Seed," she tells him, with ice in her voice.

In a daze, Tomas unclips the end of the cord from his belt. "You lying little toad," he says as the cord falls to the floor with a clang, pulling my wrist down with it.

"Step away from the Seed!" the guard barks. And when Tomas, stunned, does not move, she yells, "Now, now, *now*!"

Tomas jumps aside and I see he is shaking. I'm feeling really bad about this, but I tell myself that it was his choice to bring me here. Two more guards enter and take Tomas roughly by the arms. He winces and I see how much his shoulders hurt him. But I am not going to feel bad about Tomas. I am not. *I am not.*

I fix the guard with what I hope is an earnest gaze. "I'd like to put these good people's minds at rest," I say, and with my tie-free hand I indicate the crowd outside, who are staring in at us with horrified fascination. "I want to tell them how much the chance to be on the SilverShip means to me. Would you allow me to go and talk to them?" Oh, I feel like such a creep. But I can't stop now.

The guard frowns. "It is most irregular," she says.

I nod, as if accepting it. "I understand," I say. "And anyway, what I really want to do is get back to my crew." I do a huge smile and make sure it goes to my eyes too. "I'm just *so* happy to be back and I wanted to share it."

I see Tomas staring at me with a grudging admiration. He's worked out what I'm doing, and he is not going to stop me. In fact, to my amazement, he is going to help me. "She's the best advert for the SilverShip you'll ever get," he tells the guard. "She talks of nothing else. You're lucky to have her."

The guard is listening to her headset. "Okay. Sure. We'll go with it," she murmurs into her microphone. She nods curtly to Tomas. "Remove the Seed's wrist tie." Tomas does just that and I take care not to meet his eye while he cuts the tie, as I'm afraid the cameras will see something between us. The cable falls to the floor and I am free. But I don't move. Not yet. The guard is way too close.

"Silver Seed one-nine-five-two," the guard addresses me by my crew number.

"Yes, ma'am?" I say, all bright and happy.

"You have clearance to speak," the guard says. "Out you go now. And well done." I'm shocked. She sounds so *human*.

And so I walk out into the sunshine to the waiting audience, which has grown to maybe fifty now. And I lie to them with all my heart and soul.

T

I'm watching my sister give the performance of her life. She tells the people all the usual stuff about the camaraderie of the SilverShip crew and the exciting prospect of the new life waiting for them on the Island. It is the stuff they hear all the time from the Bartizan, but it is so much more powerful coming from the mouth of a bedraggled kid who just glows with pride at being part of it. I don't know how she does it. And I am astounded at her ruthlessness.

My commander enters the fish tank. She strides up to me with a face like thunder. "Marne," she barks. "The remains of one of your crew were retrieved from the foot of the Silo at first light. The other was found dead with a knife wound to the heart at the entrance to Thin Murk. And all the while you were hiding like the pathetic little coward you are."

I gasp. "No! I was prisoner. Of a Roach." I don't know why I bother. Nothing I say now will make any difference.

The comm looks right through me. "Tomas Marne," she says in her official drone. "You are now designated sole survivor of Enforcer group Kilo Tango. And you know what that makes you, don't you?"

Of course I know. It's the first thing we learn at induction. If you lose both your crew, you're a traitor. Don't ask me why. That is just the way it is. "Traitor," I whisper. "It makes me a traitor."

While my sister is still acting her heart out, I am marched out of the fish tank into a network of corridors. And I know exactly where they are leading me: to the Astro Room.

K

To my amazement, people listen to me. I tell them how wonderful it is to be a SilverSeed, how happy we all are, the camaraderie, the sense of purpose . . . *blah, blah, blah* . . . and then before they have a chance to lose interest, I stop. I say I must go, that I cannot wait to go back to my crew.

And now my moment has come. It is time to run. Time to get back to Jonno and tell him everything is all right. Time to thank Maximillian for all he did for us. Time for Jonno and I to take our chance together. Out of the corner of my eye I see that Tomas has gone and there is only one guard left. She is leaning against the wall, relaxed and pleased to be part of this. The crowd are murmuring among themselves, casting glances my way. I can run now and I know they will help me. Now is my chance. *Take it, Kaitlin, take it. Now!*

But I don't take it. After all that, *I don't take it.* Instead, I turn around and walk back into the fish tank. "Take me to my crew," I tell the guard. The doors slide closed behind me, and as the sunlight vanishes, I think that maybe I have gone crazy.

Chapter 14

SUN BISCUITS

M

I, Maximillian Fly, am on my way to my dear friend Andronicus. I am running low through the Underground with the smell of the blood in my head and fear for my young Wingless one in my heart. I cannot help but imagine her terror as the Vermin took her away. How the Vermin got free I do not know. Do *you* know, young watcher? Yes, I know you're here. I can feel you following me through the darkness. You do know, don't you?

I am in the most ancient part of the Underground now, on a crossing where the well-worn cobbles tell of many hundreds of years of footfall. I turn left beneath a brick-lined archway into a wide, low tunnel and, with my goggles casting their two green pools of light before me, I begin to climb upward again. This is a very civilized tunnel, lined with pleasing little brick archways at regular intervals, numbered for the houses they lead to above. The house of Andronicus is number twelve and it is toward the end. I reach his barred gate and, on two legs now, I flip open the catch. I hurry through the earthy cellar, up the rickety wooden steps and pull hard on a lever. The hatch above flies open and I hear a shrill scream on the other side. I stick my head up and the scream is repeated. It is Minna Simms. I apologize and then I wonder why it is I who apologize, for it is *my* delicate ear tubes that are buzzing, not hers.

Minna recovers herself and gives a little simper. "Oh, Maxie, it is you in your silly glasses. You are such a tease."

I do not reply.

It is considered good manners to help someone out of a hatch, but Minna merely turns on her heel and stomps away down the passage on her sturdy beige tree-trunk legs. I wait until the kitchen door is firmly closed behind her and then I begin the task of extricating myself. It is not easy due to the fact that someone has added extra beading around the inside of the opening. Given that Andronicus would not know a hammer if it hit him—I push that thought quickly to one side—I know this must be Minna's work and done this morning by the look of it. She is both petty and thorough.

As I slowly pull myself upward, I reflect that despite the pall that the presence of Minna Simms casts over the house of Andronicus, I still love to come here. I have learned so much of the world from my dear friend and I regard him as a person of great insight, which is why I do not trouble him with my doubts about Minna Simms. Andronicus clearly considers her to be a trustworthy person—she is his sister after all—and I must be content with that. Oh, this hatch is a trial. But I will not call for help. *I will not.* Aha! I now have my middle limb free.

As I wriggle my way upward, easing my wing cases through the infernally narrow gap, I feel that you are still watching me. But it is not with amusement—which would be understandable—but with disapproval. I suppose it is because the affinity you young ones feel for one another. I believe you are anxious about the small fugitive who is still in my house. Alone. I shall confess to you that I too was concerned about leaving him. But he was sleeping soundly and I feared that if I woke him and he found that his sister was gone and he was alone with me, he would panic. I have left him supplied with water and fruit. I have also locked his door so he does not wander and come to harm. So he is safe enough for now, unlike his poor sister. I need to find a Rat to take him to safety and Andronicus will know how to contact one.

But first I must . . . get . . . out of . . . this hatch. I am stuck with my lower segment in the chill of the cellar and my top two segments and three limbs sticking up into the passageway. It is utterly ridiculous. It is also suspiciously quiet in the kitchen and I have the distinct feeling that Minna Simms is watching me through the keyhole. The thought of this spurs me on. Using my two powerful lower limbs to push against the steps below, I lever myself upward, and suddenly I shoot out of the hatch and land with a clatter upon the floor. It is most undignified. I dust myself down, refold my underwings, and as I set off up the stairs, I hear a splutter of laughter from the kitchen.

On the first floor I open the door to Andronicus's private room and find a monstrosity. Like the Vermin, it is superficially attractive. It is tall with a healthy shine and is even the possessor of six delightful, delicately slim, bowed legs. "What," I ask Andronicus, "is *that*?" However, I know full well what it is, and I also know why it is there.

Andronicus has the grace to look embarrassed. "It is a dining table. A gift from my sister," he says in his soft, deep voice.

"I am shocked you accepted it, Andronicus," I say.

My friend pulls out one of the four-legged, high-backed ancillary creatures that accessorize this thing and are kept tucked neatly beneath its flat carapace. I believe they are called dining chairs. "Try it, Maximillian," he says. "It really is not so bad."

I regard the creature with disgust. "This is not respectful of us, Andronicus," I tell him. "This custom does not suit us. I see no reason to use this . . . *eating equipment.* It is an insult."

"It's a dining table, Maximillian, not an attack," Andronicus protests.

"It is both," I tell him. "But mainly, it is an attack."

I see hurt and confusion in Andronicus's eyes and I feel bad, especially when I remember how he saved me last night. "Forgive me, my friend," I say. "I am a little overwrought."

"Forgiven," Andronicus replies with a sparkle in his eyes and he quietly shuts the door. "I am humoring her, Maximillian," he whispers as he leads me into the room. "Minna is leaving tomorrow and I do not wish to part on bad terms."

I at once feel better. "Leaving *tomorrow*?"

"Indeed. First thing in the morning."

I am very pleased with this news—so pleased in fact that I agree, against all my better judgment, to have lunch sitting at the eating apparatus. Among friends we Roaches prefer to lie upon rugs and cushions. In mixed company we sit upon stools, for our wing cases need to be free to drop down behind us when we sit, and a chair back does not accommodate this. I wince as I bend my carapace in order to fit upon what Andronicus calls a

Chippendale dining chair. I gingerly arrange my wing cases so they hang down either side of its bony back and their tips graze the floor, and then I place my three upper limbs upon the table's high carapace in order to keep me steady—until Andronicus tells me this is bad form and I should put them in my "lap."

I do not like the word "lap." It sounds unsavory. I feel my temper fraying. "What, pray," I demand, "is my *lap*? Where might it be situated? On top of my head? Folded inside my underwings? Precisely *where* do I find it, Andronicus?"

Andronicus sighs. "Please, Maximillian, this is only for today. Your lap is the inner lower half of your segment that is now bent forward. Just rest your upper limbs on there."

This feels rather unhygienic to me, for it is in close proximity to our exit valves, but I have given up any protest. I do as Andronicus asks and I am grateful for one thing only—that Mama cannot see me now.

The door opens and Minna strides in carrying a tray with two bowls of steaming sludge, which she places in front of us with an exaggerated flourish. With a filthy cloth she wipes the edges of the bowls where the sludge has spilled, and with that most annoying of instructions, "Enjoy," she sashays out of the room.

Reluctantly, I pick up the eating implement that Minna

has provided—a long, fat dropper with a brown rubber bulb on the end. It smells vile. I dread to think what it has been used for in the past. I wait until Minna's creeping footsteps have gone all the way down to the kitchen and then I speak. "Andronicus, dear friend," I say. "I do not wish you to think I am ungrateful for your delightful luncheon invitation, but surely you must see, this thing"—I hold up the dropper between my thumb and forefinger with some disdain—"is most disrespectful toward us."

Andronicus sighs. "I know. I can only apologize, Maximillian. But Minna will be gone soon and there is no point upsetting her now."

Personally I can see many good points to upsetting Minna right now. However, Andronicus is a considerate person—if he were not I would have been left out on the roof last night and by now might very well be an exoskeleton at the foot of the Night Roach Silo—and I must respect that. I poke my finger into the lukewarm bowl of thick, lumpy sludge, which although Minna knows we are vegetarian, has an unpleasantly meaty smell.

"Give that muck to me," Andronicus says. He gets up awkwardly from the eating accessory and disappears with the bowls. I hear him emptying them into the dry waste composter in the bathroom. He returns with the empty bowls and two paper bags from our favorite shop, Parminter's Pantry, the small bread-and-vegetable emporium run by Parminter and her mother using produce from their farm. "I knew lunch would be vile," he says. "It always is. I've been living on Parminter's takeouts ever since Minna arrived. It's lucky for me she can't bear to see me eat." He giggles. "Although I must admit to being particularly revolted the first time she stayed for supper."

I laugh. I am so happy that my dear friend has not been completely cowed by his sister. I extricate myself from the dining equipment and join Andronicus beside his tall bay window, where there is an array of sumptuous velvet cushions on a delightful silk rug. My dear friend has exquisite taste. In this happy state we graze our way through the finely seasoned strips of vegetables and at last I get the chance to tell him of my terrible discovery this morning—and of all my foolish misjudgments that have led up to it.

Andronicus does not berate me for my recklessness in taking in my young fugitives—indeed, he praises my bravery. He says that if you stand aside and allow barbarity to happen you become part of it yourself. Which I believe to be true.

But something is troubling me. "Andronicus," I say, "you talk about barbarity, but last night, before I arrived, Cassius and two of our group voted to effectively murder that young Vermin. What has happened to us?"

Andronicus nods sadly. “Things have changed since Cassius joined,” he says sadly. “People seem . . .”

“Nastier,” I finish for him.

“You’re not wrong.” Andronicus sighs.

“The thing is, Andronicus,” I tell him, “I *like* the young Wingless ones. Yes, they are noisy and unpredictable, but they are passionate and remarkably brave. I admire how they have overcome their inability to fly. They are damp, soft creatures, but they have good hearts and they make me smile. And now I find I am very worried for my young Kaitlin.”

Andronicus is gloomy. “If the Vermin has taken her, it will surely return her to the SilverShip. And then she will be gone.” He leans toward me, while keeping an eye on the door as if he thinks Minna Simms might be listening. “Do you believe what they say?” he asks. “That there truly is an island over the ocean where the SilverShip colony thrives?”

I shake my head. “Parminter says that if they are thriving, why doesn’t the ship bring back messages from them? Which is a good point. She says it is a disgusting form of population control. And terror.”

Andronicus smiles. “And what do *you* say, Maximillian?” he asks.

“I say that if it was so good, why would those young SilverSeeds be so desperate to escape?”

Andronicus nods. "My thoughts exactly."

"I wish I could help my Kaitlin Drew," I say.

"I do not know how you can," Andronicus says sadly. "But at least the brother is still with you."

"Yes. I wanted to ask you about him. I need to find a Rat to take him to a safe house."

"*Shhh* . . . ," Andronicus hisses. Minna's slow and heavy footsteps are coming up the stairs.

We hide the Parminter's Pantry bags beneath the cushions and, with some difficulty, seat ourselves at the dining apparatus. I feel my segments lock painfully but I manage to take up the position just in time for Minna to swan in bearing a large plate covered with a cloth, which she proudly places upon the table and with a flourish pulls off the cloth. We both gasp with pleasure—and this time it is genuine. For upon the plate lie an excitingly large array of round golden sun biscuits. My mouth waters in appreciation.

"Don't say I don't spoil you, Andy," Minna says gaily as she takes the empty bowls and their revolting brown droppers. "Now, you boys enjoy yourselves. I've plenty more in the kitchen."

"Oh, Minna," Andronicus says, looking as thrilled as I feel, "you really shouldn't have."

Minna stops at the door and swings around to look at us. "Oh, yes I should," she replies with a creepy smile that seems to have a peculiar air of victory about it. I feel uneasy but I tell myself that Minna is merely pleased with the biscuits, which are not easy to make. Sun biscuits are a great favorite of the Roach community. They are bright yellow, crispy and a joy to eat.

We retreat to the cushions with the sun biscuits. "Cheers," Andronicus says, raising his delightfully round biscuit to mine, and we drop them into our mouths in perfect synchrony. They do not disappoint. The explosion of spices is intense, the sensation of melting fills my mouth and as the biscuit dissolves my head swims with joy. These are the very best I have ever tasted. Andronicus's eyes are shining. "Another?" he asks. I believe this is called a rhetorical question.

We clink biscuits—they have a beautiful tinkling sound—and throw them into our open mouths. The taste detonates inside our heads. We cannot stop. My dear Andronicus is a greedy eater and I do believe I see two biscuits for every one of mine disappearing into his welcoming mouth. But I do not begrudge a crumb. He is my beautiful friend.

I do believe these are the strangest sun biscuits I have ever eaten. With each one that dissolves like a starburst upon my tongue, I feel increasingly dizzy. A high-pitched ringing settles into my ear tubes and I begin to wonder why dear Andronicus is looking so fuzzy around the edges. Something is not right. . . .

And now there is but one biscuit left. Andronicus picks up the last ray of sunshine and waves it playfully beneath my nostrils. "For you, Maximillian. For my beloved friend. It is for you. *You.*" He giggles dreamily.

I shake my head. "No more," I tell him. "There is something bad in them. Oh, Andronicus, oh dear . . ."

Andronicus smiles. "Dear Maximillian, my *best* friend . . . my best, best friend *ever.* Cheers!" He opens his mouth, throws the last biscuit in and then collapses upon the cushion.

"Andronicus," I say. "Wake up. . . ."

But the room is spinning and I cannot focus upon my dearest, my darlingest Andronicus: friend of my heart, biscuit of my soul. . . .

Chapter 15

GOING UP

K

I am in a small, brightly lit cell somewhere beneath the Bartizan. I've been here for what feels like hours and I've had plenty of time to ponder the totally dumb thing I've done. What was I thinking of? I try to recapture the feeling I had at the moment I turned around and walked back in though the Gateway to the Future. I see now that it was, weirdly, because everyone was listening to me and I'm not used to that. The people outside and even the guards were hanging on every word I said and suddenly I wasn't acting anymore, I actually believed what I was saying. It all went to my head.

I don't know what I'm doing in this cell. It doesn't look good. I thought they'd send me back to the Silver-Ship crew quarters, but now I'm beginning to wonder if they've put me in Oblivion. How could I have been so *stupid*?

Oh! The door's opening. A guard, a stocky woman in a fancy black-and-gold Bartizan jacket, comes in. She is carrying a plate of sandwiches and a bottle of juice balanced on a big box, which she carefully puts down beside me. "Food, drink and clean uniform," she says. She walks to the wall and pulls back a sliding panel. "Bathroom and shower in there. Put your old uniform in the basket. I'll be back in half an hour." And then she's gone.

I feel weak with relief—they don't feed you in Oblivion and they certainly don't bring you clean clothes. The sudden absence of dread brings my appetite back. The sandwiches are the usual spicy yellow paste—cat sick, the little kids call them—and the juice is the usual neon sweet sludge. I feel like I'm back with the crew already. I gulp down the gloop; then I open the uniform box and pull out new everything. I take out my jacket and find three gold stars embroidered above my number. *Three gold stars.* I'm shocked. In my whole six months I never got a star because I wouldn't play their game. Jonno had one star and was hoping for a second. I smile: this is really going to annoy Jonno. And then I remember that Jonno is alone in Maximillian's house, that I will probably never see him again, and I feel my smile fall off my face. But there is no point thinking like that. I get cleaned up and put on the new stuff. I try not to feel proud of the three stars, but I do. I wonder if I'm quite the rebel I thought I was.

In no time at all, the guard returns. I'm so back in SilverSeed mode that I stand up at once. "Kaitlin Marne, come with me, please," she says.

Marne. My stomach lurches. They are using Dad's old name—this feels ominous. But on the plus side I have three stars and she said "please." Also she doesn't grab my arm and frog-march me out. She trusts me to walk beside her, which I do, like the good three-star SilverSeed I have so easily become.

We head down a wide wood-paneled corridor and stop outside an impressive pair of double doors flanked by black marble columns. She throws open the doors like a magician proudly showing the success of a trick, and reveals the fabled Bartizan tower elevator. It is a ramshackle affair with a sliding concertina cage-like door that she heaves open with a loud clattering. She indicates for me to step inside, follows me in and repeats the process with the doors. Then she keys in a code—which I make sure to remember—and we begin to move slowly upward, accompanied by a loud clanking and the occasional disconcerting judder. I know how the elevator works—we learned it at school—but even though

I know we can't fall because a safety ratchet will stop us, the higher we go, the more anxious I feel. Because I now suspect that I am on my way to the very top of the Bartizan tower, and everyone knows there are only two reasons for that—either you're headed for an Astro or the Guardian. As the lighted numbers for the floors flash steadily up, I begin to panic. There is no way the Guardian would want to see *me*, so it must be an Astro. Those cat sick sandwiches were my last meal.

The elevator comes to a juddering halt and an illuminated *TOP* appears above the column of numbers. My legs feel like water as we step out into a circular space flooded with light from a dome of colored glass that casts dancing rainbows onto the dark wood floor. The smell of beeswax polish suffuses the air and the atmosphere is hushed. I've read about temples and sacred spaces and this is how I imagine they would be. There are three hefty dark wood doors leading off the space: one has a huge silver number *9*, one a giant silver *A* and the third, which I now see are double doors, has no label but is flanked by two men in Bartizan black-and-gold jackets, standing to attention. But all I can see is the shining silver *A*. *A* for Astro. Not so long ago Mom walked through that very door, and now it is my turn. I feel dizzy and close my eyes and I see a big green *A*. There is no escape.

I feel my guard's hand beneath my elbow, walking me forward. "Come on," she says impatiently. "Your appointment is in thirty seconds." Thirty seconds. Is that all I have left? The Bartizan guards step forward. "Kaitlin Marne for Madam Guardian," my escort says.

Madam Guardian? I don't understand.

One of the bodyguards knocks softly on the polished, blank door. I hear the lock disengage and he reverently presses down the brass handle. The door swings open and he indicates for me to go in. My escort nudges me forward and follows me inside. The door closes behind us and I feel weak with relief. This is no Astro room.

It is sparse but opulent all at once. A shining slate floor, polished wood-paneled walls and a long line of sparkling windows that look out onto the misty rooftops of the city and, dimly, to the fields beyond. And sitting in front of those windows, behind a long mahogany desk in a high-backed black leather chair is a small, almost-gaunt woman who is regarding me with a steady gaze. She looks so perfect that she seems unreal. Her hair is a rigid pewter-gray bob like a helmet; she wears a black velvet high-necked jacket with three gold flashes upon its rigid, upright, collar. Her manicured hands slowly tap the top of an old-fashioned pen on the leather insert of the desk and where her delicate wrists emerge from her cuffs I see the triple gold banding that signifies an actual *Guardian*.

I really should stop staring but I can't.

She returns my stare with her cold, hooded eyes. "Well, well," she says in a lazy drawl of a voice, "Marne. Not a name I've heard for some time, I am pleased to say. But today, Kaitlin Marne, I have the misfortune to hear it twice." Still tapping her pen top, she looks at me as though expecting a reply, but I have no idea what to say. "Well, Kaitlin Marne, no doubt you think you have been very clever to abscond from our wonderful project that brings so much hope to this beleaguered city?"

My terror of the Astro room is fading, as is my shock at seeing the Guardian. I begin to think again and I understand that I have a choice. I can either act dumb or I can play along with it. I decided to play along. "Madam Guardian," I say, "I apologize. I have been misguided."

The Guardian gives an infinitesimal twist to her long, thin mouth. "Oh, I wouldn't put it quite like that," she says, leaning forward, almost confidentially. "You have been a *traitor*. Indeed, you *are* a traitor."

I feel like she's punched me. Traitors are put in Astros. It's what we learn at school: Traitor = Astro. One inevitably leads to the other. Cause and effect.

"You seem surprised," the Guardian observes coolly. "As though you did not know you are a traitor."

"I . . . I didn't know," I say.

"Well, Kaitlin Marne. Let me elucidate. We have

reason to believe that you ran away from the SilverShip crew quarters with a security device essential for the well-being of our city. We know that your mother stole this device. Which is why your mother"—she leans forward and eyeballs me—"is dead."

I refuse to react. Instead, I focus on her perfect fingers tapping the pen top as she continues. "Despite searches of all your family's *many* places of residence, this security device has not been found. How it escaped detection I have no idea. However, we now have reason to believe you somehow smuggled this object into the crew quarters."

I stay silent. There is no way I am going to tell her anything whatsoever.

"However, as you do not have it upon your person—you were scanned as you came in—you clearly have hidden it somewhere while you were at large. I had you brought up here so that you can redeem yourself by telling me where it is. *Right now.*"

Her oddly blank eyes stare into mine but I don't blink. If this is a stare-off then she's not going to win. But she does. Because she says, "You do look remarkably like your father. Your *dead* father." And I close my eyes. She gives a bitter little laugh. "Unfortunately for you."

Since I've been in this stuffy, overblown room I feel like I've gone through a lifetime of emotions: shock, fear, grief and now I feel so angry that I want to punch her.

Maybe she senses that because she leans back in her soft leather chair so that she is well out of arm's length. And then she says, almost languidly, "So, Kaitlin Marne, tell me where you have hidden the device and nothing more will be said about it. You will keep your three stars and go back to your crew as, *apparently*, you wish so very much to do."

"I'm sorry to disappoint you, Madam Guardian," I say, "but I really don't know what device you mean."

She stands up but stays safely behind her desk. "Foolish girl. I'll give you one last chance. I must make clear to you that another refusal will have irreversible consequences. And not necessarily for you."

I'm so angry I don't listen. (Later, I will wish I had listened. But I didn't and that's how it is. You can't change the past however much you'd like to.) "I have absolutely no idea what you are talking about," I tell her.

She smiles and I get the feeling that she is about to do something she's been looking forward to. She tells my guard to cuff my wrist to a ring that I now notice in the wall. I begin to feel very scared. While the guard is doing this, the Guardian leans forward and speaks into a small grille in the wall. "Proceed," she says.

This feels very, very bad, but I try to stay calm by telling myself that nothing has happened to me yet. I must be brave enough to wait and see what it is that she means to proceed with. Madam Guardian tells me to face an ornate gold frame bristling with cherubs and a fine harvest of grapes set around a pane of dark glass. I look into it and see my reflection, wide-eyed and scared, and I hear Madam Guardian say into the grille: "Turn the prisoner this way. I want to see his face." And then she barks, "Lights!"

Tomas! There on the other side of the glass is Tomas in an orange Astro suit without the helmet. He is staring right at me, but I don't think he can see me. He looks as though he has seen a ghost. No, that is not true—he looks as though he *is* a ghost. I feel sick.

"Please, Madam Guardian . . . ," I say, hating how I sound so pathetic. "Please don't do this to him. *Please don't.*"

And then, at that very moment, something extraordinary happens—a Sunstrike. This is when a small ray of pure sunlight breaks through the haze of the Orb. It's something to do with the angle of the sun hitting a particular wavelength in the force field. It rarely happens but when it does it is a wonderful thing. People always smile. Older ones call it a Benison and techies talk about an Orb fissure. But mostly we call it a Sunstrike.

The Sunstrike flashes through Madam Guardian's window. It bathes the room in brilliance and I see a shock of recognition in Tomas's eyes. He has seen me.

And soon he is saying my name, telling me goodbye and that it is okay. Angrily, the Guardian switches off the intercom. "I warned you, Kaitlin Marne. I told you your refusal would have irreversible consequences. And so it does. This is what happens to traitors. Watch and learn."

So I watch Tomas being Astroed.

And I learn that I am powerless.

Chapter 16

THE SNEAK

J

Me and Tedward are prisoners again. We are locked in a room at the top of the house with the Roach in it, and even though I keep shouting no one comes. I really miss my tribe on the SilverShip. We are the Bears because we are the youngest. Then there are the Wolves and then the Lions. Katie is a Lion even though she doesn't want to be. Today we are doing fishing practice for when we get to the Island. I really wish I was there too with my friends. Katie did a bad thing running away. Tedward is really angry with her. She tried to take him away on his own, but he wouldn't go. He wanted to stay with the Bears too, because he is a bear. Tedward is much lighter today. I hope he is feeling all right.

Me and Tedward are looking out of the window. In the street below there is a lady staring up at me. She is square-shaped and looks a bit weird. Tedward doesn't like her so we go and sit in Katie's corner in her blankets. I hope she will come back soon.

I can hear footsteps coming up the stairs. But they are not Katie's. They are heavy and slow. Tedward is scared. And now they are outside the door and I hear the key in the lock turning and the door is opening. The square lady from the street comes in. I have seen her before. It was when Katie and me first arrived at the SilverShip.

"Have you come to take me back?" I ask.

"I am here on behalf of the Bartizan to arrest a fugitive," she says.

I don't know what she means. I point to the badge on my shirt and I say, "I'm a SilverSeed and I want to go back. You remember me. You gave me my uniform."

She looks annoyed. "I don't do that anymore," she says. "I have a much more important job now. I am undercover."

I suppose she means under the blanket thing she is wearing, which is a big cover. I am afraid she will go away and leave me behind, so I ask again and this time I use what Mom calls the "magic word." "Please," I say, "please will you take me back to the SilverShip?" And just for luck I do the magic word a third time. "*Please?*"

She looks surprised. "You *want* to go back?" she asks.

"Oh, yes!" I tell her. "My sister made me come here.

I didn't want to. Will you take me back? Please, *please*?"

I get up and, even though my foot still hurts, me and Tedward go over to her and I grab her hand so she can't get away.

She sniffs. "You're a smelly little boy, aren't you?"

She is a rude lady but Mom told me that I must not be rude back. "It's not me, it's Tedward," I explain. "He's got sick on him." And then she does something horrible. She grabs Tedward and throws him into Katie's corner.

"No!" I shout, and I try to pull away but she squeezes my hand so hard it hurts.

"Not so chirpy now, are we?" she mutters. And she pulls me out of the room and all the way down the stairs and out into the street and Tedward is left all alone in the Roach house. I look up at the window to see if Tedward is watching me go, but he isn't there.

She pulls me along the road really fast and I have to run to keep up and I've got no shoes and my foot hurts. And we don't go to the Gateway to the Future. We go down a lot of dark alleys and I get more and more scared because I think she is taking me somewhere horrible. And then I think about Tedward all scared on his own in the Roach house and I start crying, even though I don't want to.

"It's no good crying at *me*," she says. "You can blame your sister. Sisters are nothing but trouble. I had one once. Until she fell, ha-ha. Off a roof. Oh yes. Oh yes." She looks down at me and her eyes look a bit crazy. She is very scary. "You got a brother too?" she asks.

I nod.

"Roach?" she asks.

I shake my head and she pulls my arm so it hurts. "Well, aren't you the lucky one?" she says. "I've got a Roach one but I won't have it for much longer. You want to know why?"

I shake my head. I don't want to know anything about her at all. She is a horrible person. But she takes out a thing like a giant ladybug with six suckers for feet. "Know what this is?" she asks.

I shake my head again.

She laughs. "This, little boy, is called a 'bug'! It listens to everything you say."

"Is it listening to us?" I ask.

"Don't be silly, why would it do that? But it listened to my Roach brother. I stuck it under the table when he was having lunch with his nasty Roach friend and it has recorded everything they said. You would not believe what those filthy Roaches have been up to—oh, there are so many treasons to choose from. It was a joy to hear. I had such a lovely time in the kitchen listening to it after they ate themselves silly with my spiked biscuits and snored their stupid heads off. How did you think I knew where to find you, eh?"

I don't understand what she is saying, but I know it is nasty. Suddenly we stop outside a dirty old door. Above it is a sign, which I can read. It says *Dancing until 2 a.m. No Roaches.* She pushes open the door and we go inside. She pulls me along dark and smelly corridors and then through some big metal doors into a huge circular room with lots more doors leading off it. In the middle is a little hut made of metal with a guard in it. She pulls me over to the hut and the floor is wet because someone is washing it and I skid along. It would be fun if I wasn't with *her.*

She is talking to the guard in the booth now and my hand hurts because she is squeezing it so tight. I bite my lip to stop crying and I listen to what she is saying: "I am returning an absconded SilverSeed and I claim my reward."

The guard peers down at me from his little window and I think he has kind eyes—much kinder than the square lady's. "We don't pay out on under-tens," he says. "I'll have someone fetch him."

"Oh no, you won't," she says. "Not until I've been paid."

Now I am afraid she will take me away. So I say to the guard, "Please let me stay. *Please.* I never wanted to go. She *made* me." I mean that Katie made me, but it comes out wrong.

The guard smiles down at me. "Of course you can stay, sonny." He gives the square lady a bad stare and says, "Looks like you've taken him away against his will. We'll be investigating that. He's injured too. What have you done to him?"

"Nothing!" she says in a high, squeaky voice. "It's not like that. Not at all. I found him in an attic." She scrabbles in her pocket and takes out the big red bug with suckers. "Look!" she says. "I've brought this back. I have recorded evidence of Roach Treason: Conspiracy, Murder and the Imprisoning of an Officer of the State."

The guard takes the bug and zips it into a bag. He gets out a pen to write on the bag. "Name?" he asks.

"Minna Simms," the square lady says.

"Good name for a traitor," the guard says, writing the name on the bag.

"No!" The square lady's voice goes even higher. "Cross it out, cross it out! I misunderstood. I thought you meant my name."

The guard sighs. "No. I meant the traitor's name. We know very well who *you* are."

"Andronicus Thrip and Maximillian Fly," she gabbles. "Write them down. On the bag. Now. The proof is in that bug, I tell you. They are at present at number twelve, Cat Trap Cartwheel. I have drugged them. They are insensible."

The guard nods. "I see. A case for fumigation."

"Yes! Oh, yes. A perfect case!" she says.

And now I am in the guard's hut waiting to be collected. Soon I will be back with the Bears. I hope I am not too late for the fishing. The guard is nice. I am sitting on his stool because my foot is hurting and he has given me some candy and let me look out of his window. The square lady is sitting on the long bench that runs around the walls of the big room. The man with the mop and bucket is cleaning the floor. She has to lift her feet up so he can clean under the bench. She doesn't look happy. Oh. Two guards are coming over to her. She is standing up and they have grabbed her arms. She is trying to pull away, but they don't let her. And now they are marching her through a door with a big silver O on it. She is screaming.

"Why is she screaming?" I ask the nice guard.

He chuckles. "Sneaks are trouble," he says. "We use them once only. Can't trust 'em a second time. She's off to Oblivion."

"What's Oblivion?" I ask.

"I forget," he says and then laughs like he has made a really funny joke. "Aha, here's the nursie coming to fetch you. She'll look after your foot. Time for you to go, young man." He pats my shoulder. "Good luck, kid. Good luck."

I walk away with one of the nurses who look after us Bears when we are sick. I look back and wave goodbye to the man in the booth and I think he looks sad. He waves to me and then turns away.

Chapter 17

KILL GAS

M

I, Maximillian Fly, am sick. Oh, I am *so* sick. Something is inside my head banging it with a hammer, trying to get out. No . . . wait . . . it is outside my head, trying to get in. *Get off my head. Get off!* I hear deep echoing groans and now I understand that I am in a cavern with a sheep . . . a flock of sheep. Inside a dark, dark cavern . . . it is good . . . I like sheep . . . all is well . . . sheep . . . sleep.

"Maximillian!" Noise screams into my ear tubes. "Wake up! For pity's sake, wake up!" Two hammers hit me on either side of my face and they keep hitting, hitting, hitting, until I open my eyes. "Thank goodness," says a voice, which I believe belongs to the hitting thing that swims in front of me. The thing is not a sheep, which I confess I find confusing.

"Maximillian!" The voice is high and squeaky with a

sharp edge of panic. It makes me uneasy. I prefer sheep. "Wake up, you great nurdle," it yells at me. "Wake up! It's me. It's Parminter!"

Parminter. This is a familiar thing. A Parminter. I know one of those. I blink to focus and see, through hazy darkness, the broad face of my dear friend Parminter. Her lovely golden eyes are brimming with tears and her antennae are drooping with concern. She is, bizarrely, wearing a headlamp, and in its beam of light I see her bending over the body—*oh no, not the body, oh please, no*—of Andronicus. "Andronicus." My voice comes out as a faint whistling thing. "Oh, Andronicus, my dearest one . . ."

"Shut up, Maximillian, and help me," Parminter snaps. I am shocked. Parminter is such a gentle, softly spoken person.

I do as commanded. With the help of Parminter, I heave the deadweight of my friend to a sitting position and then with great difficulty we stand him up. Andronicus opens his eyes and looks bewildered. "Gerr," he says. "Perr? Werr yerr err?"

I believe he is asking Parminter why she is here. I add my foolish questions to his. "And why are you wearing a headlamp? What's going on?"

Her reply is short and yet much to the point. "You're being fumigated, you twits. You've just sat here and let them seal the house and you've not even bothered to move. I really don't know what's got into you."

But I know exactly what's got into us: sun biscuits—*spiked* sun biscuits, baked by Minna Simms. I now see that the darkness outside is not nighttime but tarred hemp stuck to the windows. Yes, the house of Andronicus has been sealed and we knew nothing of it.

Parminter is pulling and pushing us out of the room. "Get a move on, you two. Any minute now they'll be pumping in the kill gas. We've got to get out of here *right now*."

We stagger up the stairs but as we reach the top landing I hear a loud clunking noise. I turn to see a huge ribbed tube, like a giant trunk of an elephant, snaking along the landing below. From it comes a puff of dense yellow gas. This truly is a thing of nightmares.

"Kill gas," Parminter hisses. *"Hurry."* I do not need to be told. We haul Andronicus into the attic, where the meeting was last night. He groans as he goes, lurching from side to side and I fear that one of his antennae is torn off. But this is no time for gentleness. I glance back to see the giant tube pushing up the stairs, puffs of yellow gas issuing from its gaping maw, which is lined with shiny red cloth so that it glistens like a monstrous, salivating mouth. Waving tendrils surround the mouth, feeling where to go, pulling the tube upward, guiding it through the house. I hear it scrape along the floor as the tendrils walk it into each room to dispense its lethal dose.

I slam the door fast and Parminter places cushions along the gap beneath it. I see she has already smashed the skylight and cut the sticky black hemp to make an opening. On the rug smears of Vermin blood are now covered with splinters of glass.

Parminter drags the ladder over to the skylight, springs up it and pulls herself out onto the roof. Then, she leans down, her stick-thin upper limbs ready to grab Andronicus. "Push him up to me," she commands.

Together we push and pull Andronicus up the ladder. He clatters and slips and I hear the scrape of the tube outside on the landing and the scuttling of its tendrils. At last Andronicus is out and I am up the ladder after him like a rat up a drainpipe. As I haul myself into the fresh air, a wisp of yellow swirls into the room below.

I sit on the ridge of the roof taking deep breaths, but Parminter is impatient. "Kill gas rises. It will be out any second now," she says. "Fly-lift!"

Andronicus is lying straddled across the ridge tiles, limp as an old rug. "Andronicus!" I say, close to his ear tubes. "We will fly-lift you. Understand?"

Andronicus looks at me blearily, "Yerr," he mumbles. He does not resist as Parminter and I gently spread his wing cases while trying to keep his underwings neatly folded. Then, with some difficulty on the slippery roof, we place ourselves on either side of him, below his outstretched wings.

Suddenly a yell comes up from the street. "Roof escape!" Panicked, I look at Parminter—*they've seen us*. But then I see a long yellow tendril of kill gas drift up from the skylight and I realize they are not talking about us; they mean the gas.

"Count to three and go," Parminter says. And so we do. Using only one wing each, Parminter and I rise up awkwardly: a three-headed monstrosity lurching into the sky. This is my first fly-lift for real. Parminter says that a fly-lift is something all young Roaches practice, but I in my lonely state never spoke to another Roach until Mama left last year and Parminter found me. Recently Parminter has been instructing me in the art of flying. She told me that the fly-lift is about trust and communication, and said it would be good for me. Last week we practiced for the first time with a sack of flaxseed—much to her mama's dismay. I found it terrifying until I understood that the trick is to think as one person, not two. But I am still a novice. Luckily, Parminter flies smoothly and with great strength and, as in many things, she gives me confidence.

The voices we heard came from the front of Andronicus's house, so we head for the back, where he has a long, narrow yard full of ancient apple trees. It is a place where he and I have spent many enjoyable summer evenings together, but today it is far less welcoming, for as we lurch above it, trying desperately to gain height, a shout goes up from below: "Roach! Roach! Roach!"

I look down to see the yard is infested with Vermin and slugs. The slugs are shiny, fat black capsules of kill gas, which a Vermin is feeding into the fumigator—a large yellow barrel from which that sinister trunk snakes out, heading across the grass and into the house through a smashed window, now sealed with a metal plate. The house itself looks blind and scared with all its windows covered with tar and hemp cloth. I feel sorry for it.

Parminter flashes me a look of warning and points downward. I now see one of the Vermin positioning a weapon upon her shoulder; it is always the females who shoot—they are more accurate and deadly. Any minute now we shall be blown out of the sky in a ball of flames and there is nothing we can do about it, encumbered as we are with Andronicus. And then I hear his dear voice whispering, "Save yourselves. Drop me."

I have no desire to live even a second of life with the image of my dear friend falling to his death, knowing that it was I who let him go. However, I cannot sacrifice Parminter to my conscience. I look into her eyes and I see my answer. "Shut up, Andronicus," she says. "Just *shut up.*"

I fear those uncouth words will be her last, for below in the yard I hear the clunk of the safety catch release on the Vermin's weapon and I await the moment of extinction. I am telling myself that the conflagration will be so sudden and all-consuming that I shall have no awareness of it and that it will be a happiness that my journey to the next world will be in the company of two dear friends, when an altercation breaks out in the yard below.

Another Vermin—from its bulk I believe it to be a male—has thrown the missile-wielding Vermin to the ground and is shouting, "Don't do it! Stop, stop!" Yes, it is indeed a deep-voiced male.

The Vermin with the missile launcher is not amused. She screams abuse at the male, making Parminter in comparison appear the very essence of politeness. And so, unmolested, we fly laboriously upward, and as we go the words of their fight pursue us, loud and clear.

"Let me go!" the missile Vermin is yelling.

Then comes the male, sounding desperate. "Please, Tana. Please, just *leave* it. *Ouch, that hurt!* You don't understand. One of the Roaches—the big one—is a P.P.!"

"So why've we just gassed it, then?"

"It's a terrible mistake. I just got the call. I was about to go in and pull it out of there."

"Liar! Whoever heard of a Roach being a P.P.?"

"Okay, then, *do* it, Tana. You'll be in an Astro tomorrow and see if I care. We're through."

I look down in dismay to see the male Vermin striding away and the female Vermin repositioning the weapon. I know that this time no one is going to stop her.

"Drop me!" croaks Andronicus.

"Shut up, Andronicus!" both Parminter and I tell him.

Far below I see the Vermin steady herself and take careful aim. A second later I hear the whoosh of the missile and I ready myself for our journey to the next world. I feel its heat upon my abdomen and I hear Parminter gasp in pain. I was wrong, I think. This fireball does not consume so fast that we do not feel it. We are going to be aware of every second of our destruction. However, I am curious as to how it is that we are still managing to fly and I see that our wings have yet to catch fire. I find I am watching my beautiful indigo wing case and bidding it farewell. I wonder if it will just quietly melt or will it splutter and sizzle? And then a shout from Parminter breaks into my thoughts: "We've done it! Oh, Maximillian, Andronicus, look! Look down!"

I do as Parminter tells me—for have I not learned that Parminter always knows best? I see the ball of flame dropping back toward the ground. We have outflown it. It must have reached its zenith immediately beneath us, and now it is returning to base. I see the female Vermin staring up in disbelief as the fireball drops down to greet her. I hear a deep-voiced yell: "Tana! Tana! Run, run!" But Tana does not run, and in a moment she is the conflagration that we were meant to be.

We continue our flight in silence. It is surprisingly upsetting, this Vermin incident. It is a full ten minutes later, as we are approaching my own dear rooftop with its yellow chimney that Parminter speaks. The words are not welcome: "Maximillian. They have sealed your house too."

It is true. The shine on my skylight is not the gentleness of rain; it is the suffocation of tar. I think of Mama's teapot, alone upon its little cushion in a dark house full of gas. *It is but a teapot, Maximillian,* I tell myself severely. *It will survive. Indeed it will utterly unaffected. Kill gas does not affect teapots.* And then I remember there is something else, just as—no, even more—precious as the teapot in the house. *The little boy, Jonno.* I think of him lying in the room where I so neglectfully left him. I imagine the gas creeping beneath his door. I imagine his choking terror, and I despair.

Chapter 18

PARMINTER'S PANTRY

M

Andronicus is a deadweight. My wing aches and my heart is heavy for the little boy and his bear left behind in my attic. I tell myself that there is nothing I can do for him now, that I must think only about getting Andronicus to safety, but it is hard to think that way.

Ah, it's you again. So once more, young watcher, you are with me on a flight? Like all Wingless you seem fascinated by the art of flying. Very well, I shall try to take my mind off the poor child I have deserted and talk to you.

We are flying to Parminter's farm. Parminter lives with her mama on the opposite side of the city, where the fields go all the way out to the edge of the Orb. The farm is a truly wonderful place; they grow flax and hemp on the long outer fields and all kinds of vegetables on the short fields near the farmhouse. I was amazed when I first saw food growing in the earth. Until then I had truly believed that food grew itself inside small cylindrical cans. You may laugh at my ignorance, but one does believe what one's own mama says. It is only natural.

Perhaps you wonder why I know so much about Parminter's farm? It is because I love to go there. I do not go as often as I would like for I do not wish to become a nuisance. I do not want Parminter's mama thinking, *Oh, not that tedious Maximillian again, always hanging around like a bad smell,* as my mama used to say—even though I know that is not the kind of thing that Parminter's mama would ever think. For she does not believe that a Roach child is a shameful thing. Indeed, she has even named their farm shop just for Parminter, whom she calls "Parmie darling" or "sweetheart." Since I have come to know Parminter I have been very surprised to discover how much a mama can love her Roach child. Very surprised indeed.

We fly slowly onward through the soft afternoon light and I think how beautiful it is up here. The Orb shimmers like a pearl and we can even see the hazy ball of the sun glowing through the misty whiteness. Below us is our city, a sprawling mass of dusty buildings with a sea of vegetation sprouting from rooftops, hanging nets, extending balconies—anywhere that will catch the precious rays of light. It is a soft and subtle array of color, ranging from dark purples through all shades of green to deep reds and oranges. It really does look beautiful.

But now I see something truly terrible: a tiny distended figure tumbling through the sky, dark against the brightness. It is a new Astro, cartwheeling out of the Bartizan hundreds of feet up in the air, and inside that fat orange suit is a poor, doomed person. It is a despicable practice, designed by the Bartizan to remind all in the city below of the consequences of being a so-called traitor. Beneath its soft colors our city has a rotten core.

Suddenly a shout comes from Parminter. "Maximillian. Look down. We're being tracked."

We are flying now over a warren of alleyways deep in shadow and I can see nothing within them, but over on Parminter's side is the Inner Circle, a much wider road that encircles the center of the city, along which the bigger houses—mine included—stand. And it is there that I now see three Enforcers jogging along at a steady pace, keeping up with us. Parminter is right: they are tracking us. "What to do?" I shout. Far below, the Enforcers stop and one of them points up at us.

"Drop down," Parminter says. It may sound odd to lose height in order to escape detection, but she is right. The closer we get to the rooftops the harder it will be to see us from the ground. "Turning now!" Parminter shouts.

She wheels sharply to the left and I just about manage to keep pace with her and hold Andronicus steady. But oh, my aching wings . . . We drop ever lower until we can't see the Enforcers—and they can't see us—and at last, in the distance I see the bright red roof of Parminter's farmhouse.

Unfortunately our detour has brought us close to the Night Roach Steeple. The gaunt, gray spire rises up from a decrepit old church and is utterly devoid of greenery—a sure sign that it is inhabited by Night Roaches. Any high structure in our city is used for cultivation to make best use of the light. The ingenuity of humans to grow and tend greenery never ceases to amaze me, but naturally they do not cultivate anything on a Night Roach Roost. And this is how, in daylight at least, you can tell the dangerous high places. If there are green things growing, you are safe.

I used to fly by the steeple on my way to Parminter's farm—it is generally safe during the day—and once, coming from deep within, I heard the sound of a flute playing the saddest tune I have ever heard. I felt as though I had heard it long, long ago in a different world. It made me feel very strange, but oddly happy too. I flew back the next day and heard it again. But on the third day it was gone and I felt so bereft that I decided I would never go near the steeple again. But now I must. We fly quickly by, and all is silent within.

I keep my eye on the telltale holes cut from the masonry where the Night Roaches enter and exit. The brightness of the afternoon should be enough to keep its inhabitants safely inside, but Night Roaches are a wakeful bunch and the sight of three struggling creatures might prove very tempting to any who are watching. However, I avoid looking at the large exit on the south side, where those who have personally offended the Guardian are left. That, I suppose, was the fate of the sad flute player.

But, unlike the flute player, we are lucky. We fly safely by and begin a slow descent toward Parminter's farmhouse and its red roof, which was painted especially by Parminter's mama so that her daughter could easily find her way home. We glide in slowly, but it is hard to keep control with the weight of dear Andronicus and our tiring wings feel as though they are on fire. We are very thankful for the farmyard's deep pile of grass for emergency landings.

Andronicus is lying on the grassy heap with his wings stuck out and Parminter and I are trying to fold our one flying wing back, when Parminter's mama rushes out to us. "Parmie!" she cries out. "Maximillian! Goodness, what is this? Let me help." Parminter's mama does not berate us or tell us we are fools. Instead she helps us carry Andronicus into the storage barn, which is the only place he will fit, because his wings are so stiff from the flight that they will not fold back. She sends Parminter off to get some hot honey water for us all and sets about trying to rub the circulation back into Andronicus's wing muscles.

I try to help but I am suddenly very weak and useless. Even so, Parminter's mama—who I am supposed to call Lizzie—does not tell me that I am a lazy good-for-nothing. She tells me to "rest, Maximillian dear, and wait for the honey water."

The honey water is warm, sweet and reviving and soon I am able to help Andronicus fold his wings back. While I tend Andronicus, Parminter describes to her mama our escape from the fumigators and the three Enforcers who were tracking us. I see a look of fear creep across her mama's features. "Oh, Parmie," she says anxiously. "That does not sound good. I think you had all best go into the safe room, don't you?"

Parminter nods. "Ma, I am sorry. We've put you in danger too."

"Now don't you worry about me, sweetheart," Parminter's mama says briskly. Parminter reaches out and takes her mama's hand and I see that her mama does not flinch or look revolted. Indeed, quite the opposite: she wraps her arms around Parminter and kisses the top of her head. "Parmie," she says. "You are a brave girl and I am proud of you."

I am shocked to hear Parminter called a girl, just as if she were a Wingless one. I learn new things every time I see Parminter and her mama together.

A faint croak from Andronicus sends us dropping to the ground to hear what he has to say. "Not Maximillian. He doesn't need to hide."

"Of course he does," Parminter says.

"No," says Andronicus, "when they saw Maximillian they held their fire."

"I don't think that is so," I say. "It was a squabble between Wingless ones, which is not unusual."

Andronicus makes a soft clattering noise with his wings. It means, I think, that he disagrees but is too tired to speak.

Out of respect to Parminter's mama, who does not find it easy to crouch upon the ground, Parminter and I stand up. "I think Andronicus is right, Maximillian," Parminter says. "They said the big one was a P.P. And that's you."

I laugh. P.P. means a Protected Person—someone who has a powerful relative in the Bartizan. "Why ever would I be a P.P.?" I ask. "I have no relatives apart from Mama." Parminter and her mama exchange what I believe are called meaningful glances, but I do not know why. "Anyway, I cannot be a Protected Person," I say. "They were fumigating my house."

Parminter shakes her head. "I saw something you did not. The fumigators were packing up and leaving before they had begun. Someone had called them off. Just as the Vermin tried to call off his mate."

I am silent, for suddenly I have something to consider—one small boy to be precise. If my house has not been fumigated, then the boy Jonno is still alive! I am so happy at this thought but soon another less welcome one arrives—that by now the little boy must be terrified. I remember when I was his age how frightened I used to be when Mama left me alone in the house all day, and that was without it being dark and sealed with tar.

I think about this while I help Parminter and her mama take down hay bales that are stacked up against a wall inside the barn, and by the time Parminter's mama is sliding back a panel in the wall, I know what I must do.

"I must fly back to my house now," I say.

"Are you crazy?" Parminter looks at me like she thinks this is a distinct possibility.

"Maybe. But I have left a child there."

"A child?" Parminter and her mama both gasp. "What child?"

I do my best to explain and Parminter looks at me in despair. "Maximillian, please. You can't go back. It is too dangerous. And you are exhausted. You cannot fly all that way after a fly-lift."

"Parmie, sweetheart," her mama interrupts. "You must let Maximillian do what he feels is right. And if he is a Protected Person, then he will most likely be safe."

Parminter will not give in. "But the Night Roaches . . . ," she protests.

"I will be flying in daylight," I say.

Parminter's mama turns to me. "Maximillian, you must rest for a while. Sleep. I will wake you an hour before sunset. That will give you enough time to get home safely."

I do indeed feel very tired and my right wing aches as though it is about to fall off. "Very well," I agree.

"I think, my dears," Parminter's mama says seriously, "that it might be best if you all go into the safe room now."

We help Andronicus through the gap in the wall and find ourselves in a small room with a tented ceiling. It is remarkably warm. "We're behind the oven," Parminter explains. "We can get out into the shop through a false wall, but that's got sacks of seeds stacked in front of it. We're totally hidden. You'd never know."

Parminter and her mama fetch rugs and cushions, we make ourselves comfortable and Parminter's mama leaves. I hear the sound of the hay bales being stacked back up and I feel bad. I have brought trouble to the door of Parminter now. I am, as Mama used to say, "bad news." However, I know that Parminter would not be pleased if she knew I was thinking of Mama and so I try my best to get Mama's voice out of my head. Andronicus is already asleep and I settle down beside him.

Parminter sits opposite, her knees drawn up to her chin, her lovely delicate wings, which have a soft purple glint to them, spread out behind her like a shimmering cloak. She looks beautiful. But also worried. "Maximillian," she says, "you will come back, won't you?"

"Of course," I say. "But I must help the boy first. I'll come back as soon as I've found a safe place for him."

Parminter is not happy about this, I can tell. "But that could take days. *Weeks* maybe," she says.

I do not know what to say. I have made everyone sad now. I lie down beside Andronicus and close my eyes, conscious that Parminter is watching me.

And she is not the only one. For there is also you, who are watching this sorry tale unfold in ways that I never expected. Yesterday I believed that I, Maximillian Fly, was an angel of goodness flying to the rescue of not one but two of your kind. Now I know that I am nothing of the sort. Indeed, I have been a disaster for my two young fugitives. Thanks to me one is now alone and terrified, locked in the attic room of a dark house sealed with tar, while the other has been taken away against her wishes by the very Vermin I brought into my home without a care for the danger it posed.

But I will try to make amends. I hope you will return with me to my house and see that I am doing my best to help my Kaitlin Drew's little brother. Even though I confess, I would far rather stay here. But I must not think only of myself. Oh, how right Mama was: I am a selfish creature. I am a waste of space and bring sorrow to all I meet. But I shall sleep now. . . . I shall sleep.

Chapter 19

BURIED ALIVE

P

It's Parminter here.

Now look here, you young one who is watching us, I don't know who you are or where you are but I am not happy about this. Not happy at all. I thought you were just another disapproving voice in Maximillian's head but now he's asleep I can feel you staring at *me*. It's creepy. And this is not helpful to Maximillian. He has enough trouble with his mother, always trying hopelessly to get her approval, without him doing the same thing all over again with you.

What gives you the right to judge this good and honest person whom you have never even met? My Maximillian is a much put-upon angel. He always tries to make things right, so often to his own disadvantage.

So let me tell you how it stands right now, seeing

you are still hanging around watching us and will not go away. Maximillian and Andronicus are safe—for now. Andronicus is lying flat on his back, mouth open, snoring at the tented ceiling, and my poor Maximillian is folded into his wing cases, asleep. But soon Ma will be back to wake him, as she has promised, and then I shall have to watch him fly away, alone and helpless to his dark and creepy house, where he has known so much misery—and I blame you. Yes, *you*. For some reason my dearest Maximillian thinks he has something to prove to you. Why, I have no idea. I wish you would just go away and find something else to do. Read a book or something, why don't you? But you don't. You are still here, watching, waiting for Maximillian to wake up so you can torment him again. Why? *What do you want?*

You don't respond. I can see why it drove Maximillian to such extremes. Here you are, watching us, despite me telling you to go. I assume you are Wingless, for I have noticed that the young Wingless have a confidence that a young Roach lacks. I suspect it is a confidence born of winning the lottery of life—for, let us be truthful, no one would freely choose the life of a Roach. Oh, we make the best of it, but deep down there is a profound sorrow at our loss of what we might have been. So, tenacious young Wingless one, I will tell you Maximillian's story, so that if you persist in shadowing him you will at least understand what has made him who he is. And I shall enjoy the telling of it too, for I love talking about Maximillian. So, are you sitting comfortably? Good. And now I shall begin. . . .

About nineteen years ago, Maximillian was born to a young couple who lived in the center of the city in the wife's old family home. He was their first child. He had his own nursery at the top of the house and a nurse too, who later became a good friend of my mother.

Maximillian was a delightfully lovely baby. Once, in a rare and precious moment of confiding in me, he showed me an old, creased photograph of himself as a still Wingless baby, which he had found folded and stuffed into a gap between the floorboards. He had a few wispy dark curls, big twinkling gray eyes and the sweetest little dimpled smile. He would have been a handsome Wingless man, no doubt about it.

Maximillian's mother was adamant that there was no "Roach taint" in her family or that of her husband, whom she had chosen for that very reason. However, her own mother had never told her that her twin sisters had been disposed of while cocooned. It happened a lot back then and I suspect it still does. There are many poor little souls buried in backyards, having obligingly spun themselves into their own coffins. It is traditional to plant an apple tree over them, and at the end of Maximillian's yard you will find a pair of ancient apple trees that lean toward one another for support.

Maximillian's parents were out at an important dinner when he cocooned. My mother's friend, the nurse, watched it happening. She was frozen with horror. By the time Maximillian's parents returned home, he was a little lozenge of shimmering gray silk, tough as steel. Maximillian's mother was frantic. She took a knife to the cocoon and pushed the point deep into it, trying to cut away the strands. This is the reason, should you wonder, why Maximillian has only three upper limbs.

I suppose it was then that Maximillian's mother realized there was nothing she could do. Coolly, she instructed the nurse to "do what must be done." The nurse asked what she meant and Maximillian's mother told her, very deliberately and coldly, "Bury. It." The nurse refused.

Maximillian's father was a good man, but he did not stand up to his wife. And so he allowed his baby son to be taken to the yard and buried alive. From the nursery window at the top of the house, the nurse watched Maximillian's mother dig the grave while his father cradled his son's cocoon and then she watched in tears as the baby she had loved as her own was buried in the cold soil and left alone in the darkness to await death.

You may not know this, but a cocooned baby is not killed immediately by being buried. Because they are in a state of suspension the lack of air does not matter, neither does the cold. But until the hard chrysalis grows beneath the cocoon they are vulnerable. They will be eaten by worms and rats, dug up by dogs, taken by foxes.

But that is not the worst that can happen to them.

Did you know that Night Roaches are created from stolen cocoons? Well, I didn't either until Ma told me. She said that when I was a cocoon she was constantly terrified that a Night Roach would swoop down and take me to the Steeple nursery. Ma says that the Bartizan has found a way of modifying the little ones as they sleep in their cocoons so that they emerge with talons and compound eyes. And then they keep these poor creatures in total darkness so that they learn to see and hunt in the dark. As a consequence they lose all their beautiful pigment and turn as white as the blind worms beneath the earth. By the time they are teens they have become murderous cannibals, corrupted forever by the Bartizan.

The night that Maximillian cocooned the fog was late, and as the nurse stood at the window watching Maximillian's mother and father walking slowly back to the house, she saw the very sight she had feared—the pale shape of a Night Roach circling like a vulture. She waited until she heard the bedroom door close and then she was out of the nursery, racing silently down the stairs. She was very brave, for a lone Wingless adult is easy pickings for any Night Roach.

She ran into the yard, waving her arms, and the Night Roach went off, to get reinforcements she guessed. Frantically, she threw herself onto the grave and began scrabbling at the earth, determined to take Maximillian away to safety. And then she heard footsteps behind her. She leapt up, ready to fight for Maximillian and found herself face-to-face with his father. One look told her all she needed to know and together they dug up the cocoon. Luckily for them, as they dug the night fog came down and they were safe.

They fled to the other side of the city and rented a tiny room in a ramshackle house at the end of our street. The nurse, whose name was Joanna, helped out in our farm shop and she and my mother became friends. By then Maximillian was out of his chrysalis and my mother said he was the sweetest, happiest little toddler you could imagine. She told me she loved to watch him jumping into the air on his sturdy little legs, trying out his baby wings. Indeed, Maximillian was the reason why Ma was not upset in the slightest when I cocooned—she knew that a Roach child is a blessing.

I suppose you are wondering how, after all this, Maximillian came to be living with his mother back in his old family home? Well, you can imagine that Maximillian's mother was not pleased when she found her husband and the nurse gone, and it did not take her long to discover the empty grave in the yard either. She hired a Sneak and set about tracking the runaways down. It took a while and by the time she found them Maximillian's father and the nurse were expecting a child of their own. In revenge, Maximillian's mother got custody of her son, which was easily done, as even then she was a powerful woman.

And so, one terrible day she sent a Bartizan official to collect little Maximillian. My mother said she heard Joanna's screams from here. Fearing a terrible accident, she rushed to help and saw the little Maximillian bundled into a Roach bag—a barbarous thing—and being taken away.

Maximillian became his mother's prisoner. She refused his father any access to his son although I believe he managed a few clandestine visits when she was at official functions. They were snatched, miserable affairs and he would return home in despair.

But life goes on. Fearing his wife's vengeance—for she was becoming increasingly powerful within the Bartizan—Maximillian's father changed his surname to Drew and he and Joanna moved to the little house next door to our farm. They had three children of their own and not one cocooned, for they were both from poor families who had never been able to afford the modification.

Ah, the modification. You're puzzled now, I can feel it.

So Maximillian hasn't told you why some of us cocoon, but most don't? I am not surprised—it is not something he likes to talk about. He still feels a failure for being a Roach and disappointing his dreadful "Mama." I shall explain. Maximillian has told you about the Contagion that destroyed virtually all human life on Earth? Oh. I see that he hasn't mentioned that little detail either. Sometimes I think Maximillian is still hiding in his cocoon, afraid to look at the world around him.

So here's the thing. About two hundred years ago Hope was just a normal city open to the sky and the world outside—and then, somewhere, the Contagion began. It spread fast and was devastating. They say you woke in the morning fit and well, felt a little feverish at lunchtime and were dead by nighttime, boiled in your own body heat. It spread like fire across the world but because Hope is isolated at the end of a long peninsula—and because we were lucky—the Contagion did not reach us. But everyone knew it was coming. And so our scientists began a daring experiment. Knowing that cockroaches could survive pretty much anything, they decided to introduce just a tiny bit of cockroach DNA into people, thinking that then maybe we too could survive anything.

It was an expensive process but people were desperate and most of the richer families tried it. It didn't work. A group with the modification left the city and caught the Contagion. Others went to find them and they caught it too. So people stopped having the Roach modification and thought no more about it. Until the first baby went into a cocoon and a month later emerged as a beautiful new kind of human.

I will have to wake Maximillian in a few minutes, but before I do there is just one more thing I want to tell you, because you won't hear it from him. It is how we met. His mother walked out on him just over a year ago. Ma has a weird and scary theory about why she went, which I am beginning to think could be right. . . .

Anyway, I first met Maximillian a few weeks after his vile Mama had left. I found him wandering along our street, painfully thin and so nervous that he could hardly speak. I took him back to our shop—I could tell he was hungry—and gave him a pile of flax cakes and some spicy vegetable strips. He refused to take them, but I told him it was an uncollected order and he would be doing me a favor.

Seven days later, when Maximillian very shyly walked into our shop, I have to confess I squealed with excitement. He turned and walked straight out again, and I ran after him. I apologized for scaring him. I told him I'd been frightened by a mouse. He said he assumed it was he who had scared me, as he knew that he was not pleasant to look at. I told him, quite truthfully, that he was very pleasant to look at indeed and he laughed as though I'd made a joke. I walked with him, trying to think of something to say and not succeeding. I expected him to tell me to go away but he didn't, so I just stuck by his side. It was a long way to his house, right across the city, and I wondered why he didn't fly it. It was only later that I found out he didn't know how to fly. And that I was the very first Roach he had ever spoken to.

I was amazed to see that he lived in a grand old house on the Inner Circle. Of course it was falling to bits, but they all are now. We stood on his doorstep for what felt like hours. I hoped he would ask me in but he didn't, so in the end I had to go.

After that Maximillian came to the shop about once a week and I would always find him a "lost" order or add more vegetables or flax cakes. After a while he stopped protesting and even began to smile at me. At last I was brave enough to ask him for supper and to my surprise, he accepted. We had many happy times eating flaxseed cakes and soup beside the stove and one day I found the courage to ask him if I could show him how to fly. He agreed! Of course he was a natural. I think that this was when he began to accept his Roach heritage.

I finally got to see inside his house when I took around some genuinely uncollected orders. Even then

I had to throw a fake coughing fit and ask for a glass of water in order to get over the threshold. As soon as I was inside I understood his reluctance. The house was a squalid mess. It seems his mother had delighted in chaos. Maximillian had made little walkways through the towering piles of “Mama’s treasures” and he lived in a tiny, remarkably neat space that he had kept clear at the very top of the house. The only other island of order was the room in the basement where his mother kept her collection of Meissen china, upon which she had lavished all the love and attention that she should have given to her son.

Over the months I helped Maximillian clear the chaos. This was not easy, because although he is by nature an orderly person he could not bring himself to touch anything of “dear Mama’s.” In the end we compromised and placed all her things into the rooms on the floor beneath his attic; then I locked them and hid the keys. So at last Maximillian had the clean and tidy space he deserved—although as you may have noticed, he doesn’t believe he deserves anything. And he most certainly does not understand that his precious “Mama” is a monster who has tried her best to ruin his life. But I will not let her do that. *I will not.*

But now I must wake him, so I’ll be off. I just wanted to show you the Maximillian you do not see. Please be nice to him. And understand that no one can judge him more harshly that he does himself. That's all from me.

M

I wake and wonder where I am. I blink to focus my eyes, and Parminter comes into focus. She is gazing at me with a very strange expression. I suspect I have been emitting unpleasant sounds while I sleep and I feel mortified. Mama always said I was a repugnant sleeper. I apologize for my noises and Parminter sighs. "There is nothing you need to apologize for, Maximillian," she says, still looking at me in this strange manner. "And there never was," she adds. "*Ever.* Just remember that."

I nod, even though I do not understand what she is talking about. Parminter gets up and brushes down her lovely, shiny wing cases. They are very neat and well formed, with a perfect curve to them. And the soft purple color sets off her deep golden eyes beautifully. She tilts her head and asks what I am thinking. I deny that I am thinking anything at all and she laughs. And then very quickly, because I know she does not want to tell me, she says, "It is an hour before sundown. You will have time to reach your house before dark if you go now."

And so, with some reluctance, I leave Parminter and set off into the low light of the late afternoon, heading for my poor sealed house and the terrified boy who lies within. I fear that my sudden arrival will not do much to calm him but I cannot in all conscience leave him there a moment longer.

The hour before sunset is a magical time to fly. The Orb diffuses the rays of the setting sun and I find myself flying beneath a vast bubble of shimmering pink. I give the Night Roach Steeple a wide berth, and head across the city. Sounds travel far in the stillness of the end of the day and from the streets below a cry of "Roach!" drifts up but it does not upset me as it once would have done. I wonder if some of Parminter's confidence is rubbing off on me?

I fly slowly, for my right wing is still sore from the fly-lift, and as I go I listen happily to the distant shouts of children at play, a sudden wild burst of laughter from a woman and the slow drumbeat from a rooftop far below where a group of young Rats have gathered to drum for the invisible sunset. I think of all the unknowable lives being lived beneath our Orb and how Hope is still full of good people, despite all its troubles. I am feeling very heartened by this, when a movement far above me catches my eye and I see the Astro again.

Shining orange in the low glow of the sun, it hangs in the sky and there is no movement to it at all. I toy with the idea of flying up to it, to show the poor soul inside it that they are not alone, but I decide that the kindest thing is to leave them in peace. And so I continue crossing the city, but now the sounds that rise up to greet me seem tinged with sadness and I think how fragile is the happiness of the people below, for the Astro above is there to remind them that a knock on their door can put any one of them up there too.

Roach and Wingless alike, we are all prisoners of Hope.

Chapter 20

ASTRO

T

I'm floating over the evening city, which is bathed in a sea of pink, the last throw of the sun before twilight falls. The fire in my lungs has subsided to a dull burn and now, at last, I feel a strange kind of peace.

Far below I see a Roach in flight. It is a large one, about six feet long at least, and it is flying slowly, almost gliding. Its shimmering wing cases glint with a sheen of pink reflected from the Orb—it is almost beautiful. A sudden feeling of loneliness sweeps over me and I very nearly put myself into a dive to go down and surprise it. But my fear of being unable to control the Astro and hurtling into the streets far below stops me. I am floating just fine right now. Let's leave it at that.

I allow my mind to wander and it takes me back to the slow and clunking ride in the elevator up to the top of the Bartizan. It felt frighteningly precarious, as though at any moment it could plunge to the ground and—although now it seems ridiculous—I was actually relieved when we reached the top. I was surprised how fancy it was up there, so colorful with all those dancing lights coming in through the dome. And that wonderful smell of beeswax from the shining wood floor. It made me realize how run-down and dirty our poor city is. I think I was in a strange state of mind by then, with every sensation heightened. I kept thinking of Mom and how all this had happened to her too. I felt I was in a dream, following in her footsteps. It sounds crazy, but that made me feel quite calm, almost as if she was walking by my side. I remember the big silver *A* on the door and how I couldn't stop looking at it. And then walking through the door and knowing I had crossed over from being alive to being very nearly dead.

The Astro Room was surprisingly small. The Astro technician who was waiting for me seemed to take up most of the space. He was kind of blank: with dark glasses, a shaved head, smooth, raw skin like it had been scrubbed with sandpaper, and soft pink hands like a mole. I felt overwhelmed by tiny details—I was desperately drinking in everything to do with being alive. I looked at the orange circle painted on the floor with some of the paint rubbed off the middle and I wondered how many people it had taken to do that. And then the long glass door with fingerprints on it. I thought if I were the Astro Tech I would have cleaned it. I saw the launch ledge stuck out like a diving board. It looked a bit flimsy and that bothered me. The light was dim, just dull daylight filtering in, and I wondered how the Astro Tech could see anything with his glasses. But maybe that was the point; maybe he didn't want to. But most of all what I remember is the silence. Soft. Slow. Gentle, like a dream.

My guards guided me onto the orange circle on the floor and turned me so I was facing the long glass door and the diving board. I heard the *zip* of a tape measure and I knew the tech was measuring me. Then, out of the corner of my eye, I saw him sliding open a panel and I caught a glimpse of Astros hanging up like a row of fat orange slugs. And then he brought it out: my orange coffin.

The suit was made of much stiffer stuff than I'd expected; it was reinforced with fine steel threads, and stood up on its own. It was headless with a metal ring holding the neck open. It looked like the spacewalk suits from way back, but much plainer and with no life support pack. Of course. They put the helmet on the ground and I saw to my relief that it was the new kind, with a tiny slit of a window. I want to see as much of this world as possible for every last second I'm in it.

The Astro Tech slit open the back of the suit with a heat-knife; then my guards took my elbows and lifted me in feetfirst. My feet touched the soles of the boots and I felt a cuff snap around each ankle. That was a bad moment. I hadn't figured on that happening and it made me feel more trapped than I'd expected. They guided my arms into the blind end sleeves and the same thing happened with my hands: cuffs snapped tight around my wrists so I couldn't pull my arms back. I took a deep breath to stop the panic rising and focused on the helmet that sat waiting on the floor, its dead eye staring back at me. A guard ran a glue gun down the back of the suit to seal it and I smelled hot plastic and metal. Nothing felt real by then.

After Mom got Astroed I made a point of finding out exactly what would have happened to her. But the trouble with knowing the Astro Protocol is that you can't get it out of your mind. So every night I'd have nightmares about it. First it was about Mom, but later I'd dream it was happening to me. I'd wake up fighting to get out of the suit and discover my sheets knotted around me. I think that was why I was so dazed—I felt as though I was still dreaming.

And then I heard a woman's voice right in the middle of the room. "Proceed," it said. And the Astro Tech jumped to attention and picked up the helmet. I forced myself to stay calm and took a deep breath in, knowing it would be my very last of fresh air. I wonder if Mom did that too? Of course she did. I expect everyone does. We're all the same deep down, aren't we? Anyway, I saw the tiny dark strip of reinforced visor glass in the helmet and I got a sudden fear that they would put it on back to front so I couldn't see out. I was wondering whether to beg them to put it the right way around, when the voice came again: "Turn the prisoner this way. I want to see his face." And so my last breath got delayed. They swung me around to face a blank piece of dark glass set into the paneling, which was, I could tell, a one-way glass. And it didn't take much to guess who was on the other side of it. The Guardian. Whoever she was.

"Lights!" said the Guardian's voice, and the Astro Tech pulled a lever and the room was flooded with a blaze of light. I went to shield my eyes from the brightness and of course I couldn't move my arms. That was a bad moment; I realized I would never be able to touch my face again.

I was staring at myself in the glass—white-faced and wild-eyed as if I was already a ghost—when something amazing happened: a Sunstrike. For those few seconds of brilliance I saw who was behind the glass: a short, thin woman with hair like an iron helmet. And standing beside her was my sister with her big, shining gray eyes staring at me. Terrified. And then the Sunstrike was over and once again I was looking at a dark glass.

I was so stunned by what I'd seen that the next snappy instruction piped into the Astro Room I heard only in my head, a few beats later. "Confirm the name of the prisoner," it said.

The guard holding my right arm cleared his throat nervously. "Tomas Harston Marne, formerly Drew, Madam Guardian."

This was weird. Why would the Guardian be interested in my name?

And then another snappy command. "Confirm the prisoner's siblings."

In the reflection I could see the guards behind me glancing at one another and I realized that they didn't know what siblings were. So, I spoke for myself. "Kaitlin Sian Drew, Jonathan Digby Drew." It felt right that the last words anyone heard me say were the names of my sister and brother.

"Silence!" the guards shouted in unison. "Prisoners are forbidden to speak."

I smiled. Because, forbidden or not, I *had* spoken. And then I spoke again, for what I knew would be the last time. Ever. "Goodbye, Kaitlin," I said. "It's okay."

They slammed the helmet onto me pretty fast after that and to my great relief the window slit was in front of my eyes. I felt the back of the helmet being fiddled with and the clang of something being attached to it. I knew that was the pipe for the ReBreethe air. The idea is that they inflate the whole suit with ReBreethe so it blows up like a balloon and floats. ReBreethe is an enriched breathable gas and it works along with the filters in the suit that slow down the buildup of carbon dioxide, so you can keep breathing it for days. It is also very light, so until the gas becomes exhausted, the Astro will float.

They shoved the ReBreethe in as fast as they could. I think they were showing off to the Guardian. It was a terrifying few minutes. The gas smelled vile and my lungs felt like they were burning up. I coughed and retched until I discovered that holding in the ReBreethe was the thing to do: the burning sensation calmed and soon became an almost-pleasant warmth—or it would have been if I hadn't known what awaited me with my next breath.

And so it went on.

The Astro suit swelled up until I no longer had any contact with its inside surface, apart from my tethered wrists and ankles. I felt it gently lift off the ground and then the rushing hiss of gas stopped. I heard the clang as the nozzle was unclipped and a faint click as they fastened the input valve cover back in place. I had become an independent ecosystem—planet Tomas Drew.

I caught sight of the Astro Tech clipping on his safety harnesses and then, through my feet rooted in their boots, I felt the vibrations as he slid back the glass door. It happened very quickly after that: one push and I was stumbling out onto the diving board. Another jolt from behind and I was gone, tumbling into the air, with nothing below me for hundreds of feet. The suit went spinning like a leaf that had fallen too soon from its tree. But it was okay. I spread-eagled myself like a flying squirrel, got back in control and began to float.

And now, hours later, here I am high above the city, ReBreething *in . . . out, in . . . out, in . . . out, in . . . out, in . . . out.* Head pounding like a hammer, lungs scorched, ears ringing, throat raw, just peed down my leg. I watch the Roach fly steadily away from me until it is no more than a small dot in the sky and I am alone. Twilight is falling now and lights are flickering far below. The chill of the oncoming night is beginning to seep through the suit. I clench and unclench my hands to force some circulation into them and slowly, slowly, sleep creeps up on me.

Chapter 21

ON THE OTHER SIDE OF THE GLASS

K,

I watched Tomas being Astroed. The whole thing. However much I wanted to look away, I knew I couldn't. It was so hard. I told myself that Tomas would have been Astroed anyway, because he had lost his crew, but I knew I had sealed his fate with my lies.

He said it was okay. But it isn't, is it?

When Tomas had gone and I was staring at the empty ledge where he had stood, the Guardian said, "Your brother looks like your mother, who was also a traitor. As was your father. It seems to run in the family, does it not?"

I couldn't let that go. "We are *not* traitors," I told her.

"You will find that it is *I* who decide who is a traitor, not you," she said. "And there are consequences to being a traitor, as you have observed. But unlike your brother you, Kaitlin *Marne*, have a chance to redeem yourself." I noticed how she liked saying Dad's old name, "Marne," as though it was a battle she had won. "We know you absconded with the security device that your mother stole by abusing her position as a trusted member of the medical team here in the Bartizan. There is no point in you denying it any longer. However, if you tell me where it is, I will be merciful and allow you to resume your place on the SilverShip as a three-star SilverSeed, which brings not inconsiderable privileges, so I am told. If you do not tell me where this device is, you will follow your brother into the Astro Room. Right now."

I knew she meant it. And I couldn't face that. I just couldn't. I'm not as brave as Tomas, I know that now. "It's hidden inside my little brother's bear," I lied. "In Tedward."

"And where is this traitorous bear?" she asked.

I might have smiled if I hadn't been so scared. So even Tedward was a traitor. The Guardian was right; it clearly does run in our family.

"With my brother Jonno," I said. "He never lets go of it. I can take you to him. And I just want to say that Jonno didn't want to escape. I made him come with me because he wouldn't let go of his bear." At least I can do this one thing for Jonno, get him back to the SilverShip where he wanted to be.

The Guardian swiveled on her heel and marched off to sit behind her desk. Her dark eyes were little slits of anger. "If you lie to me one more time, I will have you sent next door this minute."

"I'm not lying," I say desperately. "I'm not. I promise. Tedward is with Jonno. Truly he is."

"The bear is not with your brother Jonathan," she said with a nasty little laugh. "Your brother Jonathan has been returned by an informant and is back in the SilverShip crew quarters. The bear, however, is not."

I couldn't make sense of that at all. Who had returned Jonno? Surely not Maximillian? I push that thought from my mind—I know Maximillian would never do such a thing. And then I realize who it must be: the owner of those sneaky footsteps. "Then someone must have made him leave it behind," I say. "Because he takes that bear everywhere."

The Guardian nodded slowly. I could see that made sense to her. "Very well. So tell me, where exactly *did* he leave it?"

"In a house on the Inner Circle," I say. "I don't know the number, but I know which one it is."

Madam Guardian nods. "So the Sneak said. Very well, you will take us there. We shall go and collect the bear."

"*We?*" I was totally shocked. Surely Madam Guardian

didn't mean that she would come with me?

But that was exactly what she did mean. And so, in one of the strangest days of my life I find myself—in my three-star SilverSeed uniform—walking out of the massive pillared front entrance of the Bartizan three paces behind the Guardian in her black velvet finery and gold-banded hems. I wait while she steps into a glossy black-and-gold box with lattice windows and a long, sturdy pole running out from each corner. I know this is a walking chair but only because I've seen a picture, I've never seen one for real. It is made from a smooth lacquered wood with a shine that reminds me of Maximillian's wing cases.

Four hefty chair-carriers pick up the poles and set off briskly in step along the white marble pavement. The light tinkle of a bell comes from inside the walking chair and the carriers stop. One of the bodyguards leans down to hear what is being said from the other side of the lattice; then he comes over to me and tells me I am to walk in front of the chair and lead the way.

And so, flanked by four guards of my own, I set off. As we pass by, people fall silent; they step back and I noticed that some make the sign to ward off the evil eye. Twilight is falling now and the brilliant white facades surrounding the square look dark and false. Which of course, they are. The Inner Circle is a wide street leading off the far end of the square and as I head into it I focus on my shiny new deck shoes as they take me ever onward toward Maximillian's house. One step and then another—sometimes that is all you can do.

Chapter 22

UNDER ONE ROOF

M

I land on my roof, clumsy with tiredness, and there is that rat again, watching me lose my footing and slide backward down the slope. It reminds me of Mama, always catching me at my most embarrassing moments. I glare at the rat, grab hold of the chimney stack and hang there for a few minutes to allow my wing muscles to recover. Then, like a crab, I inch my way back up until I am by the skylight. From beneath my underwings, I take my dagger and cut into the thick blanket of tarred hemp that has been plastered over it; then I roll it back, flip open the skylight and drop down into the cool darkness of my house.

I lie low on my landing mat in the soft silence and at once I know that I am the only creature inside my house. The boy has gone. We who are Roach are sensitive to vibrations caused by movement, even breathing, and I feel none at all. The house is as still as a stone. I decide to check through every room to allay my fear that the young human has come to harm and is lying somewhere unconscious—or worse. I flip down my goggles so that I can see in the dark and head for the room he was sleeping in, even though the door is open and it is clear that the bird has flown. Inside it is empty apart from the pile of blankets in the middle and the little nest under the eaves where Kaitlin Drew was sleeping. It is on these that I now see the sad sight of the boy's bear lying facedown, which makes me fear that someone has taken him by force. I sit the putrid bear up on the blankets so that it is able to observe the room and creep out, but as I close the door the wretched doorknob falls upon my foot. I hop along the landing in pain and collapse onto my nest, holding my foot.

Feeling very sad about the boy, I gaze at the golden eagle teapot and I think of Mama who always said I brooded too much: *like a fat old hen on a stale egg, Maximillian*, I hear her voice drilling inside my head. Oh. This house is still full of Mama. There is no escape from her here. I long to fly back to Parminter, but I cannot leave until I have searched every room just to be sure. And so I get up from my nest and begin.

The floor below the attic has three locked rooms full

of Mama's things, so I go straight down to the floor above the entrance hall. I check the large room at the front and then the smaller one at the back, both deep in thick blackness. My poor house feels so strange. The tarry windows deaden the sounds from outside and the silence inside is eerie. I find I am creeping on tiptoe as though I am an intruder who expects to be discovered at any moment. Memories of Mama haunt me. I hear her taunting words and her laugh, so sharp it cuts the air. I stop dead. I think I am going crazy. Because I swear Mama's laugh is *for real.*

No. It cannot be.

My legs have lost all strength and I lean against the wall, trembling. I talk to myself sternly in the brave voice of Parminter. *Maximillian, it is nothing. The silence and darkness of the house has unbalanced you. That is all.* And then I hear Mama's laugh again. It is like the smashing of china: bright, sharp and oh-so-full of destruction. It is Mama's laugh. *It is real.* And it is just outside the front door.

K

We are outside Maximillian's house and someone has stuck thick, tarry cloth over all the windows. Across the steps leading up to the front door, which is also covered in tarry cloth, is a strip of yellow tape with the word

Fumigation written on it. I feel sick. I think of Maximillian lying in there, alone, and . . . *dead.* And all because we came to his house and he helped us. I do not believe things can get any worse now. I really don't.

Madam Guardian is out of her box and staring up at the house. "So you really were *here*?"

"Yes," I tell her. "But it wasn't like this." I point at the blind, tarred windows. "It was just . . . a normal house." I am finding it hard to speak. I can't stop thinking about Maximillian.

Naturally Madam Guardian does not notice. "So how do you know this is the right one?" she asks sharply.

"The blood." I point to the splodge by the entrance to the alley by the corner. "That's from Jonno's foot. We ran up the alley there at the side. To a gate."

She laughs a little crazily and I think of a cracked bell lying at the bottom of an empty well. "Why should I be surprised?" she mutters to herself. "Filthy Roach. Nasty little two-faced traitor."

I am pleased to hear that Maximillian too is a traitor. It makes him feel almost part of the family.

She sniffs. "I can't smell anything. Was this house actually fumigated?" she asks her bodyguards.

"No, madam," the taller one replies. "It was sealed in error. Apparently it is the house of a Protected Person."

She laughs. "Well, he's not protected now, that's for

sure." She tells the bodyguards to free the door, and they run up the steps, expertly split the tarry cloth and peel it back. They wait, alert for trouble, as Madam Guardian walks up the steps, pulls a key from her pocket and opens the front door like she's done it a thousand times before. A bodyguard hands her a flashlight and she strides inside. A moment later she pokes her head out and says to me, "Don't stand there like a gaping fool. Get up those steps. Now."

And so I walk up the front steps, and once again, I am inside Maximillian's house.

M

I hear the key in the lock, fast and efficient, not bumbling like Minna Simms. *Clickety-click* the lock turns and the front door opens. I feel the disturbance of air sweep into the house and see the glare of a flashlight beam shine up through the balustrades, throwing their giant shadows upon the wall in front of me. And then I hear it: the voice of Mama *inside.* "Don't stand there like a gaping fool. Get up those steps. Now." I feel ill. How many times has she said those very words to me? I hear quick, light steps and someone else walks in. "So. This is definitely the house?" I hear Mama ask.

"Yes, madam, it is," comes the reply. If the voice of Mama was not shock enough, the second voice sends me into turmoil. For who do you suppose it might belong to? My Kaitlin Drew.

I am in a whirl of confusion. *What is Mama doing here? Why has she brought my Kaitlin Drew with her?* I am now lying in the corner of the landing in a state of near collapse. Those of you with good mamas, like Parminter, will not understand my dismay, so let me explain what is in my thoughts.

First: I do not wish to see Mama.

Second: Mama is not a kind person and I am very afraid for my Kaitlin Drew.

Third: I am jealous. Kaitlin Drew was *my* friend. *Mine*. But now Mama has taken her away from me, just as she has taken so many other things.

Fourth: This is the most terrifying thought and it blanks out all the others. In a moment Mama will go down to the basement. This is always the first place she goes when she comes home, for there dwell the things she loves the best. And then she will discover what I dread the most.

K

Madam Guardian is acting very oddly. She is going down to the basement even though I have said that Tedward is in the attic. I stand in the darkness watching her flashlight beam moving down the stairs and I think of this morning, when I too was going down those stairs. I remember how free I had felt, how daring, how in control of my life. Now I know how stupid I was to think that, because no one is free in this city. *No one.* Not even Madam Guardian.

There is a strange silence in the house as though all is suspended. And in that silence I hear the soft Roach rasp of breath. And suddenly I know—*Maximillian is here. Alive!* I long to call out his name but I don't, because it seems to me he is hiding from something he is very afraid of. And it doesn't take much to guess who that might be: Madam Guardian.

Suddenly, from the basement, I hear a piercing, blood-chilling scream. And from the landing above comes a soft, low groan.

M

I cover my ear tubes and fold myself into my wing cases. *I cannot bear it.* I hear Mama telling my Kaitlin Drew that she will search the house "for that filthy Roach" from top to toe and she will find me and when she does I will regret the finding of me for the rest of my life. Which will not be long. And then, as I rock in my carapace trying to blank out the drilling of her voice, I hear my Kaitlin

Drew say, "Madam. It was Enforcers who smashed the pots. Not a Roach."

"Pots?" Mama screeches. "*Pots?* They are irreplaceable eighteenth-century Meissen porcelain. They are works of art, girl. Irreplaceable works of art. They are . . . they were . . . my *life.* All I asked of him was to keep them safe. That is all. Just one little thing. I will kill him for this. I will *kill* him. Where is he? Lurking in some nasty little dark corner like the sly, underhanded Roach he is, no doubt." I see the flashlight beam wave crazily around the ceiling and I know that Mama is making the windmill thing with her arms that she does before she hits something. I shrink farther into my carapace and hope that Mama will kill me soon. I cannot bear this. *I cannot.*

K

A cold shiver runs through me. Suddenly I understand why Madam Guardian was so shocked that this was the house Jonno and I had come to, and why she ran off to the basement as soon as we got inside. I particularly understand why Maximillian is hiding in the darkness in abject terror. It is because *Madam Guardian is Maximillian's mother.* This is the woman he calls Mama. When he told me last night, with tears in his eyes, that his "Mama" will kill him because of the smashed pots I thought he was being melodramatic. But now I understand. He was right.

I think of Maximillian being so alone and frightened and my heart is breaking. Even though I have lost my family, I will always know they loved me. Maximillian has never had that. I don't know why I care so much about him, but I do—and right now I would do anything to protect him. And so, yet again, I lie to his awful mother. "Madam," I say. "There was no Roach here. The house was empty."

"Don't lie to me, girl," Madam Guardian almost spits in fury. "Your brother Tomas, the traitor Enforcer, reported a Roach in residence who fed upon your brother Jonathan."

And this time I don't need to lie. "But my brother Jonathan is alive and back in the SilverShip crew quarters," I say. "As you know."

Madam Guardian is quiet while this sinks in and I look at her, trying to catch any resemblance to Maximillian in her, but I see nothing. Then she sighs and says, "Very well, go and get what we came for. If you have brought me here under false pretenses you will regret it bitterly."

"Yes, madam," I say quickly. "Please may I borrow your flashlight?"

"Oh, for Orb's sake," Madam Guardian says irritably,

and hands it over. And then I run up the stairs. I'm going to have to move fast.

M

My Kaitlin Drew comes up the stairs, racing past me, the beam of light casting me into deep shadows. I lie low, hardly daring to breathe. There is no more than a few feet of darkness between me and Mama, and even though I know that Mama has no sense of another's presence whatsoever, I still fear that somehow she will detect that I am lying just a few feet above her head. So, like the sneaky lowdown snoop she used to call me when she would find me in a place she had not expected, I stay totally still and listen to Mama's sounds. I hear sniffs, the blowing of her nose—which is a thing that disgusts we who are Roach—and then a sobbing whisper, "My cherubs . . . oh my poor, darling cherubs . . ."

Oh, how I wish I had the golden eagle teapot by my side. I imagine walking down the stairs with it and giving it into her waiting hands. I imagine Mama gazing at me with wonder—no, I must be realistic here, gazing at the teapot with wonder. And then, I tell myself, all would be well between us. But the stern yet wise voice of Parminter comes into my head. *Maximillian,* it says.

You do not have the teapot by your side. And even if you did, it would make no difference.

That is an uncomfortable thought and so I decide not to think it. Instead I listen to the sound of my Kaitlin Drew in the attic and I wonder what she is doing.

K

I must be quick. Luckily I see Tedward at once, sitting perkily on my nest of blankets as though he is waiting for me. It's odd that Jonno seems to have quite happily left him behind. Maybe the smell got too bad even for him. I flick open my pick tool, pry out the DisK from inside the beam and then, remembering what Mom told me about who we could trust with it, I scribble a note as fast as I can, and wrap the DisK in it. Now I need something to make Tedward heavy. But *what*? And then, on the floor I see the doorknob, just lying there. I snatch up the brass ring it rests on, shove that into poor old Tedward and pull the stitches closed. Tedward's lighter than he should be with the DisK, but it's the best I can do. Then I'm out of the room with Tedward and the DisK and running down the stairs.

There is someone I have to see.

M

I hear my Kaitlin Drew running down the stairs and I am wondering if I dare make myself known to her, when her flashlight beam catches me in its glare and she very deliberately drops it so that it rolls away from us and we are in darkness. And then she is kneeling beside me, her hand upon my carapace. I am so happy to see her, despite the fact she is clutching that foul bear, the stench of which makes my head swim. She presses a small package into my hand and folds my fingers around it. Then my Kaitlin Drew kisses the top of my head and she is gone, clutching that bear, racing down the stairs to Mama.

"What were you doing up there just now?" I hear Mama say suspiciously. Like her teapot, Mama is both eagle-eyed and eagle-eared.

"I dropped the flashlight," my Kaitlin Drew replies, breathless and all eagerness. "And then I dropped Ted-ward. But here he is."

"What vile mess is that?" I hear Mama say, and for once, I cannot disagree.

"It's blood from Jonno's nosebleeds. And he was sick on it. Twice. It's so revolting that no one would touch it."

I hear a grudging admiration in Mama's voice. "Very clever. No, don't give it to me, girl. Hand it to one of the guards when we get out of here."

I listen to their footsteps along the hall, then the slam

of the front door and they are gone. I lie in the darkness for some time, not daring to move. I feel most peculiar. At first I think it is fear because of Mama's anger. But then I realize this is not so—what I feel is sadness. Sadness because my Kaitlin Drew has gone, and I will never see her again.

Chapter 23

THE RETURN OF THE PRODIGAL

K,

After I handed over Tedward, Madam Guardian took off like a rocket in her walking chair—now a sprinting chair—and I was marched back through the Gateway to the Future.

I'm in the crew quarters in my cabin now and it is weird; I feel like a completely different person from when I was last here. And yet it is only twenty-four hours ago that we were summoned to the refectory for lockdown while they searched the ship and I knew then that they were homing in on the DisK. Their mistake was to leave us in darkness. They think it subdues us, which is true. But it also gives us freedom. And time for your best friend to hide you—and your annoying little brother who will not let go of his bear—in the rubbish cart.

I didn't hear my cabin door lock, so I try it to see if it will open. To my amazement it does. This is, I guess, because of my three stars. I step out onto the deserted walkway and wonder if I can get as far as the refectory without being stopped. As I head toward its double doors at the far end I hear voices drifting up from the recreation area below. It's the Bears—Jonno's tribe—and they are singing "What Shall We Hunt Today?" I stop and listen to their song where each one adds an improbable creature to the list. It's silly, but they love it. I lean over the rail and see Jonno laughing with his friends, and I smile to see him happy.

J

"Turtle!" I shout as loud as I can and all the Bears yell back at me, "Turtle!" And I laugh and my best friend, Leon, makes a turtle face and I wave my hands like turtle flippers and we sing the hunting song. It's my favorite. And then I see Katie leaning over the walkway looking down at me and she has *three stars*. It's not fair. I've only got one. And she ran away and now she has *three*. But then Leon shouts out, "Aardvark!" and we all laugh and when I look up again Katie has gone. And I think maybe I dreamed her.

K

I am in the refectory and no one stopped me. It feels quite weird. I go to the counter and take a box of neon yellow "orange" juice and too late I see Mattie in the far corner. "Hey, Kait, come and sit down!" she calls over. So I do, with a heavy heart.

Mattie is studiedly casual. "Very impressive," she says, pointing to the stars. "You must have done something right." She grins. "For a change."

"Dunno what," I say, taking a gulp of liquid artificial sweetener.

Mattie is cryptic; she knows this is not a safe place to talk. "So the stories of your escape with Jonno are greatly exaggerated?" she says.

"Yep," I say. Because I imagine they are.

"Well, it's nice to have you back. And three stars gets you access to all cabins. So how about you come along to mine?" She leans forward and says in a loud whisper, "I have chocolate."

"Ah . . . okay, then," I say. I'm dreading it, because I am going to have to tell her about Tomas.

"It's not compulsory, Kait," Mattie says, and she gets up and strides out.

I feel bad. I sit waiting for the sweetener rush to give me some courage, and then I do what I know I must.

As I head out of the refectory, a group of younger Seeds sitting by the doors notice my three stars and a look of respect crosses their faces. I could get used to this, I think. It's seductive, being at the top of a system. I tell myself that I must savor it while it lasts, because soon enough they'll discover that Tedward contains nothing more than a bit of old doorknob. And then I will be in the kind of trouble that not even three stars can fix.

The sliding door to Mattie's cabin swishes open and I see Mattie sitting at her desk, drawing in her regulation notebook. She looks up, surprised, and smiles. "Hey, Kait. Come in." So I do.

Each cabin has a desk, a chair and a sleeping platform. I sit on the platform and Mattie puts down her pencil, leaving her book open. She has been drawing a likeness of Tomas and it's very good. "I don't want to forget what he looks like," she says in a low voice.

Tomas's face has the same distant, fixed expression that I saw only a few hours ago when he looked at me through the one-way glass. I feel tears welling and Mattie notices. "You miss him too," she murmurs. I nod. "When we were first in here, I used to feel some connection with him," she says. "I'd get a sense that, you know, he was out on patrol or sitting in some boring lecture or just asleep and dreaming of . . . of *us*. But that faded. Until today."

I take a deep breath. "Mattie . . . ," I begin, and then I lose my nerve and stop.

Mattie gets up and suddenly bizarrely cheerful, she says, "Hey, how about a game of Table-Top?" As she says this, she is picking up a ball of the bright orange sticky stuff that they use to stick up notices around here, and pulling it about to activate it.

"*Huh?*" I am confused. Table-Top is a game down in the recreation area. You have to try and get a succession of silver balls to run through a moving maze. It's okay, but it's not a thing Mattie and I do. Mattie holds my gaze and I realize she is up to something. I don't know what it is, but I play along. "Okay," I say. "Best of three?"

"Best of five." Mattie laughs as she divides the orange stuff into five little balls. "Seeing as I'm going to win the first two."

"You wish," I say.

Mattie puts her finger to her lips and then says, maybe a little too loudly, "Come on, Kait, let's get a table before they're all taken."

"You're on," I say but I don't move, because I'm watching Mattie sticking the first of the orange balls over a pinprick hole in the wall. And then I understand what she is doing—she is blocking up the listening bugs.

Mattie opens and closes the cabin door as if we are

going out and I wait silently while she finishes sticking the four remaining bits of orange over the bugs. The last one is on the sleeping platform, right where the pillow goes. *They even listen to our dreams,* I think.

Then we sit on the floor and Mattie asks me the question I am dreading. "Tomas," she says in a low voice. "Something awful happened to him a few hours ago. I suddenly felt terrified. It just . . . it just *swamped* me."

I stare at Mattie. This is creepy.

"Oh my days . . . Kait, it's true, isn't it?" Mattie whispers.

I nod.

"What . . . what happened to him?"

I shake my head. I can't find the words to tell her.

I am saved by the shrilling of the bell for campfire assembly and its accompanying announcement: "Hey, you Lions, you Wolves, you Bears! It's time for . . . *campfire circle*!" This usually makes me cringe with its happy-camping singsong voice, but for the first time ever I am glad to hear it. And for all its jollity, it is deadly serious. If you're even a second late, it is twenty-four hours in Time-Out. As I well know.

I'm out of the cabin before Mattie can speak, and heading for the recreation area. I rattle down the metal stairs, past the huge double doors, each emblazoned with a big silver *S*—which always give me the creeps—and I join Jonno and his Bears. And there we all sit, our three happy tribes of Lions, Wolves and Bears gathered around the fake gel campfire. We pretend the SilverShip has just landed on the Island, that we've found our village, hunted and cooked our supper and now have nothing better to do than sing stupid songs.

Some chance.

Chapter 24

NIGHTFALL

M

In the silence and darkness of my empty house, a wave of longing for the warmth and affection I left behind at Parminter's farm comes over me and I cannot bear to be in this dark and lonely place a moment longer. I shall fly the night and take my chance.

I go up to my room and light the lantern; then I unwrap the gift that my Kaitlin Drew has given me. It looks like a large silver coin, but when I turn it over I see bands of gold stripes on it. There is a buzz to it, as though a small bee is trapped inside. And now I see there is a message written on the flax paper. It is most peculiar. I shall show you.

Dear Max,

This is the DisK. Take it away PLEASE they will

come back for it very soon!

Sorry sorry sorry for causing you +++ trouble.

Thank you x 1000000000s. stay safe.

Kaitlin xxxxx

P.S. Give DisK to curator W.E.NE. only.

I confess I do not understand the message, but I can tell it is important and I think that maybe Parminter will understand it better.

I now consider the teapot. I look at the gold-and-white delicacy with its chained lid and nasty little red eyes and I know that I am a fool to concern myself over such a thing, and yet I cannot bear to leave it behind. I decide to use the teapot as a carrier for this disc thing. I pull some wadding from my nest, wrap the disc in it and place it carefully in the china belly of the eagle. Then I wrap the teapot in wadding too. Its beady red eyes stare at me reproachfully until I smother its beaky little features. I place the soft bundle in a pillowcase and tie it firmly onto my belt so it will hang down out of the way in flight. And now I must go.

With great care I ascend the ladder and push my head up through the skylight. I flip down my goggles and see the rat watching me mockingly. There is no night fog yet, for which I am grateful, as I do not think I could find my way blind to Parminter's house. I try not to think about Night Roaches.

Gingerly, I climb out onto the roof. "It is your house now," I tell the rat.

I extend my wings to their fullest and feel the lift of the air beneath me. A sudden surge of joy comes over me: I am going to Parminter's house. I rise up into the night sky and I think how happy I am to be able to fly and to know I am going somewhere where I will be welcome. I am also happy to have seen my Kaitlin Drew for one last time and to be doing what she has asked of me. And I have Mama's teapot too, which one day I shall give back to her.

And then all will be well.

T

A worm of ice lives in my bones. Fear squats in my heart. I cannot stop thinking of Night Roaches. Of how they tow Astros back to their Roost. And how it takes many hours for Night Roaches to bite and tear through an Astro suit. But they always get there in the end. . . .

And now, far below, I see a Roach in flight. It is heading my way. At first I think I am safe, for it looks dark but then I fear that is just because it is in shadow. And then I see the green glint of its eyes and know that it is a Night Roach. I panic. Suddenly my head is down and my feet are up and I'm going into a dive and I am terrified that this will be the end of it all. But I don't want it to end. Not yet, not yet . . . I push my leaden legs downward, I spread my arms and at last I level out and am steady once again, floating facedown, watching the city below. I follow the steady progress of the Roach and its purposeful, businesslike flight, which gives me hope that maybe it is not a Night Roach. They fly in a different way, wheeling and gliding, searching for victims. This Roach looks to me like it is merely going home as fast as it can. It is close now and I see I am safe. Its wings have a dark, iridescent sheen and it flies steadily on, intent upon its own business.

And so I watch the Roach, heading no doubt somewhere warm for the night, to a welcome from people who love it. I never thought I would envy a Roach, but tonight I do. As it moves smoothly across the sky, I see far below the flickering pinpoints of candlelight in attic rooms and I wish—*oh, how I wish*—that I was safe in a soft, warm bed.

M

That Astro is still up there and I pity the poor creature within. Soon the Night Roaches will be out hunting; I hope the fog comes quickly and protects it, although not before I have reached Parminter's farm. With that thought I pick up speed, Mama's teapot bumping angrily with every wingbeat. I take a wide detour around the Night Roach Steeple and I am relieved to see no sign of activity. And now I can see the darkness of the fields stretching out to the eastern skylon, which rises up, its tip lost in a thick white blanket. Aha! The night fog is coming down with perfect timing, for I can also see the welcoming red tin roof of Parminter's farmhouse. I drop down into a low glide and with a feeling of happiness I land in the yard. All is quiet as I walk across the cobbles and knock softly upon the back door.

It is opened by Parminter's mama, who smiles at me as though she really is pleased to see me. "Maximillian!" she exclaims. "How wonderful. We were so worried for you. Come in, come in." And she ushers me into the warm kitchen and Parminter is already on her feet and hurrying over to me. She takes my hands, which I fear are unpleasantly cold. "You are frozen," she says. "Come and sit by the stove. Mama said it was safe for us to come in here. It's been quiet since you left." She smiles. "There's no way they'll track us here now."

I hope Parminter is right, but you can never tell—maybe they have gone to get reinforcements, or are planning something for tonight. But I do not want to spoil the happiness of this moment. I allow Parminter to lead me over to the old stove and I sit on the bench next to her and begin to relax. I love this kitchen. I love the old table with its fat, bobbly legs cut short, so it is good for Roach and Wingless alike. I love the rugs, the cushions, the stools and the benches and the rocking chair for Parminter's mama. I love the warmth of the cooking stove and its little window of thick green glass that shows the soft flickering flames inside, misty and blurred like fish beneath water. And I love to look at all the pictures nailed higgledy-piggledy onto the rough plaster of the chimney.

Upon the stove is a pot of something that smells delicious and on a pile of cushions in the corner Andronicus is still sleeping off the effects of Minna's spiked sun biscuits. And now Parminter is wrapping a blanket over my wing cases, I am sipping warmed nut milk, and as my shivering slowly subsides, Parminter asks me anxiously if everything is all right. I tell her that everything is most certainly all right. That it is more all right than it has ever been in my whole life.

Chapter 25

THE BLIND CURATOR

M

Parminter is not happy to see Mama's teapot. "Maximillian," she says crossly. "Why must you bring your mother here?"

I freeze. *Mama is here?*

"It's all right, Maximillian," Parminter says gently. "I didn't mean your mother was really here. I was talking about that awful teapot."

"I know it is not to everyone's taste," I say apologetically. "But there is more to this teapot than you think."

Parminter sighs. "I know that, Maximillian. There is *much* more to that ghastly teapot." Then she smiles at me encouragingly, as though I have done something unexpectedly clever. "But the good thing is that at least you realize it now."

Once again I feel that I do not completely understand

all that Parminter is saying. Very gently, I take off the little domed lid of the teapot, hold it carefully at the end of its delicate gold chain, and pull out the bundle of wadding. "You see?" I say to Parminter. "There *is* more to the teapot—there is this!"

Parminter does not look impressed. "Oh," she says.

I peel away the wrapping, unroll the flax paper and place the DisK in her hand.

"Oh," she says again, but this time all the teapot irritation is gone and she is, I can tell, no longer disappointed in me. Indeed, she is looking at me with a mixture of admiration and surprise. "Maximillian," she says, holding the DisK between her delicate fingers, which I notice have tiny, well-tended nails that shine a beautiful deep purple. "However did you get this?"

I tell her about my terrifying experience in my poor, sealed house and Parminter listens in stunned silence. "Your mama came to the house?" she asks. "With your Escaper? But *why*?"

"She was collecting a stuffed bear," I explain.

Parminter looks at me as if I am crazy. "*A stuffed bear?*"

"She sent my Escaper upstairs to get it. It had belonged to the brother."

"The brother you went back for?"

"Yes. But he was gone. There was only his bear. All alone." I feel so sad for the bear.

Parminter sighs. "It sounds like he did not choose to leave of his own accord. Not if he left his bear."

There is something about sitting by the fire with Parminter that makes me remember things. "I had a bear once," I say. "When I was little, a man came with some books and a bear. Mama was out. I hid the books but I put the bear in my nest so it wasn't lonely. Mama took it away."

"Oh, Maximillian . . . ," Parminter murmurs, and I can tell she is thinking about whether to say something. And then she says it. "Maximillian, did you ever wonder who that man was?"

Did I wonder? I don't really remember now. But I do remember that day. It was misty outside. The house was cold and damp and I was feeling sad—why I cannot recall. I heard a key in the front door and I thought it was Mama, so I made myself neat and tidy in the corner of my nest room, just how she liked me to be. But I soon realized that the footsteps coming up the stairs were not Mama's and I became very frightened. I thought that this time she really had sent someone to take me away, just as she said she would. So I closed my eyes and I waited. I heard my bedroom door open and I was waiting for the net to be thrown over me (Mama had told me exactly how they take Roaches away), when I heard my name spoken in a soft, growly kind of voice. "Maximillian?" I opened my eyes and saw a man there with shining gray eyes and a kind but sad face. He was carrying two big bags, which he put down with a little groan and then he came over to me. He knelt down beside me and stroked my head, all the while looking at me with the strangest expression. It made me feel very peculiar. In fact thinking about it still does.

Anyway, the man told me he had brought me a set of learn-to-read books and said that it was very important to be able to read. I would have to teach myself, he said, and to keep the books a secret because Mama would not like them and it was best not to upset her. And then he said something I've never forgotten: "You're a bright boy, Max. I know you can do it." He called me a "boy," just like Parminter's mama calls her a "girl." It felt good. And I liked how he called me Max too. It made me feel happy, not angry the way I feel when Minna says "Maxie." Anyway, he showed me a secret place in my room to hide the books and he gave me the bear. And then he left.

Oh dear.

I really don't want to think about this.

I feel most peculiar and I don't like it.

So when Parminter nudges me and says, "Maximillian? Did you?"

I say rather snappily, "Did I what?"

Very patiently, Parminter repeats, "Did you—*do*

you—ever wonder who that man was?"

I don't reply.

Parminter puts her hand on top of mine and I feel a little less unsettled. "Maximillian, that man was your father. Your papa."

Something in my heart jumps.

"Would you like to know about your papa?" Parminter asks gently.

"No!" I say. And then I realize I have been impolite. "I mean, no thank you." I say this because I know that my papa is dead. Mama told me. She came back late one evening to visit her porcelain, and then she came up to see me. She was smiling and I was afraid because Mama only smiles when she is going to hurt you. She stood in the doorway of my room and she said, "Maximillian. Even though you have shown not the slightest interest in your poor father, I thought you should know that he is dead now." And she laughed. "Sleep well." And she went. Naturally I did not sleep well.

I do not tell Parminter this, because it is too hard to speak it out loud. But Parminter is very sweet. She pats my hand and changes the subject. She asks me if she can show her mama the DisK and the message and of course I agree. So she takes it to her mama, who is in the bakery making flaxseed cakes for the morning, and when they come back Parminter's mama's eyes are shining with excitement. She sits next to me and opens her hand to show the DisK nestling in her soft pink palm. "Maximillian," she whispers. "Where did your Escaper get this?"

"I don't know for sure," I whisper in return. "But I think she had hidden it in the bear. And she had to give the bear back, so she gave it to me to keep it safe. But I don't know why it is so important. And who is this Wene person who is the curator?"

"Me," Parminter's mama says in such a quiet voice that I cannot quite believe I heard her say it.

"*You?*" I say, and then I think I have been rude and immediately apologize.

Parminter's mama pats my wing cases affectionately and smiles at me. "'W.E.NE' means the West, East and North-East skylons. You know that we have the East skylon at the very end of our long field?" she asks.

I nod.

"Well, I look after it. Dear Maximillian, you could not have brought this DisK to a better place. You see, I am a Blind Curator."

I am mortified. I had no idea that Parminter's mama was blind. I am amazed how she is able to hide it so well. I suppose she knows her way around her own house and I guess that baking is something you can do by touch, but even so . . . my train of thought is broken by Parminter, who, as ever, seems to know what I am thinking. "Ma can see perfectly well, Maximillian," she says briskly. "Ma, you tell him."

And so, for the first time ever, a Wingless one talks to me as though I am someone to whom it is worth telling an important thing. "Well, Maximillian," says Parminter's mama, "you know there are eight skylons around the edge of the city and each has a curator to look after it? And that the Guardian is curator for the ninth skylon on top of the Bartizan?"

I nod. Parminter has told me this.

Parminter's mama smiles and holds up the DisK so that it catches the light from the stove. "It used to be that there was a Disk Key like this for each skylon, but many years ago they were taken away and destroyed. So although we curators still maintain our skylons we have no control over them, which is why we are called blind. But now that we have this"—Parminter's mama looks at the DisK as though she cannot quite believe it is there in her hand—"it is the Guardian who is blind. And *we* who can see."

I feel as though I too am beginning to see that there is a much bigger world outside Mama's house than I ever realized, and that maybe even I, Maximillian Fly, large and ungainly Roach that I am, can belong in it. Now Parminter's mama is asking me something and I understand that I too know useful things.

"Maximillian," she says, "your young Escaper clearly has some inside information. She is right about the curators who can be trusted, both the West and our North-East neighbors are good people. I would very much like to meet her and ask her more."

"You can't," Parminter says abruptly. "They caught her, Ma. They took her back."

"Now, Parmie, let Maximillian speak for himself," her mama says gently.

"I am happy for Parminter to speak," I say. "This is not something I want to remember. My Kaitlin Drew will be on the SilverShip now. And soon she will be gone forever."

There is an odd silence and I see that Parminter and her mama are looking at me in a very strange way. Once again I have a feeling that I have done something wrong. "Did you say *Kaitlin Drew*?" Parminter's mama asks.

I am puzzled. "Yes, it is her name. Why? What is wrong?"

"And her little brother, was his name Jonno?" Parminter's mama says so quietly that I can hardly hear.

"I believe so," I say, surprised. "How do you know?"

Parminter's mama shakes her head. "This is so strange. The Drews used to live next door. Joanna Drew was my friend. I've babysat all the kids. Tomas, Kaitlin and

Jonno . . ." She puts her head in her hands. "And you too, Maximillian . . . when you were tiny . . . oh dear, oh dear."

Parminter puts her arm around her mama's shoulders. "Ma," she murmurs. "I think we should say something."

Parminter's mama takes a deep breath. "Maybe now is not the time, Parmie," she says, and then she takes my hand in hers. It feels so soft. I don't think a Wingless has ever held my hand before. "Now, Maximillian," she says, "you must not worry too much about your Kaitlin. No one can open the Orb without this DisK, so right now she's not going anywhere on that that awful SilverShip." And then she gets up suddenly and says, "Goodness, it's late. Parmie dear, I will go and make up some beds in the safe room for you and the boys."

I smile. I love that she called Andronicus and me "the boys."

Parminter moves close to me and, as we watch the blurry flames through the little window of the stove, I take her nearest hand and hold it in all three of mine and we sit together in happy silence. I am aware of Parminter's mama coming in and then tiptoeing out again, I hear the soft ticking of the clock and over in the far corner I hear the regular breathing of Andronicus. I wish that time could be suspended and this moment could last forever, but the clock ticks relentlessly on and suddenly I hear hurried steps and the kitchen door is thrown open.

Parminter's mama rushes in.

"Hurry!" she says, her voice hoarse with fear. "There are searchlights at the end of the street. They're smashing down doors. Oh, my loves, you must hide. Quick, quick!"

We jump up and I go to get Mama's teapot from the table. "Leave it!" Parminter says, very abruptly.

"But—" I protest.

"Maximillian, there are more important things to do right now. Like getting Andronicus out of here."

Parminter's mama takes the teapot. "Don't worry, Maximillian dear," she tells me. "I will look after it for you." And while she is telling me that she is lifting off a small painting of a fat yellow bird that hangs high above the mantelshelf in the top right hand corner. There is a space in the wall behind it, just big enough for the teapot. "Now, Maximillian," she says, "we will hide the DisK inside the teapot but it would be wise to burn the note."

She gives me the note, Parminter opens the little door in the stove and I throw the note in. I feel sad as the flames flare up and the paper shrivels to nothing. My last link with my Kaitlin Drew is gone, and her five kisses too. I see the affronted stare of the eagle as it is hidden in its aerie as Parminter's mama replaces the picture. It is a good hiding place; you would never know it was different from all the other little pictures.

We hear a series of dull thuds outside—they are

breaking down a door not so far away. "Quickly now!" Parminter's mama says.

Andronicus is bleary, but he allows us to hurry him out of the warm kitchen and into the foggy yard. And then we are rushing into the barn and back into the secret room. We hear Parminter's mama shifting hay bales and then all is quiet.

But not for long.

A sudden crash comes from the shop side of the wall. Then shouts, thuds and the sound of breaking glass. Parminter looks stricken. "Oh, poor Ma," she whispers. "She will be so afraid." But Parminter's mama does not sound afraid to me. We hear her angry yells and then a series of thuds. It is quiet for a bit and we listen fearfully for the voice of Parminter's mama and at last we hear it and we smile with relief—it is even louder and even more angry. But then there is a piercing shriek and a tremendous crash comes against the wall and plaster falls from it and I think I see it move. In a very calm voice, Parminter says, "We must go. Maximillian, help me pull up the hatch."

It is now that I notice set into the stone floor a trapdoor. I help Parminter lift it and beneath us a light comes on showing a flight of metal stairs descending to a small landing and then onward for what looks like forever. I feel quite dizzy with the height of them. Another loud thud and more falling plaster tells us we must be quick. We help Andronicus through the hatch and I take him down to the landing. Above me I watch Parminter close the hatch, and then she reaches up and pulls a long cord like a bell rope that disappears up through the ceiling. "For the frass," she says.

"Frass?" I say. I am a little shocked. Frass is insect dirt. It is also a nasty word thrown at we who are Roach.

"Yes, frass. What's wrong with that?" Parminter says as she comes delicately down the steps to join me.

"It is not a nice thing to say," I tell her.

Parminter stops on the landing and looks at me with a serious expression. "Maximillian," she says, "if people call you a bad word, that is their problem, not yours. You should never be afraid of a word. Use it how *you* want to, because words belong to us all."

I think I understand what she means. It is like calling ourselves Roach, which is a bad word some Wingless use for us, but now feels to me like a good word. And right now, standing beside Parminter, I am proud to be Roach. I truly am. I smile at her and say, "So what is this frass?"

Parminter smiles back at me. "Oh, it's all kinds of things—dust, old flour, rat droppings—whatever I sweep up from the bakery floor at night. I shovel it up and put it into the tented ceiling. And I have just dropped the lot into the secret room. It will look like no one's been there for years."

"Parminter," I say, "you truly are a wonder."

And Parminter's eyes glow bright, like lovely little harvest moons.

Chapter 26

SECRETS IN THE NIGHT

M

We are in Parminter's hut, which buzzes like a swarm of bees. Andronicus is asleep, wrapped in a rug on the floor, and Parminter and I are sitting on two stools. I have pulled them close together so that I can put my two right arms around her slender wing cases, and she is leaning against me, sobbing. I would like to feel happy holding Parminter but I cannot, for we both know her mama is in grave danger. We cannot help but be very afraid for her.

As we sit together I wonder how I would feel if my own mama were in such great danger. I confess that I do not think I would be in desolate despair, as Parminter is now. Maybe this is the one good thing about having such a mama as I do—that I will never feel such sadness for her.

Parminter's sobs have turned into little hiccups now. We sit together quietly and in the softly buzzing warmth the strange events of the day catch up with me and I feel my eyes slowly closing. . . .

P

Hello, it's Parminter here. Again. Maximillian is leaning against me, asleep. He has his mouth open just a little bit and is making soft breathing sounds. I cannot sleep because I can't stop thinking about Ma, but Maximillian needs to rest. With some difficulty—Maximillian is very heavy—I get him to lie down beside Andronicus, who is snoring in what is, to be frank, a rather annoying way. And then I sit in Grandma's rocking chair, which is comfortable even for me because it has a big space at the back to tuck the end of my wings through. As I rock to and fro I think how strange it is that as soon as Maximillian falls asleep I feel your presence.

I do think you're a bit creepy, hanging around and watching Maximillian all the time. Or perhaps I'm just a little bit jealous you can be with him whenever you want? But the truth is, I would like your company tonight. It will stop me thinking too much about Ma and wondering what is happening to her right now.

So I'll talk to you, shall I? I can explain how things work here because I don't suppose Maximillian does that, does he? No, I thought not. The reason is that he really doesn't know much. His ma—or "Mama," as he calls her—shut him away like a prisoner in Oblivion for all his childhood. He knows nothing of how our world works apart from what he has found out in a few books, and the lies and half-truths that his precious mama told him. He's not even learned much in our friendship group because Cassius always stops any remotely critical discussion.

I suppose first of all, you want me to tell you where we are now? Its official name is Curator Refuge East 3, but to us Wings it has always been simply "the hut." It is a large, insulated metal box set in the middle of our underground chamber, which forms the foundations for the four huge feet of the eastern skylon. I love to think of the delicate latticed mast rising up high above us, its roots reaching out of the earth like an ancient tree, its very tip shining out of the Orb and into the Outside sky. It makes me feel in touch with the whole world.

I watch the circle of eight lights and the ninth in the middle—one for each skylon—blinking steadily on the control panel. Beside the eastern light, number three, is the DisK Lock, the indentation where our DisK used to go, now filled with an ugly plug of gray metal.

And you are *still* here. . . . So, I suppose you want me to keep talking to you? Okay, then I'll tell you about Roach names.

In my great-grandmother's time they created the Roach Register with its compulsory "approved" names. We have always had Roach in our family, and so she decided that everyone in our family would take a Roach name—not just those of us who are Roach. She chose Wing, which was one of the nicer names. This is why Ma is "Wing" too. It has disadvantages, of course, for there are places that Ma can't go with a Roach name and she can't be employed in a school, hospital, café or restaurant either. But we are lucky enough to have our own farm, so that doesn't matter.

I am telling you this because I suspect Maximillian does not understand how hard it is to be Roach in this city. He thinks that bad things have happened to him because he is a bad person, not because he is Roach. But I have to admit that it is not that great to be Wingless in this city either, unless you are part of the Bartizan Top Tier. And who would want that on their conscience? Not me.

Oh, this is most peculiar. I can feel you looking at me. Don't you want to go now? No? Okay, then, I may as well tell you about the DisK.

In the old days, when the skylons were first built, every hut controlled its own mast with its own DisK. We curators had a lot of autonomy then; we could alter the strength of the Orb to let in more sunlight if crops were failing and sometimes we weakened it enough to let in some rain. We could even—in theory— switch the Orb off. Of course no one ever did; we acted together and trusted one another completely. However, the Bartizan was growing ever more powerful, and each successive Guardian more autocratic. One night there was a raid on all the huts. The Bartizan guards took away our DisKs, welded the controls to the *on* and the *max* positions, and destroyed the DisK Locks. So now only the Bartizan controls the Orb because only *their* DisK and their DisK Lock exists. And it is that precious, surviving DisK, which is now the only breaker and maker of the Orb, that lies secretly in its bed of wadding inside Maximillian's horrible teapot. So now do you see what possibilities Maximillian has brought us?

I do wonder how Kaitlin got hold of it, but I think it must be something to do with her mother—why else would Joanna Drew have been Astroed? Ma was so upset about that. The only reason we stay here beneath the Orb is that Ma wants to help people like the Drews. She could have got them all out to safety in Grandma's place in the Outside hills if only she'd known they were in trouble.

Oh! Do I see you being surprised that Outside is safe? Well, despite what the Bartizan says—and Maximillian too—it is free of Contagion and some people even live there, my dear old grandma included. Even I've been there a few times and it is so beautiful compared with this dull and dingy city. But it is a dangerous thing to do. Going Outside makes you a traitor, like so many things in this frightened city. And being a traitor gets you Astroed. And now I can't stop thinking that that might happen to Ma.

I am not going to think about it. *I am not*.

I suppose that now you know there is no Contagion you think that the SilverShip is a good thing? That it really is taking kids from a sad, fading city to a new life? Well, it's not. They kill the kids. All of them. And do you know how they do it? They put them in a capsule, hang it beneath the SilverShip and drop it into the ocean. My grandma follows every Exit. She has seen it happen over and over again.

Why do they do such a monstrous thing? Well, I think its because they don't want any kid coming back saying it's just fine and lovely Outside and there is no need for the Orb. Because what would happen to the Bartizan's power if people were free to leave? Deep down people know that the SilverSeed kids don't survive, even if they don't know the exact reason why. So all parents of Wingless children are model citizens, because if you put a foot wrong, your child is taken to become a SilverSeed. As Ma often says, "Parmie, it is a blessing that you are Roach. I do not have to live in fear of the SilverShip."

I feel tears welling at the thought of Ma and I wipe them away. I settle down into Grandma's chair and breathe in its fragrant smell of tobacco. Grandma still comes back here. She rings the bell that goes all the way to the shop and then Ma and I walk down the long, cold passageways beneath the fields, and in the buzzing warmth of our hut, we talk and laugh and eat flaxseed cakes, while Grandma sits and smokes a pipe or two.

I push back the rug with my foot and look at the trapdoor to the secret tunnel that takes us to the Outside—that is where Maximillian, Andronicus and I will be going in the morning. We will come out into the hidden hollow way on the far side of the Orb and walk into the hills to Grandma's cottage. She will keep them safe and I will come back and search for Ma. Hmm. I am not sure why I am telling you our big secret when even Maximillian doesn't know it yet. But I suppose there is no harm in it. It's not as if you can go telling the Bartizan all about us, is it? I suspect that you are as stuck in your own bubble as we are in ours.

Anyway, I hope you are beginning to see what a truly good person Maximillian is. I think that maybe you are, because he does seem to have stopped wanting to prove himself to you, for which I am grateful. And it is strange, but since you've come on the scene, things have certainly got interesting.

I have Grandma's favorite blanket wrapped around me, and I am going to sleep now. So good night, whoever you are. Wherever you are.

K

It is one o'clock in the morning and I'm in my cabin. Even though I have the lights off—now I'm a Three Star I have control of the light switch—I still can't sleep. All I can think about is Tomas. Tomas floating. Tomas alone. Tomas dying. And for what? Nothing. Nothing, nothing, nothing.

T

I can't sleep. My bones are reamed with ice. ReBreethe scours my lungs. With each beat of my heart, a piston pounds in my head. I have been sick. Twice. It is disgusting. I thought I wanted to die then, but I don't. I don't want to die. I want to live. To live my life. To breathe fresh air. To feel warmth. I want it all so badly that I scream it out and the sound fills the helmet and hurts my ears. I hate this suit. I hate it so much. I hate it, hate it, *hate it*. . . .

Calm down, Tomas, calm down. Get back in control. Breathe slowly now, slowly, slow . . . ly. My panic begins to lift and I get back into the Astro rhythm. I hold my breath to allow the ReBreethe to disperse through my tender lungs, then expel the stuff in a short burst. It seems to work best that way. And so I begin to relax and disconnect. I am drifting facedown over darkness. Thoughts and images wander through my mind . . . a strange mixture of things I have never quite understood. Mom and Dad gazing at an old photo of a very young and smiling Dad holding a baby—a baby who I know was not any of us three, even though when I asked, they pretended it was me. And another memory . . . coming home from school early to find Dad sitting at the kitchen table, sobbing like his heart was broken. And Mom comforting him, saying, "There is nothing we can do. He's gone and we must forget him." Another time . . . me at the top of the stairs very early one morning seeing Dad creeping out of the house with a pile of books, and looking so guilty when I asked where he was taking them.

These glimpses appear and disappear, elusive in the night. They circle and swirl through my mind, forming bizarre patterns that at first make no sense. But slowly, slowly, they come together, snippets of whispered conversations: *cocoon . . . digging . . . Maximillian . . . little Max . . . our darling baby boy . . .* and so it is, with my brain connecting and sparking in a ReBreethe haze, that I at last put the puzzle that is our family together. And maybe, just maybe, I begin to understand.

Chapter 27

THE BOY NEXT DOOR

T

Bang!

Electric shock. Every bone shot through. Upside down, head slammed into top of helmet . . . spiraling, out of control, spinning down. A bird, be like a bird . . . arms out like the wings . . . legs like a tail . . . no good, no good . . . plummet, plummet . . . down, down, down.

M

Bang!

Something just hit the hut. I'm awake and yelling, "Enforcers!"

Parminter is up and flipping open the spy hatch in the door, looking out. "I can't see anything," she says anxiously. "The lights have fused."

"They've switched them off." I am not panicking. I am *not*.

There is a covered window in each wall and Parminter flips up the shutters in turn and shines her flashlight out. "I can't see anyone," she says uncertainly.

Andronicus stirs. "Wherr?" he mumbles.

Parminter kneels beside him. "It's all right, go back to sleep," she tells him. She looks up at me. "I think I should go out and check," she says.

At once I say that I will go with her and she looks relieved. "We won't be long," I tell Andronicus, but he is already asleep.

Outside the hut Parminter swings her flashlight beam around the underground chamber. The beam catches the metal latticework of the skylon feet and casts a complex network of lines, which shift and change. We who are Roach can usually detect presences but my senses are overwhelmed with the pulsating buzz of the skylon current. If there were a whole platoon of Enforcers lurking in the gloom I do not think I would know. And so I watch warily, keeping my back to the hut as Parminter's flashlight beam travels the chamber. It appears to be empty.

To the sound of soft snoring, we quietly close the door to the hut and I follow Parminter across to a small metal box set onto the far wall. She opens it, to reveal a line of levers all pointing downward except for one. She turns to me, smiling with relief. "It's okay, it was the fuse," she says. She pulls the lever down and at once the chamber is awash with light. We are both relieved to see that it is indeed empty. I feel quite in awe of this great square cavern, with thick cables snaking up the sides of its rough concrete walls. Solidly planted in each corner are the massive feet of the skylon, which I imagine rearing up above us, keeping the Orb in place—a true Atlas holding up the sky.

"I think," Parminter says, "that something has hit the skylon."

"A bird?" I say.

Parminter is thinking. "Birds don't trip the chamber lights," she says. "They frizzle up and the current goes straight through them. I think it was something a bit bigger than a bird."

"There's an Astro out," I say quietly.

Parminter looks at me. We both know what we must do.

The struts of the skylon are constructed so that they can be used as ladders. I follow Parminter's short little legs as they move quickly upward and very soon we reach the exit in the ceiling—a diaphragm made from an intricate twist of leather flaps. I follow close on Parminter's heels as she quickly pushes through and we continue climbing up a ladder set on the sides of what feels like a large pipe. Parminter's voice has a tinny echo as she tells me that we are now moving up through the exit valve.

I laugh. "So what does that make us?"

Parminter giggles. "Frass," she says.

Parminter pushes up through a second diaphragm and I follow. Suddenly I am eye level with a field of flax stubble, pale in the dawn light. I am so surprised by the change that I have stopped halfway through the valve to gaze upon the scene and now I am aware that the diaphragm is closing in on me with some force. In fact, I am stuck fast. "*Parminter,*" I say desperately, for the pressure of the thing is pushing the breath from my body and I fear I will soon be unable to breathe.

Parminter swings around to see me looking ridiculous, planted as I am in the middle of a field like a turnip. But she does not laugh. "Oh no!" she cries. "Oh, I should have told you not to stop halfway." She throws herself down beside me and says, "Maximillian, I am going to push on your head. Really, *really* hard. You have to go back down and let the valve close above you. Then come up again fast. And whatever you do, don't stop." Parminter puts both her hands onto the flat top of my head and leans down with all her weight. She is very strong and my neck feels as though it will be pushed all the way into my body. *Parminter, stop!* I want to call out but I cannot, for I can no longer breathe. Black spots dance before my eyes, I feel myself go limp and then, suddenly, like a cork pushed into a bottle I am back through the diaphragm and there is a soft *therump* as the flaps close above my head. And now I am in total darkness. I skitter down the rungs of the ladder, gasping to catch my breath and as my feet hit the lower diaphragm it too begins to open. I panic. I have fears of the vile thing snapping at my foot and imprisoning my leg like a trap. And then I will have to wrench my leg free and it will come off and then . . . oh, I cannot bear to think of it. I grab hold of the ladder, pull myself upward with all my strength and suddenly I am free and climbing, with two legs, three arms, up through the darkness. My head hits the leather of the top valve, I take a deep breath, brace myself, and then I force my way upward. I am surprised at the resistance of the diaphragm and I push, push, *push* until suddenly I feel it give and I am hurtling through and up and running, out into the stubble and the cool gray light and I see Parminter laughing, laughing, laughing, with the soft blur of the rising sun behind her. Delighting in my escape, I pick her up and swing her around until we are dizzy and fall onto the spiky stubble. "Ouch," says Parminter, sitting up and brushing the dry dirt from her wing cases.

I begin to apologize for being so thoughtless but Parminter interrupts. "Maximillian, don't you *dare* say you are sorry," she says fiercely. So I don't. Instead, feeling a little flustered, I stand up, brush my wing cases and gaze around, hoping that I will not see a telltale flash of crumpled orange lying upon the ground. To my relief I see nothing but the wide, flat fields that stretch all the way back to Parminter's red-roofed farmhouse in the distance.

Parminter is on her feet too. "That's odd," she says. "I was so sure we'd see the Astro." And then she seizes my hand. "Over there," she whispers, pointing at a line of flax-straw bales. "Look!"

I shield my eyes and see the neighboring farm's field plowed into deep, soft furrows that look like giant corduroy, its boundary marked by a wall of bales. But for all my looking, I see no Astro. I see that some of the bales are missing from the top two rows, but that means nothing to me, for I have no idea what they should look like. But of course Parminter does, and she is already setting off toward them.

It is not easy to run across stubble and I have trouble keeping up. Parminter arrives at the bales, then stops, turns and waits for me. I hurry to her and she grabs my hand. "It's behind the bales," she says. "Look."

It is there: a fat orange suit with a long black scorch mark down its back lies sprawled facedown in the soft corduroy, surrounded by an avalanche of straw. Parminter and I exchange stricken glances. "We will have to . . . look at it," Parminter says. "Just to make sure it is . . ."

"Dead . . . ," I finish for her.

We approach gingerly and I become afraid it is going to get up and lumber toward us like an undead *thing*. But it does not move. We stand respectfully by it, as you do beside a coffin, and see the great indentation it has made in the soft soil—it has landed hard.

Parminter is brave. She kneels beside the Astro and pushes on it with both hands. She looks up at me. "I can't feel much," she says. "There's still a lot of pressure there."

"I suppose that's why it bounced," I say.

"It could still be alive," she whispers.

"Oh," I say. I do not know what is worse: a dead Astro or a living one in bits.

"We must help," Parminter says.

I glance around to check that the fields truly are deserted, which they are. But there are farmhouses in the distance and anyone could be watching with a spyglass—indeed they probably are. That bang would have been heard for miles. What Parminter is suggesting is very dangerous: it is treason to tamper with an Astro. But I cannot be a coward when Parminter is so brave. "Okay," I say.

"We need to turn it over," Parminter says. "Because

if we don't, when we take the helmet off it will be face-down in the earth."

"Ah," I say. I am impressed that Parminter always thinks things through so logically, although right now I wish she didn't. So we kneel down beside the Astro and very carefully we begin to roll it over. It is extremely heavy but we are helped by the roundness of its inflated suit and with two strong pushes it now lies flat upon its back, spread-eagled on the soft earth, with its ghostly impression beside it. We listen for any sound inside the suit but there is nothing except for the strange sense of a body settling within.

"The helmet unscrews," Parminter says. "We must check it out."

I shudder at the thought of what we will find. "But there is no hope," I say. "Surely it is best to leave it as it is?"

Parminter shakes her head. "No. We must be sure."

And so I kneel down beside Parminter. "Just close your eyes and turn," she whispers. But I do not close my eyes. I will see what Parminter sees. We will do this together. I take the heavy helmet in both hands, Parminter places her small but capable hands beside mine and together we turn the cold lump of metal until it has done a half turn and then another and suddenly the monstrosity is loose in our hands. Parminter and I look at one another with great trepidation. "On the count of three?" Parminter whispers.

I nod.

"One . . . two . . . three."

Slowly, gently, we lift the helmet off.

T

My head has fallen off. The light is too bright. But it smells so sweet. The light smells so, so sweet. I am seeing double. Double Roach. They stare at me. They have their hands over their mouths and noses. They look horrified. I splutter and spit and retch and cough. I am choking, choking. . . .

Oh, I love them. I love Roaches. I do. They are trying to help me sit up but the Astro will not bend easily. They take me under the arms and together drag me to a bale and prop me up like an old scarecrow and I am gasping in sweet air. *Thank you. Oh, thank you, thank you,* I try to say but I have no voice. It is a husk of grain. It is a swirl of dust.

The small Roach takes a piece of cloth from its pocket and very gently wipes it over my face, staring at me intently as it does so. And then, when it is finished, its mouth moves. I hear nothing. I am deaf. It puts its head on one side and looks at me quizzically. Its mouth moves, but the world stays silent.

M

"*Tomas?*" Parminter says. "Tomas, is that you?"

The smell from the suit is very bad, but Parminter is brave. Tenderly, she wipes the foul sludge from the Astro occupant's face while I stare, amazed that he is alive. I am shocked too that he is little more than a boy—far too young for this kind of horror. Parminter seems to know him. And there is indeed something familiar about the face, although I am not good on Wingless facial recognition. I rely on obvious things like hair color, the wearing of glasses, that kind of thing, and all young men with short hair look the same to me. But Parminter is good at this. I suppose because she has seen so many more Wingless ones than I.

"Tomas?" she says again. "Tomas, it *is* you, isn't it?" The boy stares at her, his mouth moving, making silent words. His sunken eyes are dark in their sockets. He looks as though he has seen a ghost. No, that is not true—he looks as though he *is* a ghost.

"Do you know him?" I ask Parminter.

Parminter looks at me with tears in her eyes. "I think so. But, oh, it can't be. Surely not . . . Oh, this is so unfair. *So unfair.* That poor family."

"What poor family?" I ask.

Parminter sighs. "The Drews," she says. "I think he is Tomas Drew."

"Drew?" I ask, thinking at once of my Kaitlin Drew.

Gently, Parminter wipes the boy's face. "Tomas," she says, "it's Parminter. Do you remember me?"

And I watch the boy's lips moving. I see him struggling to make his words come out and I stare at him. And then, at last, I remember the face. "That is not a Drew," I say. "*That* is a Vermin."

T

It is Parminter Wing. She recognizes me. I struggle to speak but my voice won't work. And it seems that the other Roach knows me too. And now that my mind is clearing I realize that I also know him. He is the one who ate Jonno. I muster all my strength and I spit at him. He recoils in disgust. Good.

Now the killer Roach is talking to Parminter and she is shaking her head. He shrugs his shoulders and then glances into the distance, to where the farmhouses are. And now they hurriedly begin to put bales of flax straw behind me and I understand that they are shielding me from view. I watch, unable to move, propped up like a dummy. I long to be free of this suit but I am trapped. My wrists and ankles are held tight and no matter how hard I pull on them they will not come free. But I am breathing in beautiful fresh air, and with each breath I feel the fire in my lungs subside. I don't care that I hurt all over; I don't even care what will happen to me next. All that matters to me right now is that I can breathe.

In a silent daze I watch Parminter and the devourer of my little brother work together building their flax-bale wall. I confess that I am surprised by the company Parminter keeps. I used to think she was a good person. She helped Mom and gave us leftover food from the shop. She even went to Jonno's school on Apple Tree Day. But as they say: *you never know with a Roach.*

They have finished their wall now and they are still talking. They glance at me while they talk and I begin to feel afraid. I think they are deciding what to do with me. And whatever it is, they clearly want to keep it hidden from prying eyes. This does not feel good.

It's not good. Not good at all. The killer Roach is taking out his dagger; it has a long, thin blade with a notch halfway down. I remember it well. He is walking toward me now. Oh, this is so unfair—to have come so far only to die at the hands of that vile Roach.

I try to call to Parminter for help, but my voice will not work. But there is no point anyway. Parminter is hanging back, watching quite happily. I try to raise my arms to protect my face but I can hardly move them. I am as weak as a newborn baby. The killer Roach is taller than I remember. He is here now, leaning over me. I look up at him but his glittering gray eyes refuse to meet mine. As he places the tip of his dagger upon my chest, I at last find my voice.

"*No!*" I shout, and this time I make a sound. It is no more than a weak bleat, but I *hear* it, like faint buzzing at the end of a long tunnel. "Please . . . ," I squeak. "Let me live. Please."

M

Oh, give me patience. The Vermin thinks I'm going to kill it.

Parminter runs up behind me and kneels down beside the Vermin. "Tomas?" she asks. "You can speak?"

The Vermin croaks like a frog.

"And you can hear me?"

"Uh," it rasps.

"Tomas," says Parminter. "We are not trying to kill you. We need to slit the suit so you can get out of it." The Vermin tries to say something but its voice seems to have given up again. "So hold still and don't be scared," Parminter tells it. "We'll get you free. Okay?"

The Vermin nods, but it does not look convinced. I am not convinced either. I would be quite happy to leave it here stuck like a deflated orange slug. But with the help of Parminter, who holds the thick and remarkably stiff material away from the Vermin's body so I may safely cut into it, I manage to get the point of the blade in. But there is a steel mesh woven through the fabric and despite my best efforts sawing away—all the while watched with terror by the Vermin—I am able to make no more than a small hole.

"It's no good," I tell Parminter. "We need something stronger to get through this."

The Vermin is opening and closing its mouth and wheezing at us in a most irritating fashion. Parminter kneels down close to it and listens. "Tomas says his wrists and ankles are held in cuffs," she tells me. "So whatever we do with the suit he'll still be trapped. We need bolt cutters."

"And where do we get those from?" I ask a little tetchily.

"We have some at home," Parminter says. "I shall go and get them."

I am shocked. Parminter is risking everything for a Vermin. "No!" I say. "He is not worth it. He took my Kaitlin Drew away. Let him stay here. It serves him right."

Parminter looks at me with a strange expression. "Maximillian," she says quietly. "Tomas is Kaitlin's brother. He would not hurt her. I am sure she went with him quite happily."

But I am not sure, not at all. "No, she didn't," I say. And I see from the Vermin's expression I am correct.

Parminter sighs as if I am being annoying. But, for once, I do not think this is fair. "Before we go to all the trouble and risk of getting him free, I want to know what he did with my Kaitlin Drew," I say.

The Vermin begins to wheeze like an old bellows and Parminter listens, her ear to its mouth. She looks up at me. "He says he is sorry. He took her back to the SilverShip. But in the end, she wanted to go."

"But not in the beginning?" I say.

The Vermin shakes his head and I hear him whisper, "No."

Parminter looks at me. "Maximillian, he is sorry and that has to be enough for now. If we abandon him he will die, and we will be as guilty as you think *he* is. I am going now to get the bolt cutters. I'll be back as soon as I can."

I do not want her to leave me with this Vermin, but more than that I am worried about Parminter going alone to her home that was ransacked by guards. It will be very upsetting for her. "I'll come with you," I say. "You don't know what you're going to find."

"Ma," Parminter says in an oddly bright and brittle tone. "I will find Ma back home baking the morning flax cakes."

I do not think this will happen. "I still think I should come with you," I say.

"No," Parminter says. "Tomas is not well enough to be left alone."

"I'm sure he'll be fine," I say stiffly. "He seems to have a habit of bouncing back."

But Parminter will not be persuaded. "Maximillian," she says, "you must stay with Tomas."

"Filthy Vermin," I mutter.

I hear a nasty wheeze from the Vermin. "Killer," it croaks. "You killed my brother."

Parminter looks at us both, amused. I find this annoying. I do not think this is at all funny. "Boys, boys," she says as if we are little children, "stop fighting now. Tomas, no one has killed your brother—well, not yet anyway. He's actually back in the SilverShip crew quarters. So how about while I'm gone you both have a little talk about brothers? Hey?"

"I'm not talking to that piece of frass," I say.

Parminter is in a very strange mood now. I do not understand it at all. She gives me a weird little smile, like she knows something I don't. "You might both find it interesting. You have more in common than you realize."

"Ha!" the Vermin and I manage to say together. Then we stop and glare at one another.

"Like *what*?" I demand.

Parminter looks at us both and takes a deep breath. "Like your father," she says. And with that she turns and walks away. She raises her lovely purple wing cases, her delicate underwings unfurl and then, with two gentle beats, she is airborne. The Vermin and I watch her go and when, at last, I look down I realize who the Vermin's deep gray eyes remind me of—the sad man who gave me the books and the bear.

The Vermin returns my gaze. "She called you Maximillian . . . so are you . . . are you *him*?" he whispers. "Max? The baby?"

I sit down beside the Vermin. I feel very strange indeed. Because I was a baby once. I have a photograph.

Chapter 28

CUTTING LOOSE

P

It's Parminter here. Maximillian is a private person and I think we should leave him alone with Tomas for now. Of course, I would have loved Maximillian to come with me, but I fear for Tomas if he is left alone. He looks so frail. And I trust Maximillian to protect him, now that he has discovered the truth. I glance back and see them sitting side by side behind the bales. They make a strange pair, a broad-shouldered Roach next to the collapsed Astro suit with its wide hoop of a neck and Tomas's sad little head poking out like a bewildered tortoise. I am so shocked by what has happened to Tomas. What a brutal place Hope can be.

So, will you come with me? Please? To be perfectly frank, I would really appreciate your company. I am more frightened of going home than I let Maximillian know. I can't get the sound of Ma's scream out of my head. All last night I was hoping she would come to the hut but, as you know, she didn't. I have been telling myself that there are lots of good reasons for that; it's a long way and there would have been a lot of clearing up to do after those guards went. But deep down I know that nothing would have stopped Ma from running the two long miles down the skylon tunnel to see if we were safe and to tell me that all was well.

In my heart, I know it is bad.

But I must try to be positive. I shall tell you what a beautiful morning it is. I do love the misty haziness of dawn when you can almost forget that we are sealed beneath the Orb. Of course it's not like being Outside. When I was with Grandma we used to walk to the top of the hill and watch the sunrise. You would not believe the colors in the sky—brilliant orange, yellow and almost luminous pink and pale green—and to see the sun for real was breathtaking. It would rise up above the hill like a huge ball of orange fire. Oh, it was such a good feeling to be out there with no barriers between us and our universe, where we all belong. But then I would look down the hill at the city in the distance, where the huge white dome of the Orb squatted like a giant spider's egg sac and I would feel so sad for all those trapped inside.

I think Maximillian describes things to you as he goes,

right? So I will do the same. I'm flying a safe distance from the Orb, which is close here where it reaches all the way to the ground. I keep away because sometimes the charge will arc across to objects that go too near. If you look down to my right, you can see a deep, wide ditch between the end of the field and the scorched area beyond where the Orb meets the ground.

Because I am afraid there might be guards in our house watching the fields, I am flying to the next skylon—number two, the North-East. They are good people there and it is also away from skylon four and the farm on the other side of us, which now belongs to the Bartizan.

So I've now reached skylon two and I'm heading across the long North-East field, which has just been sown with hemp. There are a couple of people tending the field; they wave as I fly overhead and then get back to their work.

And now I'm past the fields, flying low over the rooftops and heading for our lovely red tin roof, which Ma painted especially for me. But I mustn't think of Ma. I really must not, because I'm here now, gliding in, and I must take care and concentrate. Below our yard is deserted. Silently, I drop down and land in the shadows close to the wall. I can't smell any baking. I stay very still, listening hard. I hear nothing. The back door to the kitchen is wide open and I make myself walk toward it. I step over the threshold and stop dead.

Oh.

The kitchen is trashed. Food jars smashed on the floor, pans hurled to the ground, stools overturned, their legs in the air like stranded beetles, the table strewn with papers and the soup thrown across the floor. The fire in the stove is out and the bench where only a few hours ago Maximillian and I sat holding hands has been smashed in two, by an ax by the look of it. The pictures are all pulled from the wall and from its little burrow way up in the top right hand corner I see the red-eyed eagle on the spout of Maximillian's horrible teapot staring out at me. It's creepy and I get the weird thought that the evil little eagle has engineered all this destruction and now sits, gloating over it.

I lean against the table, stunned. I hear my voice, reedy and scared, breaking through the heavy blanket of silence. "Ma?" I call out. *"Ma?"*

There is no reply.

Gingerly, I pick my way across the debris of the kitchen and go through the connecting door into the bakery. It is as I expected. The shopwindow is smashed, the floor is strewn with glass and the wall that hid our safe place is a pile of jagged wood and plaster. I peer inside and see that the frass has done its job and the hatch is undiscovered. This is good, because it means they do not know where we are—yet. Perhaps we will be able still to get to the Outside. But for now, as I survey the wreckage of our happy home, all I can think of is Ma. I am so afraid for her.

A sudden longing to be back with Maximillian comes over me. I hurry into the workshop and take the bolt cutters. They're very heavy, so I go back into the kitchen to get my flight bag. Oh, it is so horrible in here; it feels as though all our happy times have been smashed to pieces. My flight bag is still hanging by the stove, and as I make my way carefully over to get it, the nasty little teapot's red eyes watch me malevolently. A shiver runs through me, and the thing seems almost alive. *Take the DisK, Parminter,* I tell myself. *Take it away from here.*

I am lifting the eagle down from its aerie when I suddenly know that *there is someone behind me.* Slowly, I put the teapot down on the stone-cold stove and tighten my grip on the bolt cutters. And then, as though I am the wolf in the game: *What's the time, Mr. Wolf?* I suddenly swing around.

Cassius! There he is, right foot raised, frozen in the classic creeping-up-on-you pose. He looks so comical that I want to laugh. But this is no laughing matter. I take a deep breath and make my voice as calm as I can. "Cassius," I say. "What are you doing here?"

Slowly, Cassius puts his foot to the floor. "I am performing a search for wanted persons," he says. "And I am pleased to say it is now partially successful." He leaps forward and before I can do anything he has grabbed my middle left arm so hard it hurts. He leans toward me and I smell meat on his breath. "Where are you hiding him?" he snarls.

"Hiding who?" I ask as I secure my grip on the bolt cutters.

"You know who. Maximillian Fly. Liar. Thief. *Traitor.*"

Cassius is like a nasty leech I can't shake off. I don't want to do this but there is no choice. I swing the bolt cutters out from under my wing and bring them down upon his wrist. With a lightning reaction, Cassius grabs the bolt cutters just before they hit him. He hurls them aside and in a cold fury he twists my middle left limb. I feel it pop out of its socket and I'm gasping with pain.

Cassius looks smug. "It is treason to attack an officer of the Bartizan," he says.

My head is swimming, but I am not going to give Cassius the pleasure of seeing how shocked I am. "Huh," I say. "There's no way they'd let a nasty old Roach like you become an officer of the Bartizan."

Cassius will not be goaded. I get the feeling there is something he wants from me. "Parminter," he says, "let us be civilized about this. You tell me where that traitor

Fly is, and I'll do my best to keep your mother safe."

The thought of Ma makes my eyes prickle with tears, but Cassius's words give me hope. It sounds like Ma is still alive. "You have your own fate to consider too," Cassius says. "Tell me where Fly is and I'll give you a head start. Ten minutes until I call the guards."

"Maximillian left here yesterday afternoon," I tell him. "He went home."

Cassius has a really creepy smile. "Very commendable loyalty, Parminter," he says. "But, alas, not very helpful, especially not for your mother. Fly was observed leaving his house late last night, carrying a sack. We have reason to believe the sack contained stolen Bartizan property. And that he brought it here. Unfortunately, despite a thorough search, we have been unable to locate it." A nasty gleam comes into his eyes. "But you know, Parminter, I get the feeling that a bright little thing like you would know where it is, hey?"

Fool that I am, I glance at the eagle-eyed teapot, and Cassius sees me. "Ha!" he cries, and his long arms reach for the teapot.

"No!" I yell, and I dive at him. In one slick movement Cassius places a cuff on my upper right wrist and fixes the other end to the table leg. Then he saunters over to the stove and picks up the teapot. And I have to watch as, with the air of someone about to enjoy a good lunch,

Cassius pulls a stool up to the table and sits down opposite me, cradling the horrible teapot in all four of his hands. "Well, well," he says, "let's see what we have in here, shall we?" And he draws out the wadding, unwraps the DisK and holds it up triumphantly. "Just what we're looking for," he says. "So kind of you to point it out."

Parminter, I tell myself. *You are such an idiot.*

Cassius gets up and walks to the door, then turns to look back at me. "They'll be here to collect you in about ten minutes. Enjoy." And with that he is gone.

Now, you may think that getting away from a table leg is easy. Just turn the table upside down and slide the handcuff off. But our table has weird legs. They have all kinds of bumps and Cassius has fixed my cuff onto a narrow waist between two lumpy bits. However, the bolt cutters are still lying in the corner where Cassius hurled them. I don't think he knew what they were. The problem for us Roaches is that our arms are not strong and now I have only three working upper limbs. My lower left middle hangs uselessly—and very painfully—by my side. But using my body weight I manage to push the table inch by inch toward the bolt cutters. I have just reached them when, in the distance, I hear footsteps—hard, booted, hurrying steps. Cassius has wasted no time. The bolt cutters are heavy and unwieldy but desperation makes me strong and I sever the chain first go. I am free! I hear shouts from the shop, the sound of boots upon glass. I grab my flight bag and hurry into the courtyard, where I put the bolt cutters into the bag and sling it around my waist. As I rise up into the air two Bartizan guards walk into the courtyard, but I am lucky. They are looking the other way, toward the barns. I dare not fly for fear of being seen, so I land as lightly as I can upon the roof and flatten myself into the shadows of the bulky smoke filter that is wrapped around the chimney stack.

The guards are in the kitchen now and I can hear their voices coming up the chimney.

"Oh no! She's *escaped.*" This is a young one with a squeaky voice. It sounds scared.

Another, an older woman, says gruffly. "Idiot Roach, chaining her to a table leg. Why didn't he bring her in himself? I do like that teapot."

They go out into the courtyard and join the third. "Flown the roost," the woman reports. I can see her now, tall and chunky. There is no way anyone would twist one of *her* arms out of its socket.

The third guard swears.

"It's mission failure, isn't it?" says the squeaky young one, a scrawny young man who looks like he should still be in school.

"That's right, son," the guard says glumly.

"It's my third mission failure in a row," the young man

says, anxiously looking for support. He doesn't get it.

"Tut-tut," says the woman.

"I'm done for, aren't I?"

There is an awkward silence.

"We . . . we, er, don't have to report it as a failure." The young man sounds so desperate that I almost feel sorry for him.

And then the woman, the leader I think, says, "Well, we don't *have* to do anything."

"Exactly." He sounds so relieved. "We don't *have* to do their dirty work. We don't *have* to go terrorizing Roaches and locking up innocent baker-ladies."

"No, we don't," the woman says. She pauses and adds, "Not if we're *traitors*."

I can feel the young man's fear from here. "What are you *doing*?" he yelps suddenly. "Let me go! It was just a joke. Honestly. Just a stupid, stupid *joke*," he gabbles.

"A *traitorous* joke," the woman says.

There is a shout, the sound of a scuffle and I hear the squeaky voice rise even higher as its owner begs for mercy. I watch the two guards march their new victim away down the street and I do not move until the sound of boots is no more.

As I slowly fly away with the bolt cutters, I cannot but help feel guilty. I escaped, but another was sacrificed. They got their traitor after all.

M

I am sitting in the middle of a field and I think that maybe I am in a dream. The Vermin has told me so many strange things, and every single one of them makes me feel most peculiar. I have made a list for you to read because I cannot say them. Here it is in order of peculiarness:

My Kaitlin Drew is my half sister.

The Vermin is my half brother. Its name is Tomas.

Tomas and Kaitlin's papa was my papa too.

Their mother was my nurse.

Mama buried me in the yard.

Tomas's mother and my father dug me up and ran away with me.

We lived just along the street from Parminter's mother.

When I was about two years old, Mama took me away.

Papa is dead. He was sacrificed at the Steeple. He played the flute.

There are many other things that the Vermin has told me, but they are all so sad that I do not know if I can hold them inside me without bursting my carapace.

P

I am flying slow, the bolt cutters are a deadweight and the pain from my arm—which I have tucked into my waistband to stop it from flapping as I fly—makes me feel ill. It seems like forever, but at last I see Maximillian and Tomas behind their flax bales. I coast in, drop the bolt cutters a few yards away and land with a bump. Maximillian is already on his feet. "Oh, Parmie," he says. "What has happened?"

He called me Parmie. I clench my teeth and make a stern face because I will burst into tears if Maximillian is any nicer to me. "Can you put it back for me?" I ask briskly.

This is one of the good things that have come from our friendship group. Titus is an Underground nurse and one evening he taught us how to put dislocated limbs back into their sockets. Maximillian looks nervous but he grasps my useless arm firmly and with his hand on my wing cases, strong and steady, he gives my arm the *push-and-twist-and-push-and-up-and-IN* and we both hear a deep, dull *clunk* as it settles back into its home. I am so relieved that I have to sit down. It is all too much.

M

There is a security cuff on Parminter's upper right wrist and she is very shaken. Something bad has happened to her. But I must not think about that. She is here now and that is enough. "Does it still hurt?" I ask anxiously.

She looks up and tries to smile, but it doesn't quite work. "Only a little bit. Nothing like it did. Thank you, Maximillian."

I understand that we have both decided not to talk about what happened back at the farm, because there is something we must do right now. Our arms are not strong, but with both of us holding the bolt cutters we have just enough strength to cut through the steel mesh of the Astro. It is slow going.

"Free my hands," the Vermin whispers impatiently. "I can do the rest."

We can't free his hands because we can't get the heavy Astro cuffs off his wrists—we just don't have the strength to cut through the thick metal bands. But we do manage to cut the suit away from his arms and he flaps his arms like a bird, the heavy cuffs weighing him down. "Free!" he says hoarsely. He looks at me. "Maximillian, thank you. I can never repay you for what you have done." And he wraps his arms around me and holds me close, the cuffs clattering on my wing cases. I am shocked, but strangely happy.

Chapter 29

COUNTDOWN

K

It is SilverShip dawn and the sound of birdsong is being piped into my cabin. As the light slowly brightens—*look, kids, just like the rising sun*—I lie on my sleeping shelf and think how yesterday I was waking in Maximillian's house to proper daylight and those two real little birds were hopping and tweeting outside on the parapet. So much has changed since then.

I listen to the increasingly loud dawn chorus—which will end with a series of shotgun blasts—and I feel wretched. I couldn't sleep last night. I kept thinking about Tomas up there in the sky. And when I wasn't thinking about Tomas, I was expecting any minute to be marched up to the Astro Room myself. Because by now they surely must have discovered that the DisK isn't inside Tedward. So why haven't they come for me?

The birdsong is becoming increasingly frantic. The sound of the cuckoo kicks in and I know that in sixty-six seconds the shotgun blasts will begin. It is time to face the day. I am out of the cabin just before the first blast and confronted by something very weird. The walkway is lined with ground crew, blank-faced and formal, repeating in unison, "Silence, please. Proceed to the refectory. Silence, please. Proceed to the refectory. Silence, please. Proceed to the refectory. . . ."

But it's not silent. There is a low, rumbling roar filling the air and our ears. It is a little like what they call thunder in the Outside storms we sometimes hear, but unlike the thunder, it just keeps going. As we move along the walkway in anxious silence, the low-level rumbling and the impassive gaze of the ground crew add to my feeling of dread. I am convinced they are going to make an example of me. They will tell everyone that I'm a traitor and take me away to be Astroed. Later this morning both Tomas and I will be floating beneath the Orb together.

Feeling so scared that I'm shaking, I walk into the refectory and see six huge numbers projected on the blank white wall: *00:34:47.* I'm so stuck in my terror that it takes me a few seconds to get it. *Duh, Kaitlin. It's the Countdown to Exit.*

I want to sink to the floor in relief—I'm not going to be Astroed. Okay, so I'm going off into the unknown and

I'll never come back, but at least I will be with friends. And who knows, Mom might be wrong. The Island might really exist and all will be lovely. After all, no one has proved it doesn't exist, have they? I head over to the table where my tribe—the Lions—is sitting. I join Mattie and three others: twin girls, Pia and Mia, and a lanky boy, Marlon, who never speaks. We're a small tribe, us older ones. We exchange nervous smiles and I sit next to Mattie, who is watching the moving numbers counting down: *00:33:05* . . . *00:33:04* . . . *00:33:03* . . .

At *00:33:02*, with my terror gone, I begin to think straight. Unfortunately. I realize that if we are on Count-down to Exit, then they must have taken the DisK from Maximillian by force—he would never have freely handed it over. I feel Mattie's arm around my shoulders. "Hey," she says, "we'll be fine." I look up and see she is smiling and there's a new light in her eyes. "And Tomas will be fine too," she whispers.

I shake my head. "No, Mattie. He's . . . ," I begin.

Mattie puts her finger to her lips. "Don't tell me," she says. "Whatever happened to him yesterday is all right now. This morning, just before Birdsong, I suddenly knew he wasn't scared anymore. He's all right, Kait. I know he is."

I look at Mattie, doubtfully. *"Really?"*

"Yes," she says very decidedly. "So don't tell me what

happened. I don't want to have it in my head. Okay?"

"Okay," I agree. Truthfully I feel anything but okay. Because I am sure that the reason Mattie feels that Tomas is no longer scared is because he can't feel fear anymore. In fact, he can't feel anything. Because he is dead.

J

Leon and me are with the Bears in the refectory. There isn't any breakfast. I look over at Katie and she has her serious face on. There are lots of guards all around the wall and everyone is very quiet. I think we must have done something really bad.

K

The guards are standing elbow to elbow, arms folded, feet planted firmly apart. They remind me of the strings of concertina cutout figures Mom used make for us. On *00:30:00* one of them steps forward and announces the names of the Leavers—the ones who get to leave before Exit. This is where we hear our fate.

The Leavers are either kids who were taken as hostages to encourage their parents' good behavior, or whose family have paid a ransom to set them free. On the last Exit—a lifetime ago when we were still living in our house by the fields—the farming family on the other side of the Wings gave the Bartizan their entire farm in order to get their son back.

The list of Leavers is read out to hushed attention, and at our table the twins and Marlon stand up. The twins cannot stop smiling, but Marlon is glum. He once told Mattie that he was looking forward to his new life on the Island. He planned to spend his time hunting bears and living in a cave. Mattie said she was unsure whether he meant the Bear tribe or the actual animals. But now, along with the other Leavers, he files quietly out and is gone, back to his old life. The canteen is half-empty now; those of us left are what they call the core group—the bit with pips that no one wants. Mattie takes my hand and squeezes it. I give her a nervous smile.

There is an uncomfortable silence in the refectory as the reality of Exit begins to sink in. The Wolves and the Bears huddle into their depleted tribe groups and, along with Mattie and I, the last two Lions, we watch the relentlessly diminishing numbers on the wall suddenly vanish. We steal glances at one another, wondering if Countdown is canceled, but then these words appear: *A Message from Madam Guardian to her SilverSeeds.* They fade away to be replaced by an image of the woman I remember all too well. Her hair shimmers like a pewter helmet, below which a pair of intense eyes set deep in her shield-shaped face stare at us like two dagger points. One of the Bears begins to cry.

Madam Guardian's mouth is moving but no sound comes out. We watch the thin lips opening and closing, showing perfect little rat teeth, and suddenly one of the ground crew, looking terrified, races across the room and throws a switch in the sound system.

Madam Guardian's voice kicks in: ". . . ulations to you all. Today, at long last, you are leaving behind your cares and woes in our besieged city and embarking upon your journey to our Island of Hope. In the magnificent SilverShip you will soon be flying across the beautiful blue skies of our planet, passing over ruined cities, great oceans and vast deserts. On the threshold of your brilliant future you SilverSeeds are ambassadors of Hope, you are our . . ."

The spiel continues, and I disconnect myself from the words and look around the room. The kids are staring up at the screen with a dawning look of apprehension: this is for real.

And then it is over. The image of Madam Guardian dissolves into moving shapes of what we've been told are ocean waves breaking on sand. The SilverShip anthem, "This World Is Our World," begins to play and we all stand and cross our arms over our chests and watch the waves. They do look amazing, although I have trouble believing they are real. I mean, what are they *for* exactly? The anthem finishes with its rousing clash of cymbals and then all is quiet. As the waves wash silently onto a distant shore we file out of the refectory and walk into the wild roar, which is, we now understand, the noise of the SilverShip balloon being inflated.

At once we kick into Exit drill. We've done it so often that it is automatic. First we put all objects containing metal, including pens, belts and even glasses into the store capsule, which will, we are told, be attached to the ship separately, for safety reasons. But I remember Mom telling me about a friend who saw her son's glasses in a shopwindow six months after his Exit. He'd scratched his name into the bridge and when she went into the shop and asked to see them, there it was: *Derek*. She was distraught. How, she'd asked Mom, could he manage on the Island without his glasses? I said that I supposed Derek got new glasses on the Island and Mom just ruffled my hair and said, "Oh, Katie, that poor, poor boy."

As I hold my precious combi-tool, which was a present from Dad, I know it will not be coming with me, despite what they say. I am expendable—my combi is not.

J

I don't want to leave my fishing rod in the store. And I don't want to leave Nettie either. She will be scared on her own.

K

On my way to the store I see Jonno in a small group of Bears solemnly walking ahead and he glances behind him. Our eyes meet and he hangs back and waits for me. I'm unreasonably happy about this, because I've hated things being bad between us. Jonno is carrying his fishing rod and a small brown bundle with a piece of fishing twine tied around it. It looks a little like Tedward minus his arms and legs. "Hey, Jonno, what have you got there?" I ask.

Jonno smiles sheepishly. "She's Nettie," he says. "I hope Tedward won't be jealous."

"I'm sure Tedward won't mind at all," I tell him.

Jonno looks at me, anxiously. "I know Nettie is really a net, but I don't want to put her in the store. She'll be frightened. Do you think I can take her with me?"

This tears me apart. "Well, let's see, shall we?" I say and then change the subject. "Looking forward to all that fishing?" I ask, way too jovially.

Jonno grins. "When we get to the Island I'm going straight out to catch enough fish for everyone, because we'll be hungry after the flight," he says.

"Good idea," I tell him.

He looks surprised. "You don't usually say stuff like that," he says.

"I'm sorry. I'm sure you're going to catch lots of fish.

It will be really great." I don't think I sound very convincing but Jonno doesn't seem to notice.

"So you *do* believe that we're really going to be hunting and making dens and fires and catching fish and keeping pets and . . . and *everything*?" he says all in a rush.

What can I say? "Yes," I tell him. "Of course I do."

Jonno reverts to his old irritable self. "Well, you might have said so before," he grumbles. He looks down at his fishing rod, a telescopic one with a fancy reel. I don't know how he got hold of it but it's a good one, even I can see that. "I wish I didn't have to put this in store," he says, regretfully.

"I wish I didn't have to put my combi in store either," I say. "But I guess we have to."

J

Katie is being nice again, but when she smiles her eyes looks sad. I thought going on Exit would be exciting but it's not. It feels nasty and I don't like it. Everyone is rushing and the roaring noise sounds like an angry monster.

I don't want to be a Bear anymore. I want to go home.

Chapter 30

EXIT

M

The Vermin's Astro is in chopped-up pieces upon the ground and its ankle cuffs lie snapped in half. The Vermin can't manage to get the wrist cuffs off—he doesn't have enough arms—but he seems happy with that. "They're a badge of honor," he croaks. "Like yours, Parminter."

Parminter looks at her own cuff in disgust. "Not honor," she says. "Not this."

"Why, Parminter? What happened?" I ask.

Parminter sighs. "I have been such an idiot," she says. "I've ruined everything."

"Don't be silly, of course you haven't," I tell her, thinking that I am sounding a lot like Parminter myself.

But Parminter is not listening to me. Her hands fly up to her face and she gasps. "Oh no!"

"Parminter, what is it?" I ask.

Parminter looks devastated. “Listen.”

I hear it now: the distant sound of wailing sirens from the city. This is most odd. They sound like the Exit sirens warning everyone to go indoors and close their shutters and curtains to stop any Contagion seeping in.

“They are preparing to stand down the Orb,” Parminter says.

I laugh. “But they can’t. They haven’t got the DisK.” And then I see Parminter’s expression and I say no more.

“They have,” she says. “They took it. And now they are using it.”

K

The roar of the gas has stopped. All is horribly silent for a moment, and then the guards start yelling, “Sixty seconds! Sixty seconds! Boarding, boarding! Now, now, *now*!” The store is slammed shut before Jonno and I get there and we are shoved down the metal steps to the recreation area, where the double doors, each with their shining silver *S*, are wide open and gaping like the mouth of a monster about to swallow us up. Some of the younger kids hang back and the guards push them forward none too gently. I see Jonno ahead of me, clutching Nettie and his fishing rod. As he walks through the doors I think how vulnerable he looks with his thin little neck and his spiky hair. And then I think how fragile we all are, and how it is such an easy thing to destroy a human being.

J

It's not a real ship. It's not at all like they said it would be. There are no seats and no windows. The walls are all wobbly. It's horrible in here. Nettie doesn't like it and Leon is crying.

K

The capsule is unsettlingly bare. I think we'd all expected at the very least some basic seats, but it is completely empty. Mattie and I sit on the deck and when I lean back I'm shocked to feel the walls give against my weight—they appear to be made of nothing more than thick hemp cloth. Our capsule is no more substantial than the tent Dad used to take us camping on the Wings' long field. "Mattie," I whisper. "This feels bad."

Mattie nods. "Yeah," she says.

We're in now, all fourteen of us. Some of the Bears are crying and a few of the younger Wolves look close to tears. Jonno looks very serious; he is holding Nettie tight and whispering to her. I'm so pleased he didn't have to give her up.

Mattie and I, along with one of the older Wolves, Ethan, move around the capsule comforting the little ones while the canvas door flap is closed and the acrid smell of it being sealed fills our noses. We hear the clang of the doors to our old crew quarters being shut and as we are cut off from everything we have ever known, one of the Bears pipes up, "There's no toilets!" The others giggle but look concerned too.

"No need," Mattie says briskly. "We'll be there before you know it."

We listen to a series of muffled clangs and then a long rattle as though chains are being reeled in. The cabin shifts and I get the unnerving feeling that the ground is no longer beneath us.

M

A crack, loud like a pistol shot, rips out from the top of the skylon, sending out a long line of light so bright that it hurts to look at it. I peer out between my fingers and see the Vermin leaning back against a bale, looking up at the Orb, shielding his eyes with his hands. He has to press them hard against his forehead to stop them shaking. Another burst of light shoots out. It is magnificent, terrifying and fascinating all at once.

"The SilverShip!" The Vermin give a hoarse, scraping shout. "Look! There it is!"

I scramble to my feet and see in the distance a giant silver fish rising up above the rooftops.

"They're lucky," the Vermin croaks. "They can start a new life."

"They are *not* lucky," Parminter tells him angrily. "They will have no life at all."

My eyes fill with water. "Because they will die of the Contagion," I say.

But the Vermin disagrees. "No they won't. They'll be fine. The Island is free of Contagion."

"It's free of Contagion *everywhere*, dumbo," Parminter tells him. "The Contagion is long gone. It's just a story to keep us all prisoners in this nasty little city."

The Vermin laughs. "Oh, you believe those Rat tales too, do you?" he croaks. "Well, all their stories about people living Outside are total rubbish." The Vermin is cut short by another electrical surge above our heads that sets our carapaces humming.

This one lasts much longer and Parminter yells above it, "So how come my grandma has lived Outside, just over the hill there, for the last fifty-five years? How come she is just fine?"

The Vermin frowns, unsure whether to believe Parminter. But I believe her. Oh, she's told me stories about the Outside before, but that's all I thought they were—stories. Wishful thinking. She has never mentioned that her grandmama is actually *living* there. This is very different. I feel a weight of sadness lifted from me. My

Kaitlin Drew, *my sister*, will live. And even though I won't see her again, I will know that she is alive on the Island. And that will be enough for me.

"Well, good for Grandma," the Vermin says, somewhat bitterly. "So now everyone will be just fine, won't they?"

It is quiet now, apart from a low buzzing as the skylon recharges. "They won't be 'just fine' at all," Parminter tells him angrily. "Because the Bartizan puts the SilverSeeds in nothing more than a giant canvas bag. They hang it under the ship and drop it into the ocean. Grandma has seen it happen over and over again."

The Vermin stares at Parminter in shock. He has seen for himself the horrors that the Bartizan is capable of and he believes her at once. I find that I am clutching his hand and he is clutching mine. "Maximillian, we must save them," my brother Tomas croaks.

We must. But I do not know how.

K

The capsule is filled with whimpering. Most of the Bears and at least two of the Wolves are crying for their mothers, but Jonno is quiet, clutching Nettie and biting his bottom lip. I am so proud of my little brother; I want to tell him that he is a brave and good Bear.

I have the same sensation in my stomach that I had in the Bartizan elevator—we are going up fast. The walls of the cabin wobble alarmingly and the smallest Bear—a little redheaded boy called Leon—starts up a wild, ululating shriek. Another joins him. And then the oldest Wolf—a large, pimply boy called Dom—lets out a long, low howl of despair and throws himself facedown on the deck.

"Kait," whispers Mattie. "We've got to keep a lid on this."

I take a deep breath and go for it. "Hey, you Wolves and Bears! It's . . . *campfire circle*!" I trill out, mimicking the intonation of the usual odious announcement. I've always been scathing about the campfire circle with its repetitious songs and rituals, but now I see it has a use. Immediately the old habits kick in and the wails of terror subside. Jonno pulls Leon into the group and the kids shuffle together to make a circle in the middle away from the worryingly wobbly walls. We all link arms while Ethan, in a soft tenor that holds the tune beautifully, begins the hunting song. He sings it not in the usual jaunty style, but slowly and mournfully and it makes perfect sense that way.

And so, as we ascend into the unknown in our flimsy bag that feels as if it is being swung by a careless shopper, the kids add their animals to the song and we leave the place where we were born, the place where some of us still have mothers and fathers, families and friends, singing: *Turkey, tiger, caterpillar, fish . . . We'll make a rhino, dodo, dinosaur dish . . .* It's a silly, babyish song but it calms each and every one of us. Including me.

M

There is a loud *craaaack* and once again long, jagged lines of dazzling light snake across the Orb from all directions, blind fingers searching for one another. Tomas's hair stands up on end and my carapace tingles. We watch the streaks of brilliance almost touch and then fall away. Tomas's hair collapses and my carapace stops tingling.

"I think the next one will do it," Parminter whispers to me.

Now, young watcher, I have not talked to you for a while, but as you may have noticed, there has been quite a lot happening and I confess that at times I have forgotten to explain things to you. But I have not forgotten the promise I made to you when we first met: that I will give these SilverSeeds all the help they need to escape that vile SilverShip. I intend to keep it. I take Parminter's little hand and I say, "Parminter, I am going to follow the SilverShip to the Outside."

Parminter smiles like she has expected this. "Of course you are. And I am coming with you," she says.

Tomas is watching us intently, trying to work out what we are saying. He forces out his hoarse croak: "Take me with you. Please."

Parminter looks at me doubtfully. "He'll be very heavy," she says. "Those cuffs weigh a ton."

Tomas stares at his wrists in disgust. "Please. I must help them. *Please.*"

"If we don't take him," I tell Parminter, "they'll come for him and put him in another Astro."

A strangled groan comes from deep inside Tomas.

Parminter gives in. "Okay. Fly-lift. Let's get ready."

A noise like the ripping of a thousand sheets zips overhead. A myriad questing fingers of blinding flashes of light spin out from their respective skylons. They split and multiply across the sky, traveling fast and heading toward one another like iron filings to a magnet. They meet, they merge, there is an earsplitting crackle and the Orb becomes a shimmering net of light, enclosing us below like bewildered fish in a pond. The air fizzes with charge and my carapace buzzes as though a thousand bees are trapped beneath it. Tomas's hair is waving like weeds beneath water—even his eyebrows are sticking out. And then, just as I feel that my wing cases are about to explode, the lights vanish and silence enfolds us. I look up and see a clear, shining, emptiness of blue—*blue, it really is blue*—with small dabs of white fluff floating in it. It is the Outside. And it is beautiful.

"Let's go," says Parminter.

With opposite wings from the ones we used for

Andronicus we form a platform for Tomas. He scrambles up and gingerly lies flat upon us, spreading his arms across our wing cases. Parminter takes my hand. "Ready?" she asks.

"Ready," I tell her, a little nervously.

Slowly we rise up, heading toward the brilliant, breathtaking blue of the unveiled sky. We fly up past Parminter's skylon, which stands quiet and watchful, and in a few wingbeats we are Outside. The air tastes so sweet and clean and I feel Tomas take a deep, shuddering breath. We head away from the skylon as fast as we can, afraid of what will happen when the Orb is reactivated. Slow and steady, we rise into the blue and I cannot believe how bright and clear the Outside is. I feel as though I have lived my life behind a dirty pane of glass.

"You see," Parminter shouts to me. "The sky *is* blue!"

"And the clouds are so white!" I say. But the thing that truly amazes me is the sun. It sits in the sky just above the line of hills in the far distance with a ribbon of pinkish cloud lying across its middle. Parminter has told me very firmly not to look the sun in the eye, but even if she had not I would never dare, for its brilliance is awe-inspiring.

Directed by Tomas, we are heading toward the Silver-Ship. It is much closer now, a giant sky-fish with little fat fins sailing serenely above the line of fluttering silver pennants that mark its path out of Hope.

"Hurry!" I hear Tomas's anxious croak close to my ear.

He is right; we must be quick. The SilverShip has just crossed the perimeter ditch and its shadow is now a dark fish swimming through the rolling green grass of the outside plain. It is moving fast toward us and we must hurry if we are to meet it. A loud *craaaack* behind us makes me jump and I glance back to see the first jagged fingers of light shoot out from the tops of all the skylons, which surround the city like the points of a crown.

"Maximillian!" Parminter yells, her voice sharp with panic.

I have lost the rhythm of our wingbeats, and Tomas has slipped over to Parminter's side. I quickly adjust myself, and Tomas moves to the middle once more. *Don't look back, Maximillian*, I think. *From now on, look only forward.*

We hear a long, snapping crackle as the Orb reforms behind us, and we fly as fast as we can toward the oncoming SilverShip. At first I think how beautiful it is but then, hanging beneath its belly like a piece of frass, I see a small, silvery capsule, from which comes the sound of young voices singing an eerily sad song—and I know there is no beauty here. Only terror.

The SilverShip is so close now that I can see the seams on the balloon and the numbers stenciled on different parts of it. I hear a whirring sound and beneath the ship's tail I see a propeller slowly turning, sending it forward with remarkable speed. The ship is heading across our path fast and we must take care to judge our landing well. If we miss we won't get a second chance. We'll never be able to catch it.

"We'll land on the capsule roof!" Parminter shouts. "Ready?"

"Ready!"

The capsule is attached to the ship by two thick struts. It has a flat top but this is not going to be easy, especially with Tomas weighing us down. We coast in, swooping beneath the silver belly and in complete harmony, Parminter and I glide onto the roof of the capsule, which sags alarmingly beneath us. I lose my footing and we all roll into a heap in the middle beside the struts. A terrible screaming starts up from under us.

"They put them in a bag," I say, disgusted. "A flimsy little *bag*."

"Vile," Parminter says. "Just vile."

The screaming has stopped and I can hear a murmuring of anxious voices beneath. Slowly and somewhat shakily we sit up, and I think how bizarre this is: two Roaches and a Vermin perched upon the top of a bag full of young ones that is hanging beneath the fat belly of a flying silver fish. I am musing upon the strangeness that I have discovered in this world—ever since, young watcher, I began to talk to you—when something sharp pokes me in a delicate place and I leap up with a yell, only to fall backward as the canvas wobbles alarmingly beneath me.

"Look," Parminter whispers, pointing to a sharp sliver of a blade sticking up through the roof.

I smile. I have seen that businesslike little blade somewhere before.

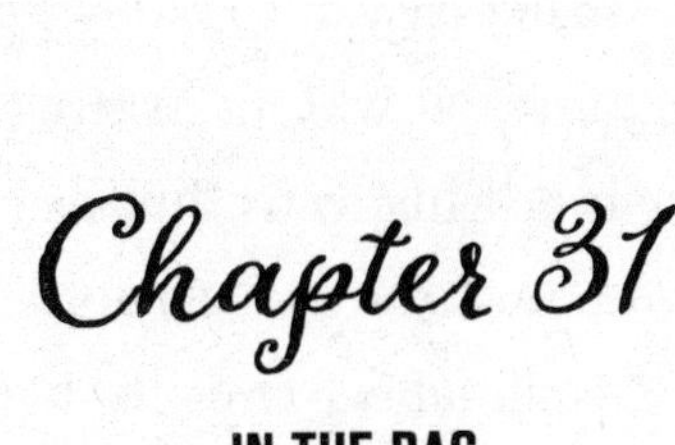

Chapter 31

IN THE BAG

K

I am sitting on Mattie's shoulders and I can just reach the roof. The tip of my blade hits the bump and I hear a strangled yelp. It is very familiar. But surely it cannot be who I think it is? "Maximillian?" I call out. "Is that you?"

And above us I hear a laugh and then the delighted voice of Maximillian. "It is I, Maximillian Fly. Your brother!"

Mattie's eyes are shining with hope. "Your brother? *Tomas?*" she whispers. "Tomas is here too?"

I have no idea what Maximillian means. How can Tomas be here? But then I hear a croak. "Kait? Mattie?" and I know it is indeed Tomas, his voice wrecked by the ReBreethe.

"Oh, Tomas," Mattie calls up. "I knew you'd come. I *knew* it." And then she looks back at me. "His voice. It was an Astro, wasn't it?"

"Yes," I say quietly, "it was an Astro."

Another voice is talking to us through the roof now, and I begin to wonder how many people are up there. This is another Roach, who I am sure I also recognize. "We're going to cut a hole in the roof," she says. "Keep out of the way, please." It is Parminter Wing, our old neighbor. I'm sure it is. This is so very peculiar that I wonder if maybe I am dreaming.

I slither down from Mattie's shoulders, lose my footing, and as I fall into the soft side of the cabin I know I'm not dreaming—there is a long, thin blade sawing a hole through the roof. "Are they going to set us free?" Jonno asks. It seems even Jonno has realized we are prisoners.

"Yes, they are," I tell him, smiling like I can't stop. A familiar head pokes down, antennae waving jauntily. "Maximillian!" I yell out. "Maximillian!"

Maximillian's round Roach face draws one or two cries of dismay—not everyone on board is comfortable with Roaches. But Maximillian does not notice. "Hello, my Kaitlin Drew," he says. "Hello, my little sister."

Whatever does he mean?

J

It is the Roach with the bent antenna. He is smiling. And so is Katie. And Nettie too. "Permission to come aboard, Captain?" Mr. Maximillian asks. This is what you say on ships.

Nettie and me stand up and I say, "Permission granted."

K

Maximillian drops down into the capsule, followed by Parminter Wing and then, amazingly, Tomas. The kids gasp—suddenly there are two Roaches and an Enforcer in this tiny space, so close they can reach out and touch them.

Tomas stares at me with the very same expression as he did through the glass. He looks awful—haggard, battered and bruised. I don't know what to do, what to say. But Tomas does. He hugs me tight, and his vile Astro cuffs stick into me. "I'm so sorry," he says.

"I'm sorry too," I tell him. And then I let him go to Mattie and she just holds his hands, staring at those terrible cuffs.

I introduce Maximillian and Parminter to the kids, but they hang back, wary of two Roaches at such close quarters. Maximillian, being so tall, is particularly overpowering in such a confined space. But to my surprise Jonno goes up to Maximillian and takes his hand. "You made my foot better," he says.

The ice is broken and in seconds the kids are bombarding Maximillian with questions and chatter. And as I listen, I find I cannot stop smiling because the Maximillian I see now, surrounded by admiring children hanging on his every word, is so wonderfully different from the Maximillian I last saw cowering in the darkness of his own home.

J

Nettie wants to see the Outside, so I ask Katie if she will cut a hole in the wall too, so we can look out. So she cuts a little triangle and I look out and I see two big white horses, just like in my picture book and there are people riding them very fast. I think they are chasing us. I stick my arm through the window and wave. Because one of them is my daddy.

K

"It's Daddy down there," Jonno says, as casually as if he is telling me that the grass is green.

I don't want to upset Jonno by telling him that his daddy is dead, so I look out of the window while I decide what to say. Below I see two horses with riders—a man and a woman—cantering along behind us. I have never seen the woman before, but . . . *no, it can't be*, I think. *But it is.*

"Dad!" I scream out through the flap. "Dad, Dad!" Suddenly Tomas is by my side looking out and he gives a loud whoop. "Look, Jonno," he says, "see the man on the horse? It's Dad!"

"I know," Jonno says. "I told you it was."

M

Kaitlin and Tomas are laughing like crazy people. And now Tomas is beside me, saying, "Maximillian, would you like to look Outside?"

The young ones also want to look. "Me too, me too!" they clamor.

"In a minute," Tomas tells them. "But first Maximillian." They don't argue with Tomas in his Enforcer's CarboNet and Astro cuffs. He really does look quite alarming.

I do as my brother asks. I crouch down to look out, and far below I see two most ugly creatures with four legs and two heads—one long, one round—apiece. I have no idea what they can possibly be. And then Tomas says the strangest thing. "Maximillian, it is our father."

Well. I am horrified. How could Tomas say that our father is one of those abominations? "He might be your father, but he is not mine, thank you very much. *My* papa does not have two heads and four legs," I say with some dignity.

Now Parminter is by my side, peering out. "Of course he doesn't have two heads and four legs, Maximillian. One of those heads and all four of those legs belong to a *horse*. Which your papa is riding."

Oh. I look again and I see that the abominable creature is indeed a man on a horse.

"Maximillian," Parminter says softly as I gaze down at the man below. "Your papa is *alive*. I wanted to tell you yesterday evening, but you didn't want to know. For the last few months he has been living with my grandma." Now Tomas and Kaitlin look as surprised as I do. "He escaped from the Night Roach Steeple," Parminter tells us. "He hypnotized the Night Roaches with his flute playing and climbed down the carvings on the Steeple. He turned up in the middle of the night at our farm begging for help. Ma took him straight out to Grandma's."

Suddenly Papa calls out, "Maximillian? Is that you?"

He knows me. Even from so far away, *he knows me*. And I call down, "Yes! Yes it is I! It is I, Maximillian Fly!"

K

We are going too fast. The wind is blowing harder now and the fishlike shadow of the SilverShip is racing over the ground. Dad and Parminter's grandma are chasing us, galloping along a dark green band that bisects the rolling plains below. But they are steadily falling behind, and already they seem so much smaller.

Tomas draws me away from the window. "Kait," he says in a low voice, "Max and Parminter can only fly two away from here. Just two. Because once they're on the ground they'll never be able to catch up with us again. How are we going to choose who they take?"

I shake my head. I don't know. I really don't. All I know is that the faster we are moving, the sooner we will reach the ocean. And then there will be no way anyone can help us.

J

Maximillian and me are watching Daddy. He has a bow and arrow and I think he is going to make a hole in the SilverShip balloon so that the air will come out and we will go down to the ground and be safe. Because we are not safe up here. I know that now.

Daddy shoots the arrow. It flies up high, chasing us fast, but it doesn't reach and it falls back down on the grass. Daddy shoots another arrow but it falls down even farther away than the last one. We are going too fast for arrows to catch us.

"You could do that with your dagger," I tell Maximillian. "It would be even better than an arrow because you could make a really big hole and lots of air would come whooshing out."

Maximillian smiles at me, and his bent antenna dances up and down. "So it would," he says.

M

Parminter and I are outside, balancing on top of wobbling canvas. Two thick wooden struts attach the bag of children to the ship and we each cling to one of them. In the distance I see a dark blue line on the horizon that sparkles. It is, Parminter tells me, the ocean—and every second it is getting closer.

I look up and see the fat silver belly of the ship. It is not far to fly, but we dare not let go of the struts because the air that whistles past would tear us away in an instant. Parminter tells me that this singing, moving air is called wind. I do not like it very much, I must confess.

Clinging to the struts, slipping and sliding, using our wings for lift, we progress upward at a snail's pace. As I climb, I cannot help but consider how only two days ago I was living my dull little life in the dull little world beneath the Orb. And now I find myself in the Outside, clinging beneath the fat belly of a flying silver fish, with the wind whistling in my ear tubes like a demon. And I would not change it for anything. I draw my dagger out from its holster beneath my wing. "Ready?" I call over to Parminter.

"Ready!" she shouts. She flips open Kaitlin's little knife and we plunge our blades into the tough skin of the SilverShip.

Nothing happens.

"There's another skin beneath!" Parminter yells. "This knife's too short. It won't reach!"

And so it is up to me. I push my dagger in deep and I feel the second skin shy away from its tip, unwilling to be caught. I think of my brothers and sister and all the little ones with fear in their eyes, I think of the wide ocean ahead that is waiting to swallow them up and I know I must do this. And so, clinging onto the strut with only my knees, keeping steady by beating my wings, with the power of all my three hands I push my dagger in deeper and deeper until at last I feel the second skin give way.

"Make a big cut so it doesn't seal up!" Parminter shouts.

With all my strength, I do just that. I saw into the stiff silver fabric, bringing my blade zigzagging down, widening the cut. My blade is sharp and I am pushing and twisting with all my strength and yet nothing is happening. Where is the gas? I begin to fear that maybe there is yet another skin to cut through.

And then I hear a ripping sound and suddenly there is gas—too much, too fast. A strange-smelling blast hits my chest and throws me back with such force that my dagger goes flying from my hands and I lose my grip on the strut. And then I am dropping backward through the air like a rock. I try to open my wings but the rush of the air prevents me. I try to right myself but without the use of my wings, I cannot. And so, limbs flailing, I hurtle toward the ground. I know what has happened, for Parminter explained it in our flying lessons. I am caught in a backstall. This is very bad. Indeed, it is fatal.

As I fall, I stare up into the ridiculous blue above me and suddenly I see Parminter, swooping down. A moment later she is gliding beneath me, tipping me over so that my wings flip out and I too am gliding, safe in the air once more. Immediately, I ascend, heading back to the ship, but it is far away now, the importunate wind sending it speeding through the sky. Parminter and I look at one another in despair. "Oh, Parminter," I whisper. "What have we done?"

We become aware of a thudding noise below and we look down to see a white horse galloping toward us. Upon it is my papa. "Wait!" he shouts. "Wait!" And so we glide down to the long grasses and we wait. The horse is an even stranger creature close up and I am not sure that I like it. It looks wild and angry and it blows noisily through its huge nostrils. But astride it is my papa. His unruly hair is dark and flecked with gray and he wears his bow slung across his shoulder along with a quiver of arrows. I take a deep breath and walk over to him. Papa smiles. "Maximillian," he says. "My boy."

And then he is off his horse and holding me tightly to him. And I lay my head upon his shoulder and we are utterly still. He is the man with the sad eyes and the books and the bear. He is my papa.

And I am his boy.

Chapter 32

NETTIE

K,

I saw Maximillian fall. If Parminter hadn't caught him he would have been killed. I can see them now, dark against a sea of green with two white horses beside them. I cannot even begin to think how much I wish I were there too.

I know this is goodbye. Tomas has told Mattie and me what will happen to us—it doesn't surprise me—but we have not told the others. We've cut more windows and the Bears and Wolves are taking turns to look out. I listen to their excited chatter and all the while I watch two people whom I love and will never see again grow ever smaller.

Tomas comes over to me. He is holding his Zip, his combi-tool, with the blade flipped up. "I am going to finish what Maximillian started," he says.

Mattie is there beside him. "Tomas, you can't," she says. "Not with those awful cuffs on."

"Tomas can't, but *we* can," I tell her. "We have no cuffs." And I hold my hand out to Tomas for Zip.

M

Parminter and I are flying low and fast. I watch our shadows racing over the waving grasses in wonder; beneath the Orb the only time we see our shadows is by lantern light.

We reach the top of a range of low hills and hover, pausing to allow Papa and Parminter's grandmama to catch up with us. We are looking down onto a wide valley with a glimmering ribbon of river winding through it, and far away, flying down the middle of the valley is the SilverShip. It is heading toward a brilliantly bright expanse of deep, dark blue that sparkles in the sunlight and spreads across the horizon for as far as we can see. That, Parminter and I both know, is the ocean—so beautiful and yet so deadly. Above it is the sky, a paler, hazy blue, but where they meet is hard to tell. It is the strangest thing I have ever seen.

Below us two white horses crest the hilltop. We drop down to join them and together we watch the SilverShip flying relentlessly toward its destination. Papa is upset. "Ever since I heard that your sister and brother were on this abomination, I've been waiting to shoot it down," he says. "But I messed up. Again."

I understand, because I often feel like this too.

"No one has messed up," Parminter tells him. "Look!"

We all look at the SilverShip and I think there is something different about it. It is a little less fat maybe. And, yes, it is moving strangely too—meandering just like the river below it, as though it cannot make up its mind which way to go. A feeling of hope steals over me. "It's losing air!" I say.

"But not fast enough, Max," Papa says. "It will be over the ocean before it touches down. All that will happen is that it will fall into the ocean sooner."

This is a terrible thought. "No, that will *not* happen," I tell him. "Parminter and I will catch it." I grab her hand and we do a double takeoff from the top of the hill, our breath swept away in the rush of air as together we soar upward; then we break our grasp and glide down the hillside and into the valley.

And you, my young watcher, are with us. Let us fly together down this impossibly green valley with a silver strip of river snaking through it. Let us swoop over this abandoned settlement where rotting boats litter the riverbank like carcasses of long-dead fish, and let us chase that indecisive giant silver fish in the sky—which I do believe is *wobbling*—before it reaches the deep, dark ocean. And then, please, let us catch it. Because now I truly believe we can.

K

It is wild up here. The wind funnels through the gap between the belly of the ship and the swaying top of the cabin. The struts are so fat and slippery that there is no way Mattie or I can climb them—but that doesn't matter, because when we look up we see a jagged hole in the fabric and feel the rush of gas coming from it. The whole underside of the ship looks soft like melting jelly. *Maximillian and Parminter have done it.*

Two large white birds with big yellow feet and crazy orange beaks glide past, free as . . . well, free as birds, while I cling to the strut taking in deep breaths of air; it is like breathing in sparkles. I watch the long, thin strip of yellow sand ahead and the white foam of the waves breaking upon it, drawing ever closer and think how strange and yet how beautiful it is, and how much I would love to be down there, barefoot with the grit of the sand beneath my toes and the softness of the water running over my feet. I want to be part of this world for as long as I possibly can. I want to be . . . *alive.*

I am so immersed in my thoughts that, when a faint and tinny voice calls my name and I wheel around to see Maximillian and Parminter clambering up beside me, I very nearly fall off in shock.

"We'll take two off now," Maximillian is saying. "And then we'll come back. And we will keep coming back until—" He is cut off by a sudden shout.

It is Tomas, his head poking out of the capsule. "Hey, you, Vermin!" Tomas yells. "Wait right there!" And he ducks back down.

J

Tomas is horrible. He has taken Nettie. "Give her back! *Give her back!*" I shout at him but he won't and they are lifting him up through the hole in the roof and Nettie has gone and no one will let me go after her. "Nettie!" I yell. "*Netteeeeee!*"

M

Tomas hands me a round squashy thing like a limbless bear. "Jonno's new attachment object. Poor kid's not had much luck with those recently," he says with a rueful smile. Puzzled, I take this attachment object. "Fishing net," Tomas explains. "A big one. Strong too. Chuck it over the propeller. I reckon it might stop us if we're lucky."

This is a very good idea indeed. "Thank you, Vermin," I say.

"Vermin yourself," Tomas says and he gives me a thumbs-up. And then he suddenly disappears with a yelp and I hear him say, "Hey, Jonno, cut it out will you?"

I open out the net and see it is indeed big and very light too; but it is a dangerous thing to fly with because it could easily entangle us. Holding it at arm's length, Parminter and I hover beneath the flabby underbelly of the ship as it moves forward above us. We watch the huge, powerful propeller slowly turning, dark in the shadows beneath the tail, the tips glinting as they catch the sunlight and I fear that it will, as Parminter would say, eat the net for breakfast. But we must try. We wait until the ship has passed over us and then, like hunters creeping up behind their prey, we fly fast toward the huge blades. And then we throw.

The net lands upon one of the blades and I am so sure it will be thrown off that I drop down, hoping to catch it for another try. But there is no need. It snags on the second blade, then the third, and in a moment the propeller is winding the net around the long shaft that disappears into the flabby silver skin of the ship. The blades slow until they are hardly moving, and then from deep inside the ship comes a long, low grinding noise and the propeller stops. There is silence. The SilverShip slows to a wafting drift above the long strip of yellow sand that meets the pale green water of the ocean.

Parminter and I stare at each other in amazement. "We did it!" she squeals with excitement. "We did it!"

I see Tomas pop up again like a rabbit from a burrow, waving his arms in triumph despite his Astro cuffs. "Great throw, Vermin!" he calls out, laughing.

"Great *idea*, Vermin!" I shout back. And I am laughing too.

K

The SilverShip is sinking gracefully, crumpling like an old paper bag. I cut a big hole in the side of the capsule so that we can easily crawl out onto Maximillian and Parminter as they hover beside us. We decide they will take the youngest ones first and work upward in age, which means that Tomas will be the last one left on board. I say that I should stay behind until last and that Tomas and Mattie should go down together—I can tell that Mattie would like that too—but Tomas insists. "Oldest last, Kait. That's only fair."

J

Me and Leon are flying. I am on Maximillian, the big Roach with the bent antenna, and Leon is on the smaller Roach, who is quite bossy. We land on the beach and I see Daddy galloping toward us through the sand dunes on a big white horse. It feels like a dream but it is real.

M

Parminter and I set the final pair, Mattie and Kaitlin, safe upon the sand, but as we rise up to get Tomas, a sudden gust of wind whistles through the gap in the dunes. It picks up the SilverShip and sends it skittering out across the waves, flip-flopping from side to side like an old paper bag.

"No!" Mattie yells out. "No, no! Tomas, Tomas!" She runs into the water with my sister chasing after her, catching her and holding her tight, stopping Mattie from throwing herself into the ocean to swim after Tomas.

"We will bring him back to you," I tell Mattie. "I promise."

Together, Parminter and I fly low over the water, the taste of salt in our mouths, the smell of the ocean in our nostrils, flying as fast as we possibly can. But all I can think of is what will happen when the SilverShip hits the water and how Tomas, with his great iron Astro cuffs, will be dropping down through the cold, dark depths of the ocean like a rock.

Chapter 33

SAND, SUN AND STARS

K

We watched Maximillian and Parminter chase the Silver-Ship until they were no more than little black dots against the blue. Maximillian said by the time they caught it, it was just a skin of fabric floating on the surface. Our capsule had already sunk. Tomas had managed to grab the edge of a tail fin, which was still inflated, but his Astro cuffs were pulling him down.

But they got him and they brought him back, and that is all that matters.

And now I am on the beach—how strange it is to be able to say that. I am looking out to sea, watching the waves, which really are like the ones they showed us at Countdown, and what Dad calls the "swell of the sea," which makes it rise and fall, up and down, like a monster breathing. I cannot quite get past the impossibility of so much water. It tastes of salt too, which is a big surprise. The beach is bigger now than when we arrived because the sea is retreating, but Dad says it will slowly come back again. The sand is soft and damp, and if I stand very still, my feet sink into its coolness and water oozes up between my toes. It feels just as wonderful as I thought it would.

The big orange ball of the sun is dropping down toward the line where the dark blue of the water meets the pale blue of the sky and the colors are so bright they make me dizzy. In the distance I can see the glint of a silver skin lying flat upon the ocean, and the sight of it makes me shudder. Beside me stand Tomas, dripping with water, and Mattie, quietly watching too. Suddenly, we see a distant flash of silver as the tail upends and the SilverShip is gone forever.

I promise myself that there will never be another. Ever. I will make sure of that.

I leave Tomas and Mattie to watch the sunset and head off toward the smell of cooking. Right now I want to be with everyone, safe by the fire, away from the great emptiness of the ocean. I crest the dunes and head down toward the dark shapes of ruined stone cottages beside the broad, shallow river where Dad and Parminter's grandma have set up our camp. As I reach the flat expanse of grass that leads to the group of people clustered around the fire in the twilight, I see a small figure break away and come running toward me, yelling, "Katie! Katie!"

It's Jonno and he sounds happy. Not whiny, not cross, not scared. Just happy.

J

"I caught three fish for supper," I tell Katie. "And us Bears are sleeping by the river. Just like we planned. Come and see!" I pull her along, trying to make her go faster. I am so happy.

But then I remember Nettie.

K

"*Kaay*-teee . . . ," Jonno says. "I asked Tomas to give Nettie back, but he won't. And he won't say why. It's not *fair.*"

It seems like Tomas has ducked that one, but I guess he's allowed. "Nettie had an important job to do, Jonno," I say. "Nettie saved our lives."

Jonno's eyes are wide. "Did she?"

"She did. And she's been very brave. But . . . well, I'm sorry, she had to go away and she won't be coming back."

Jonno's eyes fill with tears. He's been through a lot for a little boy of only six, I think. I scoop him up and carry him, and he snuggles his head into my shoulder. And as we walk toward the flickering firelight and the smell of cooking becomes ever more delicious, he says sleepily, "I told you I would catch fish for supper and we would make camp by a river, didn't I?"

"You did," I agree.

"I know you didn't believe me, but I knew we would. I just *knew* it—here." And he thumps his little balled-up fist over his heart.

Maybe, I think, *there is more to Jonno than I realize.*

M

Night has fallen and we are sitting around a fire beside the river. Entranced, we watch flames untrapped by glass leaping up into the darkness and I am amazed at the heat they give out. I find it strange to be outside after dark with no fear of Night Roaches and nothing but the vastness of the sky above. Every time I look up at the blackness I feel as though I am going to fall into a deep pit. It is most peculiar, but Parminter says I will get used to it.

In the background I hear the rhythmic rasp of a saw. Papa has found some rusty old tools in a ruined boat builder's shed. He took off Parminter's cuff first, and now he is cutting through Tomas's Astro cuffs. It is a good sound.

Parminter's grandmama—who brought cooking pots, blankets and potatoes on her horse—has made a fish stew and we dip spoons into the big pot and share it. I have never been so close to so many young Wingless ones before, and I confess I find it quite tiring. They are noisy, full of energy and say such very silly things. However, they are also charming in their squishy way and it is delightful how sweetly they sing. They have just embarked upon what Jonno tells me is the "Good-night Song." It is quiet and slow and Papa plays the tune with them on his flute. I listen to it with a strange new feeling: happiness and sadness both together. It is a not unpleasant sensation. By the end of the song some of the littlest ones, including Jonno, are already asleep. "Let them sleep by the fire, poor little mites. I'll sit with them," Parminter's grandmama says. She covers them gently with blankets and when she is finished she comes over to me and says, "Maximillian, dear. Why don't you take Parmie to see the moon over the ocean?"

And so I do. I walk through the dunes with Parminter toward the *swish-ish* sound of the waves upon the beach. At the top of the dunes we stop. I gasp—there is another sun rising over the low hills in the east. I know it must be the moon, but it is so bright and big and round just like the sun that I can hardly believe this is the dull glimmer we used to call the moon. The ocean is huge beneath it, dark and deep with a hundred thousand little moons dancing upon the wavelets. Parminter's small hand has crept into mine. "The stars," she whispers. "Look at the stars."

And away from the brightness of the moon, at last I see them: a dusting of silver as though someone has thrown a handful of glittering white sherbet across the sky. There are so many I can hardly believe it. But I find that I do. I do believe in stars.

We sit on the soft dry sand at the foot of the dunes gazing up at the indigo darkness sprinkled with silver dust. I think of how we belong to the stars and the sky and the Earth turning beneath us, and I am dizzy with happiness.

"How small we are," Parminter whispers. "Like grains of sand."

"Two grains of sand," I say. "Together."

Chapter 34

TEAPOT

M

Ah, my young watcher, here you are! I have not seen you since two evenings ago at our camp, but now I find you waiting for us in Parminter's house. You understand me too well—you knew I would come back with Parminter to find her mama. It is good to see you, but please excuse me a moment while I help Papa, Tomas and Kaitlin to immobilize the vile Cassius Crane. Yes, we found Cassius sitting here, gloating amid the destruction with poor Andronicus tied up in the corner. But now it is Cassius who wears Andronicus's bonds. And he is gloating no longer.

So, let me tell you what has happened since you disappeared. We spent another day at the camp to get our strength back and we left first thing this morning.

Mattie stayed behind with Parminter's grandmama to help out. Papa, Tomas and Kaitlin rode the horses back to their field beside Parminter's grandmama's cottage on the far side of the hills and then we all walked along the sunken lane and through the secret tunnel to Parminter's skylon hut.

Andronicus had found his way out of the hut all the way back to Parminter's house, but unfortunately he had also found Cassius Crane roosting in the kitchen. Cassius took Andronicus prisoner and it has not been a good experience for my poor friend. He has been a little flustered since our arrival and it is only now that Cassius is lying upon the floor, wound around with rope so that he resembles a giant and very angry caterpillar, that Andronicus notices Tomas. "Oh my," he says to me, "you have brought the Vermin."

"He is a good Vermin," I tell my dear friend. "A very good one indeed."

Tomas laughs and puts his arm around me. "This is a pretty good Vermin too," he says.

Andronicus looks stunned.

"Cassius, however," I say, "has turned out to be a particularly nasty kind of Vermin."

Cassius attempts a hiss, but he cannot draw a deep enough breath.

"He has indeed," Andronicus agrees. "We must consider what to do with him."

"I am already considering," Parminter says angrily as she strides over to Cassius and glares down at him. "Where is my mother?" she demands. "What have you done with her?"

"I *forget*," he says with a smirk. "As will everyone else."

We all know only too well what he means. Parminter turns away from the vile Cassius and I see tears springing into her eyes. "Parminter," I say. "Even if your mama is in Oblivion, it is has only been for three days."

"Only!" says Parminter.

"She will be all right," I tell Parminter. "We will find her, I promise."

Cassius chuckles. "Good luck with that," he says. "You'll need it."

Unfortunately Cassius is right. Oblivion is a prison maze that occupies at least five subterranean floors of the Bartizan. It is guarded and locked. Even if, somehow, we managed to get in unnoticed, we would need a whole ton of luck to find Parminter's mama. A prisoner is put into a cell at random, no records are kept of where they are and the key is, literally, thrown away. I feel Parminter looking at me in despair and I cannot face her. I fix my eyes upon the little eagle teapot that sits untouched upon the table. I stare at it, thinking how unfair it is that such a delicate, nasty thing manages to survive and Parminter's mama will not.

Papa follows my gaze. He picks up the teapot and holds it at arm's length, as though he is expecting its sharp little beak to bite him. "How did this thing get here?" he asks.

I am embarrassed to say. "I brought it with me," I tell him. "I . . . I thought that if I found Mama and gave it to her she would forgive me."

"For what, Maximillian?" Papa asks. "For being her son?"

"Perhaps," I admit. "But at the time I wanted her to forgive me for allowing her precious porcelain collection to be smashed to smithereens."

Papa's eyes fill with glee. "Really? The whole lot in pieces? She won't have liked that."

"She didn't," I agree. How strange it is, I think, to be talking like this about Mama. And how liberating too. "The teapot was a foolish idea," I say. "Even if I knew where to find her I do not think she would ever forgive me."

It is now I see my sister, Kaitlin, looking at me in a peculiar manner. "But, Maximillian, of course you know where to find your mother—I mean, your mama."

I shrug. "Why would I? She never told me. She does

not want me to find her."

My Kaitlin looks shocked. "But when she came with me to your house, *surely* you knew then?"

"Knew what?" I say. I see that my papa is looking at me with the same expression as Kaitlin. Also Tomas and Parminter. Oh dear. I think I have been foolish again. I sigh. Why is it that I am always a fool when it is anything to do with Mama?

Papa is slowly pacing the room, stepping over the mess on the floor like a heron searching for fish. No one is saying anything, but at last, Tomas breaks the silence. "No more secrets, Dad," he says sharply, and Papa looks stricken. He comes to me and takes two of my hands in his. "Maximillian," he says. "When your mama left you it was not because of anything you did or said. It was because she had become . . ." He stops and takes a deep breath. "Guardian. *The* Guardian. Up in the Bartizan."

I gasp. Behind me I hear Andronicus gasp too and I feel a little happier. At least my friend did not know either. So we are both fools together.

"That is the reason why your brother and sister were conscripted as SilverSeeds," Papa is saying. "It is why your lovely stepmother, my dearest Joanna, who loved you and looked after you when you were a baby, was put in a barbarous Astro. And it is why I was put in the

Night Roach Steeple. Because when your mama became Guardian she at last had the power to finish what she started all those years ago when she took you away from us. She had the power to destroy us."

My legs feel wobbly and I sit down upon a nearby stool. There is something I understand now. "It was *your* flute I heard in the Night Roach Steeple. I flew there every evening to listen. I thought I went because the music was so beautiful. But I see now that it was because it was . . . it was *you*. My papa."

Papa smiles at me. "Oh, Max, I wish I had known you were listening. I would have played your favorite song."

I do not know what my favorite song is, so I say nothing. Or maybe I say nothing because it is too hard to speak. I am not sure. I wonder how Mama could have done such an evil thing. Evil. This is a new word for me to think about. But it is true. Mama is evil.

Papa is pacing like a heron again. "Max, I believe you are right," he says. "You must give your mama her teapot back."

"I am sorry, Papa," I say politely, "but I do not wish to give it to her anymore. I no longer care what she thinks of me. All I wish for is to find Parminter's mama and go back to the beach and live beneath the stars."

But Papa will not take no for an answer. "Maximillian," he says a little sternly. "We must not think only of ourselves. We have a duty to set *everyone* in this city free so that they too may live beneath the stars."

I am thinking that I do not understand what Mama's teapot has to do with this when we hear the distant rumble of an explosion.

A harsh laugh comes from Cassius. "No one in this city is going to be living beneath any so-called stars. While you were away we searched your cozy little hut of conspiracy and found a most interesting tunnel. Which has been blown up. Your little moment of triumph will not last long, I can tell you. I am looking forward to a very interesting spectacle—a mass Astro launch, testing the first Roach Astros. They're all ready to go. Orange bags, in case you wondered. Nice and simple. Just like your nasty little baby cocoons." I wonder if Cassius has gone crazy, for he seems to forget that he is Roach.

"Parminter, is there anywhere we can put this unpleasantness?" Papa asks angrily, pointing to Cassius.

"We have a dung pit," Parminter says with a smile. Tomas and Papa pick Cassius up like a sack and Parminter leads the way out.

Kaitlin stays behind. She kneels down in front of me and takes my hands, just as Papa did. I think this must be a family thing. It is a little uncomfortable, for

I am not used to prolonged touch from a soft-skinned human. It feels too damp and sticky for comfort. But I do not show my unease, for my Kaitlin Drew is my dear sister now.

"Maximillian," my sister says, "everyone has the right to see the stars, don't you agree?"

How can I disagree? "Yes," I say. "Of course they do."

"So," Kaitlin says, "you must take the teapot to your mama."

Why? I wonder. *What has this nasty teapot to do with the stars?* I am beginning to wish I had never found Mama's teapot.

K

I've guessed what Dad wants to do and I think it is our only hope. I feel Maximillian trying to pull his hands away from mine, but I'm not letting him go. This is too important.

"Why?" he asks curtly.

"Because if you have the teapot she will agree to see you."

"But I do not wish to see *her*," Maximillian says stiffly.

I ignore this. "And while you are distracting her by giving her the teapot, we will take the DisK back."

"That is just crazy," he says.

"Maybe it is, but it is our only chance to open the Orb—forever. And set *everyone* free. Please. You have to do this."

"No," he says. "I cannot." And suddenly Maximillian looks just as he did when I saw him cowering in the shadows of his own home. So frightened. So *alone*.

"Maximillian, you are not alone anymore," I tell him. "You have us now, your own family who love you, and you have no need to be afraid of your mama. In fact, she is the one who will be afraid of you."

He laughs. "I don't think so."

"Oh, she will be," I tell him. "She will be afraid of us *all*." I let go of his hands and a look of relief crosses his face. I think I have imposed upon him too much, too soon. But there is so little time left; any minute now they will find us and then that will be it. Over. Finished. But Maximillian doesn't seem to understand that. So I stand up and say, "Maximillian, it is time for you to confront your mother. You know it is."

He looks at me with his big gray eyes that sparkle just like Dad's and I see that I've almost convinced him. But just as I think he is going to agree, Parminter races into the kitchen, her wings clattering in alarm. "Enforcers!" she says. "Coming up the Long Field track! We must get out of here, fast. But where can we go?"

And then Maximillian says a wonderful thing: "We will go to the Bartizan. With the teapot. To see Mama."

I want to hug him, but I let him be. He has had enough of me for now. And besides, as Parminter says, we must get out of here. Fast.

We have a teapot to deliver.

Chapter 35

FAMILY REUNION

T

We are wading through the gloom of the city, breathing its thick, muggy air with the whiteness of the Orb pressing down upon us. After only two days beneath the big blue—as Jonno calls the sky Outside—it feels unbearable to be trapped in this muggy bubble once again. I look back at my new Roach brother, who is following at a discreet distance because it is illegal to walk in a mixed group. I have never minded this before, but now, seeing Maximillian alone and trailing behind us, I mind a lot.

It is not pleasant walking through the streets. People are edgy—the SilverShip has not returned and no one knows why. They glance anxiously up at the Orb and jump at every noise, expecting the sirens to start up at any moment so that they will have to run for cover.

At last, at the end of grubby alley known as Sneak

Snoop, we arrive at a pair of battered doors, which look like the entrance to a seedy nightclub. Above them is a sign saying: *Dancing until 2 a.m. No Roaches.* But this is no club—this is the hidden way into the lower levels of the Bartizan for Sneaks and us Enforcers. "This is it," I tell Dad.

He looks surprised. "Oh! Right. We'll wait around the corner." He gives a brief, tight smile and Kaitlin and I watch him walk away. We wait while Maximillian goes by, cradling the teapot wrapped in a soft cloth like a baby, following Dad into the shadows. I glance up at the dullness of the Orb and see Parminter and Andronicus flying above, shadowing them. Everything is in place. Kaitlin and I exchange nervous glances. It all depends on us now.

We push open the doors and set off briskly down the dingy corridor. We are heading for the Enforcers' uniform store, the pass to which is still embedded in my tattered CarboNet. Every step we take brings us farther into danger and right now I can't imagine why we ever thought this was a good idea. But there is no going back. We have to do this.

K

We did it!

Tomas took two sets of CarboNets out of the automated uniform store with no trouble at all and we are now two Enforcers, marching in step. This CarboNet feels great. It's so easy to move in, and it gives you so much confidence. I could get into this. I pull down my visor and stride along the corridor, taking care to keep in step with Tomas. Suddenly we hear a shout.

"Hey, you! Marne!"

My heart does a flip of fear and I see Tomas go pale. He wheels around, salutes and stands to attention, his right fist balled over his heart. I do the same, taking care to cover up the identical *T.M.* embroidered on my left pocket. "Ma'am!" he says.

The woman's badge declares her to be a commander. She eyeballs Tomas suspiciously. "Marne. It *is* you. But you're Astroed."

My CarboNet confidence has evaporated. I want to run away screaming. Or take a chance and thump her. Or both. Anything to get out of this.

But Tomas is so calm. "A cover story, ma'am," he says smoothly. "Apologies. Can't reveal anything right now. Excuse me, ma'am. I'm expected on Top Tier."

She tries not to look impressed, but she is. "Very well, Marne. Carry on," she says. And then she is gone, her metal-tipped heels clacking away up the corridor.

We march away fast and are soon out through the doors, falling into Sneak Snoop with relief. "Tomas, you are so cool," I tell him. "She believed you!"

He looks shaken. "For now," he says. "But I know my comm. Soon enough she'll complain to someone that she wasn't told about me. And then they'll be after us."

"No time to lose, then," I say. And I stride off down the alley in search of Dad and Maximillian, my CarboNet confidence returned.

M

We are walking into the lion's den.

No matter that we have a detailed plan, that we all know what we must do, and even have a code word—"evil"—for when we must do it. No matter that I am surrounded by my family, whom I trust with my life, as I walk between soaring pillars of ebony and progress up the white marble steps into the main entrance of the Bartizan I feel as frightened as if I really am the first Roach to be Astroed.

Papa leads the way and, flanked by Tomas and Kaitlin as my guards in their smooth Enforcer carapaces, I follow him. Every step I take I fear will be my last, for this entrance is forbidden to all who are Roach. Papa says that if we walk in with enough confidence no one will challenge us, but as we reach the top of the steps, a guard in Bartizan uniform bars our way. "No Roach filth here," she barks.

"Quite right too," Papa says. "But this, here"—and he

points to me like I am a *thing*—"is our very first Roach Astro." Papa is smiling proudly. He leans forward to the guard and lowers his voice confidentially. "We're testing the bags. You can see it in about half an hour. Be worth a watch." He laughs. "Think of a giant orange sausage. Ha-ha!"

I do not know how Papa can laugh at this awful thought, but he does it so well that the guard laughs with him. "We heard Roach Astros were being planned," the guard says. "Get rid of the lot of them, I say."

"All the more money for me, ha-ha," Papa says. "Roach Astro bags are my own invention and I'm very pleased with them, even if I do say so myself." He makes a play of fumbling through his pockets. "Now, let's see, I can show you the design. It's very interesting how we . . ."

And now I see how clever Papa is. Because the last thing the guard wants to do is to listen to the mad inventor of Roach Astro bags. "Yeah, yeah. I'm sure it is," she says impatiently. "The lift is over there. Don't be late; they won't like it. You might find yourself heading out in your own little orange suit. Ha-ha."

Papa does a very good job of looking terrified. He hurries us past the guard and our "Enforcers" escort us across the lobby to two black marble pillars with a dark wooden door set between them. Tomas pulls it open and then slides a noisy concertina cage-like door across as confidently as if he has done this all his life. And now we are squashed into this strange box contraption, lurching upward, every inch taking us closer to Mama. I feel quite ill.

At last three little letters: *T-O-P* light up and the contraption stops. Tomas and Kaitlin pull back the gate, shove open the door, and we pile out into a surprisingly bright and colorful atrium. And standing there, as if she has been waiting for us, is *Mama*.

I cannot believe it. I feel dizzy at the sight of her. But there she is, wearing a black jacket with the three gold bands of the Guardian. So it is true. Mama really is the Guardian.

Mama's hands fly to her mouth and she smothers a sharp little scream. "Matt!" she squeaks.

"Marianne," Papa replies.

I wonder who Marianne is—and then I realize it is Mama. It is very unsettling to hear she has a name. And it seems that Mama finds her name unsettling too. She looks gray with shock. "But *how*?" she whispers.

Papa laughs. "Who knew Night Roaches would fall asleep to the sound of a flute? Such delightfully musical creatures . . ."

Mama gathers herself together. "Well, Matthew, you may have escaped from the idiot Roaches but you've not escaped from *me*." She clicks her fingers at the two bodyguards standing with folded arms outside a pair of double doors opposite us. They jump to attention. "Fetch the Astro Techs. Go!" she barks. The bodyguards hurl themselves into the elevator, slam the doors, and we hear them clanking downward. Mama glares at Tomas and Kaitlin. "Enforcers. Why was I not informed of this?"

Tomas's voice screen gives me a shock. "Madam Guardian, I apologize," he says smoothly. "We understood that you *were* informed."

"Well, I wasn't," she snaps. "Shame. I would have liked a few hours to look forward to this . . . event." I see a thin smile move across Mama's lips and her eyes flick across to me, like a snake. "Well, well. Matthew and Maximillian," she says. "Together again. How sweet. Just like old times, the three *M*s—remember? Quite the family reunion."

And then it hits me. This is indeed a family reunion. For the very first time in my memory, I am with both my parents. And Mama wants to kill me, just like the last time we were all together.

K

This is the moment that Maximillian is meant to tell Madam Guardian about the teapot. But he doesn't. I am holding his arm and I feel it trembling beneath my glove.

I glance at him and I see him paralyzed with fear, just as he was on the landing in the darkness of his house. This is bad. The silence lengthens and at last Dad comes to the rescue. "Marianne," he says, "Maximillian has something he would very much like to give you."

It is so weird to hear him call Madam Guardian by a normal name. And it is even weirder to think that once Dad was married to her, and that she and Max were his family. And that Tomas, Jonno and I didn't exist.

Madam Guardian laughs her brittle silvery tinkle. "I want nothing from Maximillian, thank you very much. All he has ever given me is trouble, and I have had quite enough of that." She looks at Tomas and me, "Enforcers, take them to the Astro Room," she snaps, and then she wheels around and walks toward the double doors.

We all look at Maximillian in dismay.

Now, Maximillian, Dad mouths. *Say it now!*

M

I must do it. I must speak. "Mama!" I call out as if in distress. "Oh, Mama, please wait!" Mama stops dead, like someone has pulled her on a leash. "Mama," I say quickly, "I have your teapot. Your little golden eagle. Your precious darling bird." Slowly Mama turns around. I unwrap the teapot from its cloth cocoon and see Mama's eyes widen. "Oh . . . ," she breathes.

I hold the teapot out to her as an offering. "I saved it, Mama. Just for you."

Mama reaches out for the teapot and Papa steps in front of her. "Marianne," he says. "First, a word please. In private."

Mama cannot take her eyes off the beady-eyed teapot. "Matthew. Just tell me why I would ever want to talk to you again?" she asks.

"Because I do not think that Maximillian is ready to give you the teapot until you do," Papa says very calmly.

Mama laughs. "I could have my Enforcers take it from him like *that*," she says, snapping her thin, hard fingers in Papa's face.

"You could indeed," Papa says smoothly. "But your teapot is such a delicate thing, Marianne. So very . . . *vulnerable*."

I see Mama balancing up the odds. To our great relief she says, "Very well. But make it quick. We will go into my office. And don't trip, Maximillian. You know how clumsy you are." She presses the palm pad, the double doors open and we follow her into the Guardian's chamber like the bad smell Mama thinks we are.

T

I am in Madam Guardian's office, as Enforcer with my prisoner, *who is my dad*. How did this happen? Three days ago I was on the other side of that one-way glass with all those grapes and cherubs prancing around it, being shoved into an Astro.

I glance over to Kaitlin, who stands alert and ready, grasping Maximillian's left upper limb in the approved two-handed Roach grip. He is at least a foot taller than her but my sister is totally in charge. She's a natural at this. If she were a real Enforcer she'd be a comm in a few months, no doubt about it.

The Astro Room one-way glass is giving me the creeps. I steal a glance at it and I can't see any sign of activity. Yet. I keep thinking of the Astro Techs that Madam Guardian sent for. Are they on their way up? Or maybe they are already there in the Astro Room, setting up for Dad and Maximillian. And, if this all goes wrong, for Kaitlin and me too.

This feels seriously dangerous.

I will not look at the glass again. I. Will. Not. Panic.

K

Madam Guardian is ensconced behind her giant desk, watching us as a spider would a group of foolish flies that has just fluttered into its web. "Put the teapot on the desk, Maximillian," she says.

Now is Max's big moment, but to our surprise, Dad stops him. "Not yet, Max," he says. "I have something to say first." He steps forward to the desk but Tomas, in role, pulls him sharply back.

"Enforcer. Allow the prisoner to approach," Madam Guardian says coolly.

Dad walks the few steps to the desk while Madam Guardian watches him with her heavy-lidded eyes half-closed. Nonchalantly, Dad rests his hands on the edge of the desk and leans over to her. To my surprise, she does not react. She looks at him steadily and for a fleeting second I catch a glimpse of something that was once between them; it is possible to imagine her and Dad as a happy young husband and wife with a little baby called Maximillian. And then the moment is gone and Dad is saying, with barely controlled anger, "Marianne. I would like to know how, in all conscience, you sleep at night."

"*What?*" She looks shocked, but she can't feel half as shocked as we do. This was not in our plan.

But Dad is not stopping now. "You keep a whole city imprisoned in abject terror. You murder innocent people and send children to their deaths and it really doesn't keep you awake? *Ever?*"

Madam Guardian sits back and looks at Dad with something like amusement. "What rubbish, Matthew. We are not imprisoning people; we are protecting them from the deadly Contagion. And we murder no one. We have a very fair judicial system that will, quite reasonably, not tolerate traitors to our city. And as for sending children to their deaths, what utter rubbish. The SilverSeeds are extremely privileged young people, and we go to a lot of trouble to send them off to a better life."

"Lies, lies, lies, Marianne," Dad is saying.

Stop bickering with your ex, Dad, I think. It's weird. I've never seen him like this before. He's like a dog with a bone and he won't let go.

But Madam Guardian seems to be relishing the argument as much as Dad. *Did they always fight like this?* I wonder. She folds her arms and I do believe she smirks. "Prove it," she tells him.

I am so scared. Any minute now the Astro Techs will march in and that will be the end of it for us all, but Dad just won't stop. "Very well," he says. "For the last few months I have been living Outside. And do you know who I saw walking on the hills early one morning?" Madam Guardian does not get a chance to answer, because Dad does it for her. "You, Marianne. *You.*"

At last, Madam Guardian has had enough. "Enforcers!" she shouts. "Take him."

Tomas and I are at Dad's side in an instant. We pull him back from the desk and bring his arms up sharply behind his back. Dad gasps. I feel awful doing this, but Dad told us to be realistic.

You would think that would be an end of it, but Madam Guardian, it seems, does not like to lose an argument any more than Dad does. She gets up, walks to our side of the desk and plants herself in front of Dad. She laughs in his face. "You don't fool me, Matthew. I know you're upset because two of your brats were on the last Silver-Ship Exit. Let me see, that's all of them gone now, isn't it? Not one left apart from the Roach."

Dad struggles angrily and we hold him back. The Guardian smiles like a snake would if only it could. "Oh dear," she crows. "Did you not know about the oldest one in the Astro three days ago? Cried like a baby when we put him in the suit."

I can tell that Tomas is about to explode. *Tomas. Please. Just keep calm,* I think.

Dad is calmer now. Maybe he's said all he had to. "I know very well what happened to Tomas," he says, in a low, measured voice. "You're a killer, Marianne, no doubt about it. You started early on our defenseless baby boy, and I always thought you'd have a go at my other three when you got the chance."

Madam Guardian snorts indignantly. "What did you expect, Matthew, after you ran off with that nurse?

Making me look a fool. Not to mention giving me a Roach son."

Poor Maximillian. He is clutching that awful teapot to him like a baby and looking at his parents in dismay. I think how strange it is that Maximillian actually has the full set of two parents here, with him, and yet he seems so orphaned.

"Maximillian is a fine young man," Dad is saying. "You should be proud of him. And it was *you*, Marianne, who gave him the Roach gene, not me. You may not know it, but you had twin sisters who cocooned. What do you think lies under those two old apple trees in the yard?"

This is something Madam Guardian does not want to hear. "Maximillian," she barks, "give me that teapot. Right now!"

"Max, my boy," Dad says with a sigh. "Don't keep your mother waiting. Give her the teapot."

M

I hold the little gold-and-white teapot with the beaky spout out to Mama and my hands do not tremble. Standing here with my family around me, I know that I am no longer the "poor, frightened thing" that Mama used to call me.

Mama snatches at the teapot but, just as we planned,

I do not let go. I feel Mama's sharp nails slip off the porcelain and I draw the teapot away from her clutching fingers. And then I open my hands. For a heartbeat the little eagle teapot seems to hang in the air—and then it falls to the slate floor and smashes into a thousand pieces. There is a beat of silence, a terrible stillness.

It is done.

K

"You idiot Roach!" Madam Guardian screams.

Coolly, Maximillian replies, "I am no idiot, Mama, and I never have been." He pauses and then, at last, he says our code word. "But you, Mama, you are *evil*."

Evil.

At that, Tomas and I throw back our visors. Madam Guardian stares at us, nonplussed. She looks from me to Tomas and back to me and then she recognizes us. Her jaw drops, and for the very first time I see her afraid. We step menacingly toward her—the plan is to hold her while Dad gets the DisK from its hiding place—we know exactly where it is because Mom told him. But Madam Guardian scoots past us and is out of the room before we can stop her.

"Let her go," Dad says as he hurries behind the desk and pulls open a drawer. He looks up in panic. "It's not there!" he says.

We rush to the desk and pull open all the drawers. There is no DisK to be found.

"Oh my days, supposing she keeps it with her now?" Dad says.

We stop and stare at him in horror, our plans turning to dust before our eyes. It is then that I see a small, almost unrecognizably clean bear sitting in the corner. I snatch him up. "Tedward!" I say.

Dad is snappy. "Stop messing about, Kait. We have to find that DisK."

I feel like telling Dad that I'm not the only one who's been messing about up here, but I don't because Tedward is heavy again *and he has a smart new zipper in his back*. I unzip Tedward and pull out the DisK.

We are out of there in seconds and into the atrium. It is deserted. Madam Guardian has fled. But as we head through the big door with the silver number 9, we hear the clanking sound of the elevator coming back up.

M

We are in skylon hut number nine on the roof of the Bartizan. It is different from Parminter's hut, for it has a flight of metal steps up to the control panel, and its thick glass windows look out onto the Bartizan roof. And of course there is no friendly rocking chair, warm blankets or welcoming lantern.

Its control panel is almost the same—a ring of numbered lights for each skylon is glowing steadily—but there is a small but essential difference. In the center of the ring, beneath the glowing light for skylon number nine, there is a circular indentation that is not obliterated with a splodge of gray metal. This is the only open DisK Lock in the city—neat and sharp, crisscrossed with burnished gold bands and it is just waiting for the DisK.

"The DisK will try to spring up after it has made the connection," Papa tells Kaitlin. "But you *must* hold it down until the Orb is fully open."

"Okay, Dad," Kaitlin says, and she pushes the DisK striped side down into its bed. There is a satisfying *pzzzz-ut* as the connections are made and the eight lights surrounding it begin to pulse brightly. Kaitlin keeps pressing down on the DisK and we wait, holding our breath, to see what will happen. Suddenly, through the window, we see a brilliant flash of light arc across the sky.

"The DisK," Kaitlin says. "It's getting hot."

"Keep pressing," Papa says anxiously. "We must fuse the skylon circuits so that we destroy the Orb forever. You *must* hold it down until the sky is *totally* clear."

"I know, *I know*," Kaitlin says between clenched teeth.

Tomas has climbed out through the hatch, and Papa and I peer through the thick blurry windows, watching the arcs of light traveling across the sky. They travel fast but are falling back well before they touch.

Kaitlin lets out a gasp. "Ah . . . so *hot*!"

Papa looks worried. "Katie, are you all right?"

Kaitlin is biting her lip now. "Dad, this really, *really* hurts."

"I'll take over," he says. "I've got tough old hands."

"Let me," I say. "My hands are tougher."

Papa knows this is true. "Thank you, Max," he says. "Take care it doesn't come back up. It *must* stay down until all arcing has stopped and the Orb has completely gone. I'll tell you when. Okay?"

I understand. And I am happy to be the one who frees Hope from its incarceration. I take a deep breath and then I place my hand over my sister's. I choose my middle limb, for the lower hands of a Roach have tougher skin than the more sensitive upper ones. "Pull your hand out now," I tell Kaitlin, "and I will press down." Kaitlin pulls her soft little paw out from under my armored one. I keep the pressure on the DisK, which to my relief, is still in its bed, soaking up the power and opening the Orb. But oh, it is *hot*. I keep pressing and pressing. I will not let go. *Not until our city is free.*

T

I am out on the Bartizan roof, standing beneath the skylon. My hair and skin buzz with charge but I don't care. I am here to witness the new beginning of Hope.

A long ripping sound comes from the tip of the skylon. I shield my eyes from the brilliance and see a starburst of light snaking out. Its delicate fingers race across the whiteness of the Orb, stretching out toward others that are zigzagging toward it. They hover, suspended, tantalizingly close and then just before they meet, they fall back.

Suddenly a new starburst shoots out from the tip of our skylon and its questing fingers zip across the Orb at such a speed that I know that this time they must collide.

They do. With an earsplitting crackle they meet those from the other skylons racing toward them and they fuse into a net of blindingly bright light stretched across the Orb. I watch the dull whiteness that encloses us evaporate like steam on a summer's day, to reveal a brilliant blue. Outside it is a beautiful day.

"Yes!" I punch the air. "Yes! Yes! Yes!"

K

An excited yell from Tomas fills the hut. "All clear! All clear!"

Maximillian snatches his hand away, shoves it under his armpit and jumps back from the control panel. Dad and I look at the DisK. We both want to know that there will be no going back from here. And there it is, or what is left of it: a blob of gold and silver—with a worrying swirl of indigo—fused into the control panel. Seeping out around it are dark wisps of evil-smelling smoke. "Let's get out of here," Dad mutters.

Dad and I help Maximillian up to the hatch and Tomas pulls him through.

Black smoke is spooling out from the control panel. It smells vile and catches in our throats. Suddenly, at the foot of the flight of steps that lead up to the control panel, the door crashes open—two Astro Techs hurtle in and swarm up the steps toward us. I'm terrified. There's no way we're going to get out now. But as Dad is lifting me up and Tomas is pulling me through the hatch, I hear a soft *whoomph* and a sheet of orange flame gushes from the control panel. A moment later I am on the roof and Tomas and I are pulling Dad through. An Astro Tech has hold of his ankle, but he kicks her off and we pull him free and roll across the roof away from the heat of the fire. There is a loud *bang* and a great spurt of flame shoots up from the hatch. A scream comes from the hut below. And then there is nothing but the roar of fire.

M

The Bartizan roof is on fire. Flames are licking around our feet—and my family is having an argument.

Papa is telling Kaitlin to get onto me so I can fly

her off the roof and Kaitlin is refusing and saying that Tomas must go first. Now Papa is telling Kaitlin to *do as she is told* and I am telling them both to make their minds up before we all fry to a crisp. We are all yelling at each other when out of the corner of my eye I see a wonderful sight—the sun glinting off shimmering purple wings of Parminter. Behind her comes Andronicus and together they are gliding down toward us. Never have I been more pleased to see my friends. They land lightly upon the edge of the Bartizan roof but as they hurry over to us there is a loud *craaaack* and the skylon hut is engulfed in a wall of flames. It is time to go.

We are off. I am taking Papa, Parminter has Kaitlin and Andronicus has Tomas. As we glide down past the line of windows by the Astro ledge, I am shocked to see the pale face of Mama staring blankly out at us. She is twisting the little gold chain from the lid of the teapot around her fingers, watching the family that she never wanted leave her forever. I almost feel sorry for her. Almost.

K

Wheeling through the beautiful blue sky, we glide away from the flames and the heat and the smell of burning rubber. I look down and see people running about like ants whose nest has been disturbed. They are calling to one another, shouting and pointing up at the roaring flames and smoke pouring out from the top of the Bartizan.

We land in front of the Bartizan to find people running out of the entrance shouting, "Fire! Fire!" and then suddenly stopping and staring upward in disbelief as they see the bright blueness of the sky.

Everyone is running out, but we are going in. We have to find Parminter's mother before it is too late. Going against the crowd, we push our way up the wide steps of the entrance and I am surprised how many people the Bartizan holds. Not just guards but ordinary people too: cooks, cleaners, clerks, medics. A nurse hurries by and I grab hold of her. She stops and stares at me, fear in her eyes. It takes me a second or two to remember that I'm wearing an Enforcer's uniform. But I use it to good effect. "Evacuate the hospital," I tell her. "Immediately!" She runs back and I see her heading up the stairs.

But we go down into the depths of the dark heart of the Bartizan.

Into Oblivion.

Chapter 36

OBLIVION

M

Tomas takes us down to a huge circular underground space that he calls Sneaks' Hall. In the center is an armored booth with a lone guard inside. Tomas's Vermin training is now very useful indeed—he tells us that he spent a week as a guard in Oblivion and he knows how it works. He marches up to the little window in the booth. "Week twenty-four. Which level?" he demands.

The guard eyes us all suspiciously, but Tomas has a wild look that cannot be argued with. "Level three," the guard replies nervously. Tomas leans forward to the window in a confidential manner. "By the way," he says, "I've locked you in. And just so you know, the Bartizan's on fire. Hand over the master key to the cells and I'll let you out."

The guard scrabbles for the key in panic. He flips

up the little glass window and throws the master key at Tomas. Then he is out of the booth and scuttling away as fast as he can.

"Let's go," Tomas says, but we need no telling. As we race through a door with a large silver *O* on it and hurtle into the dingy corridor beyond, Tomas explains that although no records are kept of where prisoners are put, a different level of Oblivion is used each week. "And your ma," he tells Parminter, "was taken in week twenty-four. Same week I was Astroed." Parminter shudders. "So we only have one level to search," Tomas says. "Which is a lot better than five."

Parminter has come prepared. She has a flashlight, a roll of fine cord and a flask of water. The water is for her mama when we find her. Not one of us dares say "if," although that is what we are all thinking as we career down two flights of narrow stairs to a grubby landing where there is a door with *3* scrawled on it. Parminter ties the end of her cord to the door handle and with her flashlight shining we set off into a wilderness of doom.

It is a warren of narrow passageways peppered with countless cell doors. Tomas throws open each one in turn and I shall not tell you what we see within. All I shall say is for the first ten minutes we find no one alive. At last, at the end of a corridor dripping with damp, Tomas throws open yet another cell door and something stirs within. The smell is bad. "Ma?" Parminter whispers, fearfully. "*Ma?*"

The inhabitant of the cell heaves itself off the floor with a groan and staggers toward us. It stares at us with wild eyes, then grabs Parminter's water bottle and pushes out past us at a run.

"Minna!" Andronicus says, shocked. "That was *Minna*."

"Do you want to go after her?" I ask him.

"No," Andronicus says, but then he thinks the better of it. "Yes. To stop her from cutting our cord."

We free two more wretched people but some twenty minutes later the thing we are dreading happens—we smell smoke. We speed up, with Tomas throwing open the doors faster and faster and Parminter rushing into each cell yelling, "Ma!" We are in the very last corridor when we open a door and Parminter races in. "Ma! Oh, Ma! Ma, Ma!" she screams.

It is good scream. A scream of joy.

The Sneaks' Hall is full of choking smoke, but Tomas guides us safely through it and into yet more corridors until at last we stagger out into Sneak Snoop, where Andronicus is waiting for us. "I followed her out," he tells us. "I don't know where she's gone now, and I don't care." He hands Parminter's mama a cup of water, which she drinks down in one long gulp. She has had nothing for three days.

And then arm in arm, Roach and Wingless together, supporting Parminter's mama, we walk slowly back to the farm, all the while looking up at the beautiful blue sky, which now has wisps of dark smoke drifting across it.

Behind us the Bartizan burns and ahead of us our freedom awaits.

Chapter 37

OUR HOUSE

M

Like a beacon of freedom, the Bartizan burned all night. The smoke obscured the stars and it was not until the next day dawned, with the Bartizan reduced to a smoldering stump and, to people's amazement, the sky still blue, that the city began to relax. Hope is a small place full of gossip and rumor and word soon got around that Outside was safe and the Contagion long gone. I was surprised that people believed this so readily. It was as if the collapse of the Bartizan tower had brought the teetering stack of lies down with it.

That first morning of freedom found us at Parminter's house putting it to rights. Then we all walked down the Long Field, past the Astro-shaped crater that Tomas made, past the feet of the skylon, down into the perimeter ditch, up the other side again and out into the long, luxuriant grasses of what was, only the day before, the Outside. I think it was only then that we truly understood we were free. Parminter led the way up the sunken track into the hills and down to a small settlement of cottages where her grandmama lives.

People came running to meet us, laughing, welcoming us like long-lost family. There, for the first time, but certainly not the last, we told our story. And then Tomas and Kaitlin—and Tedward of course—took the two white horses and set off for our camp at the beach with the wonderful news of our freedom.

When Parminter's mama was well enough to travel, Papa, Parminter and I made the same journey, along with the parents and relations of all the young SilverSeeds. It was such a joyful time.

We spent three happy months at the camp beneath the sky. We swam in the ocean and gazed at the moon, the sun and the stars. We walked and flew wherever we wished, we caught fish and picked fruit from the trees and took vegetables from the earth in the deserted settlements along the river. We never tired of feeling the wind on our faces and the rain too. But eventually the days grew colder and the nights longer and at last we decided to return to the city of Hope where we belonged. By then, even my little brother Jonno wanted to come back.

And now it is the depths of the very first true winter

we have ever known. We are living in my house and it is a happy place full of noise and laughter. Parminter and I share the top floor; Papa, Kaitlin and Jonno have a room each below us—they took all Mama's stuff out and gave it away—and Mattie and Tomas have the floor below them.

Today is a special day, because for the first time we have *snow*. Right now we are all sitting around the fire in the big room by the front door and Papa and Parminter's mama have arrived with a basket of flax cakes—Papa helps out on the farm now—and we are toasting the cakes over the flames. Open fires were forbidden beneath the Orb but now we can keep as warm as we please. And as I sit by the fire holding my toasting fork with a flax cake balanced precariously upon its prongs and my little brother Jonno tells us for the umpteenth time how fast he and Tedward went on their sled, I can hardly believe it is possible to feel so happy.

I hardly ever think of Mama now. When I broke the teapot I broke her hold over me. I have no idea if she survived the Bartizan blaze. Some say they have seen her wandering the streets and that she lives with a small group of diehards in the Underground. But it matters no more. The Bartizan's power went up in smoke and it cannot return now that we who live in Hope have the light of the sun shining freely upon us and the whole wide world is open.

And as for you, my young Wingless watcher, I've not seen much of you lately, have I? You have been with me through some strange times and I sometimes wonder whether, had it not been for you watching me on that extraordinary evening, any of this would have happened. Indeed, I think not. For if I had not wanted to prove my goodness to you I would never have let two Wingless fugitives into my house. And so I would never have found my brothers and sister and my own dear papa. And Hope would still be trapped in its nightmare beneath the Orb.

So I'd like to thank you from us all. And to tell you that you are welcome to drop by any time for toasted flax cakes beside the fire—with Parminter and I, Maximillian Fly.

Acknowledgments

Writing *Maximillian Fly* has been a fascinating journey with many twists and turns, and I'd like to thank all those who traveled the way with me. It takes so many people to make a book and there are many whose names I don't know who worked to help *Maximillian Fly* emerge from its cocoon. Thank you, all.

In particular I'd like to say a massive thank-you to my wonderful editor and publisher, Katherine Tegen, who helped me to step out from Max's world and take a look from the outside in. And to Eunice, my lovely agent, whose enthusiasm always brightens up the day. Also huge thanks to Mabel Hsu at HarperCollins who, with her subtle insights, steered me safely through rocky waters.

Also to the fabulous art editors Amy Ryan and David Curtis, who found Red Nose studio for the stupendous cover, thank you so much! And to Chris Sickels at Red Nose Studio for capturing Maximillian so perfectly.

Thanks too to production editor Kathryn Silsand and copy editor Jacqueline Hornburger for their attention to detail and their understanding of Max's world that helped put the delicate finishing touches to the manuscript. And to Lisa Lester Kelly for those oh-so-important last-minute tweaks for which I am very grateful.

To Rhodri, who was and is always here to read, talk, make cups of coffee and talk some more, thank you for your endless patience and scientific insights about weird insect stuff. And to Thomasin for her powers of brainstorming—thank you too. And lastly to Maximillian Fly himself, who appeared out of nowhere one day and just would not go away—thank you, Max.

More books by ANGIE SAGE

SEPTIMUS HEAP

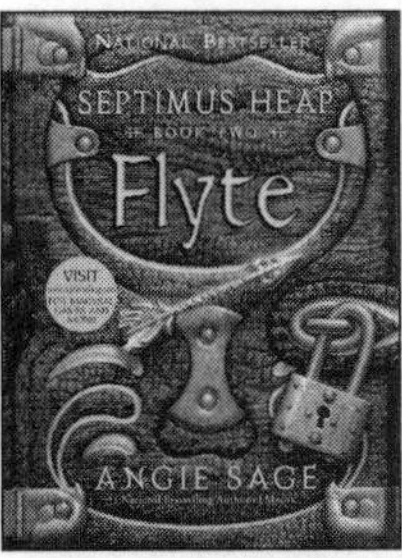

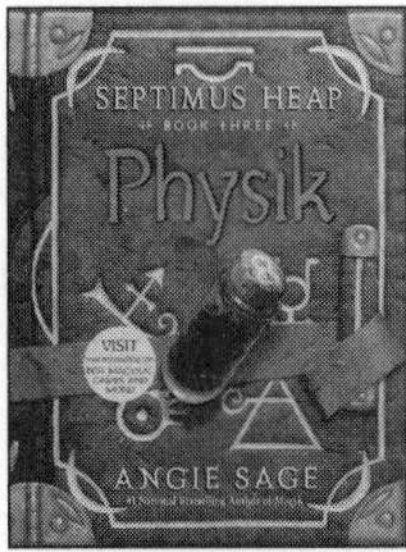

TODHUNTER MOON

KT KATHERINE TEGEN BOOKS
An Imprint of HarperCollinsPublishers

www.harpercollinschildrens.com